THE HIGHLANDER'S ENGLISH ROSE

Sisters of Ember Hall
Book 4

Elizabeth Heights

ARE YOU SIGNED UP FOR DRAGONBLADE'S BLOG?

You'll get the latest news and information on exclusive giveaways, exclusive excerpts, coming releases, sales, free books, cover reveals and more.

Check out our complete list of authors, too!

No spam, no junk. That's a promise!

Sign Up Here

www.dragonbladepublishing.com

Dearest Reader;

Thank you for your support of a small press. At Dragonblade Publishing, we strive to bring you the highest quality Historical Romance from some of the best authors in the business. Without your support, there is no 'us', so we sincerely hope you adore these stories and find some new favorite authors along the way.

Happy Reading!

CEO, Dragonblade Publishing

Additional Dragonblade books by Author Elizabeth Heights

Sisters of Ember Hall Series
The Scot's Secret Love (Book 1)
The Lord's Reluctant Lady (Book 2)
The Earl's Indifferent Daughter (Book 3)
The Highlander's English Rose (Book 4)

The Earls of the North Series
Gambling with the Earl (Book 1)
Forced to Marry the Earl (Book 2)
Taming the Earl (Book 3)

PROLOGUE

Year of Our Lord 1333
Din Eidyn, Scotland

THE SKY ABOVE Din Eidyn remained resolutely grey and a fine mist hung over the hills and valleys which Lord Gaunt had heard tell were beautiful.

Damp and dismal, he decided for himself, curling his lip at the muddy ground and bare trees.

He walked carefully along the wall walk, negotiating slippery cobbles, buffeting winds and a sore head from overindulgence in poor quality wine. Once he had reached the highest point, he flung back his hood and gazed up at the broken ramparts of the mighty fortress.

Mighty, my arse, he thought.

Shaking his head and ignoring the steady drip of rain, he turned to survey the sweeping landscape beyond the castle, including the smoldering rafters of the old town. A smile played around his thin lips, even as he ruminated on the ruin of his surroundings.

The English had proven their superiority over Scotland once and for all.

And best of all, he, Gaunt, continued to rise in the young King's favor.

A strong gust of wind swept along the wall and Gaunt was obliged to grasp hold of the slimy stone battlements until it eased. He cursed as he re-arranged his hood, and a cold trickle of water found its way down his neck.

It was time to head inside. To a fire and such meagre comforts as Din Eidyn could offer.

Gaunt pulled his woolen mantle further over his shoulders and stalked back to the castle gates. Men-at-arms bowed and moved out of his path as he approached. He had amassed a strong army to join Edward's journey north, his ranks swelled by virtue of association with the young King. It still gave him a jolt to see his family's red and gold crest blazoned across so many shields and tunics.

If only his father were still alive to witness how far he had risen.

He barked a command at a tall, narrow-shouldered lad who was about to duck beneath a low doorway.

"Where are you taking that?"

The youth all but dropped his tray.

"To the dungeons, milord."

"Food for the prisoner?" Gaunt raised his eyebrows, enjoying the lad's obvious discomfort. He took a step closer and lifted the linen cloth covering a wooden bowl of thin broth.

"Aye."

"To Lady Elena McIvor?" Gaunt clarified.

The lad nodded, eager to please.

Gaunt struck the tray so the broth spilled and the bowl bounced across the cobbles. Ignoring the servant's recoil and the curious stare of the guards, Gaunt continued on his way, ascending the wide steps to the western tower and shrugging off his mantle as soon as he stood by the small fire in the anteroom that had been set aside for him.

It was warm here, and a relief to be out of the biting wind, though the furnishings were shabby and the walls were bare. He perched on the edge of a hard chair and tried not to dwell on the lack of tapestries and cushions. Nor on the likelihood of his journey's end offering even less in the way of creature comforts. His current dampness and distress were necessary bumps along the path to prosperity. He would show everyone that Gaunt was a name to be reckoned with; gone were the days of meek subservience to his alleged superiors.

A knock sounded on the panel. Gaunt waited a moment before replying.

"Come."

A messenger boy stepped inside, handed over a roll of parchment and took his leave. Word had spread around the castle that the man of short stature had an even shorter temper.

Gaunt's heartbeat quickened when he recognized the seal.

A log hissed in the fire as he unfurled the parchment and quickly scanned the information it contained. His bark of laughter reverberated around the small chamber.

God's bones, he would show them all!

Gaunt sat back in the hard wooden chair and closed his eyes. For a moment, he imagined himself far from his sparse surroundings. Instead, he pictured the gilded feasting hall of Wolvesley Castle, lavishly decorated for a yuletide ball with boughs of pine and blazing candelabras. He recalled the golden-haired beauty of Isabella de Neville, how her jewels had sparkled, and how her slanting gaze had slid with disinterest over a titled baron from the marshes.

He sighed with deep satisfaction, stretching his legs toward the fire. Aye, he had been right to follow Edward north and feign pleasure in the acquisition of godforsaken lands. His new title meant that he would soon be joined in marriage to the most powerful family in England.

Once they had looked down upon Lord Gaunt. But as the Laird of Greenock, he would bring the de Nevilles to their knees.

CHAPTER ONE

Glen Greenock, Highlands of Scotland
Six days later

THE SKY WAS as dark as his mood.

Hamish sat atop his charger at the pinnacle of the rocky outcrop to the south of the castle, screened from view by heavy clouds and the few sparse pine trees strong enough to survive the harsh, highland climate. His horse, Luar, stayed as still as the ancient stones all around them. She had been his favorite since youth and was well-tuned to his thoughts and wishes.

Hamish was a proud warrior, not a coward. But just this once, he deliberately blended into the background.

Though not even one of these English usurpers had the good sense to lift their heads and scan the hills for enemy surveillance. They marched into Greenock Castle as if they had every right to be there. As if their ranks were so strong—and so righteous—that they could never be threatened.

Hamish tightened his grip on the reins, making Luar's black ears flicker backward nervously. He would show these English bastards the true meaning of Scottish vengeance, if it stole the last breath from his body.

"There is no call for such melodrama," quipped a lilting female voice.

Brianne.

Hamish turned to see her familiar impish smile. Her chestnut curls glistened with the first slow drops of rain. She sat easily astride her dapple-grey destrier; the one he had picked out for her himself.

She was oft-times his only companion.

He spoke softly, his words floating on the heavy mist which curled up from the valley.

"I will reclaim our family home. Greenock is nay an English stronghold. 'Tis ours." Despite his calm intentions, he could not contain the emotion which reverberated through his final words. Luar shifted beneath him, but Brianne was unperturbed.

"Aye. Ye have done it before, and ye will do it again. I have every faith in ye, Hamish."

Faith that I do not deserve.

This time, the grief rising inside him was answered by a loud crack of thunder. Luar whinnied and shied to the side as Hamish forced himself back to the present moment. He could not afford to be seen. Speaking quiet words of comfort to the horse, he backed into the trees until the beloved ramparts of Greenock Castle were no longer visible. Heavy rain lashed down through the branches, finding an easy path beneath the neckline of his cloak. Luar's ears flattened as rivulets of water coursed over her flanks. However much Hamish might wish to stay up here and keep watch, it would be madness to stay out in this weather.

He had not caught sight of Alaric, but that did not mean he wasn't there—marching amongst the English soldiers as if he was one of them. God willing, he would bring long-awaited news back to Hamish before the day was over.

Moving silently, man and horse turned away from the valley and trotted deeper into the hills; the paths they took as familiar as the McIvor standard which was engraved into the stone archway above the castle gates.

For now.

Hamish's temper worsened still when he imagined the English usurper ordering a stone mason to remove all traces of his family's history. Replacing them with the standard of a minor English baron of no renown whatsoever.

Lord Gaunt.

The name echoed around his head as Luar picked her way along the river; the shallow waters erasing any trace of their mission. Hamish had first heard that name a sennight prior; though it seemed to him now that this man had always been his sworn enemy—eclipsing even his father's brother in the crimes he'd committed against all who lived and loved in Greenock Castle.

At least Uncle Donald had fought for his own victories, swinging his broad sword and roaring battle cries as he stormed the keep some two years prior. Hamish shut his eyes, only narrowly avoiding a low-hanging branch. He could not bring himself to revisit that harrowing day, not even for the briefest moment, despite the passage of time.

His mother had always told her three children that time was the greatest healer of all. But Hamish had yet to feel the benefits of it.

Mayhap two years was not long enough, he mused, giving Luar a long rein so she could better balance herself on the steep and stony track.

Or mayhap the fact that history had all but repeated itself—with Hamish and his dwindling followers once again obliged to take shelter in the little-known caves of Greenock Crags—obliterated any healing that had somehow, against the odds, managed to take place.

When will I stop losing the people I love the most?

The anguished question ripped through his mind before he could better direct his thoughts. Self-pity had no place in a warrior's arsenal. Hamish shook his head, dislodging rainwater from his shoulder-length, russet-colored curls and then ducking once again, so that overhanging holly did not prickle him as Luar picked her way through the narrow gap in the thickly-growing bushes which cloaked the entrance to their hiding place.

Two years earlier, he would have had to shout a password to a lookout, else risk an arrow in his chest before coming through the holly. He would have emerged into a clearing that was busy with families cooking and playing, whilst loyal men sharpened their blades and prepared to follow Hamish and his father in retaliation against Donald.

All of that was gone now. The clearing was large and empty, loud only with the deluge of rain. However, smoke from a cooking fire drifted from the entrance of the caves, together with a faint scent of roasting meat.

The smallest of smiles played across Hamish's rugged face.

Thank all that was holy for old Siegfried and his unshifting loyalty.

He led Luar to a high overhang of rock and tethered her beneath it, removing her saddle and rubbing her down as best he could with a twist of cloth. Her breath plumed in front of them, as steam from her flanks rose up to mingle with the mist and woodsmoke. He found the stubby end of a carrot in a saddlebag and presented it with a mumbled apology.

"Ye deserve better, Luar."

Luar did not seem to mind. She munched the carrot and nudged at his stomach. Hamish gave her neck a final pat before stepping out into the rain and jogging over to the cave entrance, his leather boots squelching through the mud.

"Yer back safe then," Siegfried greeted him, his watery blue gaze never lifting from the cooking pot.

"Aye." Hamish shook out his cloak. "'Tis a pity the weather did not choose to turn before the English ended their journey. We could have taken them out, one by one." He mimed shooting arrows, but his companion was not amused.

"One of ye, against ten score of them?"

"There are two of us." Hamish seated himself upon a log which was positioned near the fire, glad of the warmth as he stretched out his long legs. "Three, if you count Alaric."

Siegfried made a noncommittal noise. He had never hidden his distrust of Alaric, ever since the young laborer had arrived at the cave and pledged allegiance to Hamish's father, two summers earlier. Alaric had proven himself to be a strong and valiant warrior, not once giving Hamish good cause to doubt him. But deep down, Hamish shared Siegfried's disquiet. There was something about the expression in Alaric's sharp brown eyes that made him uneasy.

"This is nay the time to be picky about our comrades," he reminded the older man.

"Indeed, it is not. Especially since you sent the bulk of them away." Siegfried stirred his pot, before lifting the ladle to his lips and tasting the stew. His thick grey hair was neatly combed, despite the roughness of their surroundings. Siegfried was a man who believed in upholding standards.

"I had nay choice." Hamish kept his voice level. Siegfried may be an old curmudgeon, but he spoke the truth. "We have not the provisions to see ourselves through the winter. I canna ask men to serve me and then watch them all starve." He flexed his fingers and held them over the blaze, deliberately looking away from the dank and shadowy cave behind his friend.

It was no place to spend the winter.

They had managed it once, aye. But that was with troops of men, and many months to prepare before the snow set in. Things were very different.

"Ye do ken, Siegfried, that ye are also free to leave whene'er ye wish to."

This time, the aging warrior met his gaze across the fire. "I'll serve ye until ma dying day, just as I promised yer father I would." He nodded sharply, one hand going to the simple cross he wore over his good woolen cloak.

Hamish gulped down a lump of emotion. "I'll see ye back as the Seneschal of Greenock before then. I swear it, Siegfried."

"Aye, well." He smiled, transforming instantly into the good-humored mentor that Hamish had revered as a child. "I'll not pretend I dinna miss the comfort of my own bed, but we have ter make the best of things."

Hamish found his hands clenching into fists. "I'll not rest until Greenock is back under my control."

"Then ye'll charge straight onto the sharp end of an English man's sword." Siegfried unceremoniously ladled out the stew and handed a roughly hewn bowl to Hamish. "Eat this. 'Tis the last of the meat."

"I'll go hunting on the morrow." Hamish gazed down at the unappetizing stew with little pleasure.

"Only if this weather breaks." Siegfried settled on the far side of the log and considered his own bowl with comparable disinterest.

Hamish gazed out at the sheets of rain falling beyond the mouth of the cave. His friend was right. Few animals would be about in this.

"I should not ha brought ye back here." He spooned stew into his mouth and chewed. "'Twas selfish of me."

"Ye had no choice."

"And now I have no plan. Save launching an attack at the man who calls himself the Laird of Greenock." Bile rose in his throat.

"If ye kill him, he'll only be replaced by another." Siegfried shrugged expansively. He had seen more than fifty summers, but his shoulders were as broad and muscular as any younger warrior's.

"What would you have me do then? Kill the King of England?" Hamish was only half joking. His back ached and the fur of his cloak had been damp for days.

Beside him, Brianne tossed back her hair and declared that, at last, things were getting interesting.

But Siegfried was less easily swayed by hyperbole. "Ye need something over him." He put down his bowl and gazed into the orange flames. "What do ye know of the man? This Lord Gaunt?"

"Naught." Hamish shrugged. "Save he is short and weak. He looks hardly able to lift his own broadsword."

"He has nay need to. He commands an army," Siegfried reminded him.

Hamish spat into the fire. His mother had raised him as a

gentleman, but at that moment he cared little for the fine manners she had instilled in him. "A man who canna fight his own battles is not worthy to be called Laird of Greenock."

"Nor is a man who canna think before he acts."

Hamish bristled at the reprimand. Siegfried had taught him much, aye, but that didna give the man the right to speak to him as if he was a green youngling.

"He has taken Elena," he growled, clenching the wooden spoon so tight he thought it might splinter.

"I have nay forgotten that." Siegfried's eyes were calm.

"I canna bide here whilst a weakling takes my castle and holds my sister hostage." Hamish's voice shook with the rage he had been holding inside since the fateful siege.

"She is of noble blood. He will treat her as such."

"Are ye certain of that?" Hamish rose to his feet and loomed over his companion, straightening up when he saw a flicker of apprehension in his blue eyes. "Forgive me, Siegfried. None of this is yer fault. But heaven knows I must take my revenge."

Siegfried lifted his chin so he could meet Hamish's gaze. "Then ye risk losing another sister."

His words carried a note of finality. For a while, the only sound was the crackling of logs in the fire and the incessant rushing of the rain. Hamish looked for Brianne, to see what she made of this, but she had gone.

She was never really here in the first place. Except in his memory and heart and very soul.

A wave of loss made his knees buckle. He fought for breath as if he was winded.

"Brianne's death was not yer fault," Siegfried said softly.

"Dinna speak of it." Hamish held up a warning hand. He wanted to sit back down on the log but could not find his way for the tears that momentarily blinded him.

When his elderly father insisted on fighting beside him during the battle to retake Greenock from Donald, Hamish had no choice but to comply. The fighting was hard and bloody, with both sides suffering heavy losses. Compelled to keep one eye on his father, Hamish had lost sight of Brianne. He'd told himself that she would be okay; that she was a warrior as fierce as any other.

Aye, Brianne had fought like a warrior. In the end, she died like a warrior. But that knowledge brought him no comfort. His spirited sister haunted his every thought and Hamish knew that however long he lived, he would never forgive himself for leaving her side on that fateful day.

"Elena lives still. All this is but temporary." Siegfried gestured behind him at the comfortless cave. "But ye must choose yer next move with care."

Hamish stumbled back to the log, breathing deeply to dispel the despair rising within his breast. His hands gripped the rough bark, rooting him in the here and now.

He had prevailed once, against those who would take his family home away from him and spill the blood of the innocent.

Ye Gods, he would prevail again.

But how?

Siegfried quirked a bushy eyebrow. "Ye dinna fancy strumming a tune on yon lute?"

Hamish guffawed with unexpected laughter, not even glancing toward the rocky shelf in the back of the cave where he had stowed his beloved instrument. "Now is not the time, but I thank ye for lightening the mood."

Siegfried sat up straighter, one hand going to the hilt of the sword at his hip. "Someone is coming."

Hamish held out a palm for silence. He crept around to stand beside Siegfried and liberated his hunting knife from its hidden pocket. He heard the snap of a twig and a muffled curse, perchance caused by the sharp holly.

Hamish raised his eyebrows toward Siegfried. If this was an enemy, he had no skills in subterfuge.

A throat was cleared, then a familiar voice rang through the clearing. "'Tis I, Alaric."

Siegfried visibly relaxed, but Hamish felt a new wave of anxiety. Why was he back so soon?

"We were not expecting ye until nightfall," he said in greeting, sheathing his knife as the tall, dark-haired warrior strode toward them.

Alaric nodded his head in a gesture of submission, though his narrow eyes gleamed with triumph.

"I have news for ye, Hamish. News ye will be glad to hear."

Hamish was winded again, this time by hope. "Is it Elena?"

"Nay." Alaric did not appear sorry to have raised false hope. "The news concerns a lady ye have ne'er met." He stood with his feet apart, his hands resting on his hips. His sodden cloak dripped onto the earth floor, but Alaric was apparently unconcerned by either the rain or the cold. "The new Lady of Greenock."

Hamish snorted, before tipping the remains of his stew on the fire and wrinkling his nose at the pungent smoke. "Ye will have to explain yerself further, Alaric. I canna see how this news is of interest to me."

Instead of answering, Alaric swiveled to face Siegfried. "Is there more of that stew? I have nay eaten since sunrise."

Wordlessly, Siegfried ladled some into a fresh wooden bowl and passed it over. Alaric sat down and tucked in with enthusiasm. After waiting a moment, Hamish too sat down, rubbing his hands on his damp braies. He thought he might be prepared to sign over the rights to Greenock Castle in exchange for a hot bath and a skin of strong wine, so long as the safety of his sister was assured.

"The English soldiers are free with their chatter." Alaric spoke through a mouth full of meat. "They changed their horses at Din Eidyn, just as ye thought they might. I put meself amongst the stable hands and none thought to question me."

"So ye did not infiltrate the soldiers?" Hamish interrupted.

Alaric paused, his spoon midway to his mouth, and flashed him a smile. "I didna have to. I heard all I needed at Din Eidyn."

With that, the man resumed his supper, causing Hamish to

gnash his teeth with impatience. "God's Bones, Alaric, spill yer news afore I spill yer stew."

Alaric gulped and belched, causing Hamish to wonder if his mother had ever taken the time to teach him manners. "Lord Gaunt is thought to be a great man, now that he is Laird of Greenock. So much so that he has negotiated for the hand of a woman recently made a widow."

Hamish gestured angrily. "What care have I for this?"

"Listen now." Alaric was placatory. "This widow is a great prize. Young, beautiful, and wealthy to boot. They call her the Rose of England. She and Lord Gaunt are to be wed the very day she arrives in Greenock."

Hamish leaned forward, fixing the warrior with a menacing gaze. "Is there any sort of point to yer tale?"

"This woman. The Countess of Felsham. She will be escorted to Greenock by three of Gaunt's men." Alaric paused for emphasis, and Hamish sat back, finally able to see where he was headed. Beyond the cave mouth, the rain began to slow. Frail shafts of late afternoon sunlight permeated the heavy cloud.

"Three?" He raised an eyebrow.

"Three." Alaric nodded sagely. "And there are three of us." He opened his arms wide to encompass both Hamish and Siegfried, as if neither of them was capable of counting so high.

"And where will this rescue party meet our Rose of England?" Hamish's fingers beat a tattoo on his knees as a plan began to form.

"A place called Ember Hall. 'Tis located south of the border." Alaric scraped up his last spoonful of stew, looking well pleased with himself. "'Tis a fine plan, is it not?"

"'Tis a fool's plan," Siegfried scoffed, folding his arms across his chest. "Ember Hall belongs to the Earl of Wolvesley. There is no richer man in England. Mark my words, they will be well-defended."

"Ye know the place?" Hamish turned to him.

"I know *of* it. I have ne'er been." Siegfried shook his head.

"The lands nearby are dangerous with raids."

Hamish pursed his lips. He had never been one to run from danger.

"'Tis the beginning of a plan," he mused. When Siegfried appeared to contradict him, he spoke up quickly. "You said yerself Siegfried that we need something over Gaunt. We need something that he wants, something we can bargain with." He stretched out his legs to the warmth of the fire as a slow smile stretched across his face. "And when all's said and done, if this woman is to be the Lady of Greenock, then by rights she belongs to me."

Alaric leaned closer, so that Hamish winced at the sourness of his breath. "That is exactly what I thought." He fished inside his cloak and produced a flask with a flourish. "Let us drink to the Lady of Greenock."

Hamish accepted the flask and drank deeply. The wine was rich and warming. In that moment, he could have hugged Alaric, sour breath or no. "To the Lady of Greenock," he echoed, holding the flask high. "Whomever she may be."

CHAPTER TWO

Westchester Hall
North of England

ISABELLA BREATHED A sigh of relief as she crept through the hidden door set into the glossy paneling of the long gallery.

Safe at last!

Well, *peace* at last, anyway. Even Lady Catherine's piercing shrieks of displeasure would not permeate the heavy stone of these ancient walls.

Isabella picked up her taffeta skirts and began to climb the steep, spiral staircase which led to the tower room of Westchester Hall; the room she had come to consider her own private sanctuary.

Hardly anyone knew of the secret door in the long gallery, and the only other entrance to the tower was outside, accessed via a long walk through the rose gardens. Given that the last of the roses had given up their blooms long before Michaelmas, Isabella thought it unlikely that the fastidious Lady Catherine would risk getting her slippers muddy.

The circular room at the top of the tower was hung with silken drapes and tapestries bedecked with flowers. Isabella had spent years ensuring the elegant furnishings inside complemented the lovely views outside. Six well-spaced windows ran from the floor to the ceiling and flooded the space with light, even today, when the weak winter sunlight was obscured by heavy clouds. However, six windows meant a chilly draught, especially with the fireplace left unlit. Isabella drew her soft woolen shawl further over her shoulders, shivering in her fine gown. Perchance she should have chosen something more practical, but to Isabella, appearance was everything.

Whenever possible, she dressed in deep blue silk, the same hue as her eyes. Her golden hair was pinned neatly atop her head, just as if this was a normal day for the Countess of Felsham.

But she was no longer the Countess of Felsham and this wasn't a normal day.

This was goodbye.

As she gazed out at the immaculate rolling lawns and the woodland beyond, Isabella was enveloped by a wave of sadness. The weight of it pressed down on her shoulders and made it hard to breathe. Panic flared in her chest and tears filled her eyes.

The truth was, she didn't want to leave.

She twisted a heavily jeweled ring around her finger and tried to stop herself from repeating what had become a familiar refrain. *If only things had been different.*

Isabella had learned the hard way that there was naught to be gained by wishing or hoping or praying. She'd been doing all that and more for eight long years; but wishes weren't enough to put a babe in a cradle, nor to have a half-grown heir ready to take on the title of Earl of Felsham.

Instead, the day her husband had breathed his last, his title—and all that went with it—had passed to his nephew, Edward.

Edward was the new Earl of Felsham. His wife, Catherine, was the new countess who waltzed around Westchester Hall as if she owned the place.

Which she did, Isabella reflected wryly, fixing her gaze on the barren branches of the distant trees. At least she had seen the splendid red and gold display of Westchester's woodland for one last time. Her home looked glorious in the autumn, with the ancient trees basking in the slanting sunlight. It was the same in the springtime, as pretty flowers unfurled their first, tentative petals, as well as in the long, lazy days of high summer when fluffy white clouds scudded over the battlements. In fact, it was a beautiful home year-round. Now that she was obliged to leave, Isabella reflected on all of it fondly. Even her marriage, which had never been happy, had never been exactly *unhappy* either. Many years her senior and grappling with ill health from the first days of her marriage, Charles had left her well enough alone.

What will my new husband be like?

Isabella gulped, imagining for a moment the sallow face of Lord Gaunt; a man she had met only once at a long-ago yuletide ball. They had talked little and in truth she had found his conversation dull. When Edward told her of his offer, her first instinct had been to laugh.

She was Isabella de Neville. The Rose of England!

He was baron of some poor estate in the east. An overseer of farmland which yielded little. A man with greasy, greying hair, a pointed chin and a glint of something that was at best, disinterest, and at worst, cruelty, in his dark eyes.

What right did he have to offer for *her*?

But then Edward commented, mildly, that Lord Gaunt was now Laird of Greenock and a favorite of the young King.

And suddenly his suit had grown more interesting.

Isabella reflected that Lord Gaunt was barely more than ten summers her senior. A man that age could still father many children.

He had land, coin and a title. All Isabella had was her de Neville charm and golden good looks. Looks which would not last for many more years.

All she wanted—*all she had ever wanted*—was a child.

Isabella put a hand to her heart, careful to avoid brushing her fingers against her collarbone which surely protruded more than ever before. Perchance, within the year she would be a mother!

She had been raised to accomplish such a task.

Sighing deeply, she gazed at the tapestried armchairs and low wooden tables, all of which could be pushed easily aside for dancing. Such life and energy had flowed through this chamber. She had once imagined her own sons and daughters excitedly climbing the spiral staircase. But soon it would be as if her years at Westchester had never been. She would leave no legacy here, save this beautiful room and memories of the beautiful music which had once rippled around the silk-clad walls.

The sound of actual footsteps ascending the spiral staircase made her turn in surprise. No servant would dare interrupt her repose; and neither Catherine nor Edward knew of the secret door.

Did they?

A smile broke over her face when she recognized the tall man who bowed gracefully on the threshold, his dark winter cloak pooling on the polished floor behind him.

"Will, how lovely. Have you come to play for me one last time?" Isabella straightened her shoulders, ensuring that her shawl fell in flattering folds over her tightly fitting gown.

Will had once been a travelling bard and lute player. Isabella had first encountered his dry wit and artful music-making when she was staying as a guest at Windsor. She had beckoned to the talented youth—then no older than a squire—and invited him to perform for them at Westchester.

That was five winters ago. And Will had never left.

Isabella oft-times fancied that Will was the closest thing she had to a friend. They had certainly spent many pleasant hours talking and laughing together. But something must now be amiss, for his blue eyes were no longer alight with merriment and his smiling mouth had turned down at the corners.

"Alas, no, milady." He stepped forward and she saw, with alarm, that his long fingers were trembling. "Forgive the interruption, but I have come to bid you farewell."

Isabella frowned. "I am not due to leave until the morrow. Surely, I will see you this night? Will you not perform for us in the feasting hall, as usual?"

Two spots of red appeared on Will's pale cheeks.

"That would give me great pleasure." He paused, awkwardly. "These last years have been full of pleasure. It has been my honor to serve you."

Isabella's alarm increased at his stammering, but her years of experience as a hostess quickly came to the fore. "Come and sit down." She took his arm and led him to an overstuffed armchair positioned by the unlit fireplace, sitting beside him and crossing her ankles gracefully. "Tell me what has occurred."

Will took a deep breath. Now a man of more than twenty summers, his frame had never filled out so though he was tall, he was as slender as a willow branch.

"Lady Catherine has declared that she no longer requires my services."

Isabella blinked as her mind tried to process this. "She has no need of a musician?"

Will linked his fingers together, possibly in an attempt to control their trembling. "She says she will hire her own musicians."

Isabella's confusion was washed away in a hot flush of anger. "But that is foolish indeed. 'Twas one thing for her to bring her own maids. But this!" She jumped up from her chair and began pacing over the rugs. "I swear I will not stand for it. Wait here. I shall go and speak to her this instant."

"Nay, pray do not do that." Will rose unsteadily from his chair and stood before her, his arms wavering entreatingly. "Truth be told, I would not have wanted to stay at Westchester without you, milady."

"Oh." Isabella blinked. "But what about coin, Will? How are you to live?" Concern for the young man's wellbeing flooded through her.

"I have some coin set by." Will tried to smile. "And I can make a living just as I always did, with my wit and my lute. Thanks to your patronage, doors will open to me where'er I go."

"You must go to my father's castle at Wolvesley." Isabella snapped her fingers as the thought occurred to her.

"Thank you, I shall." Will nodded, though his eyes were wild. "May I speak freely, milady?"

"Of course." Isabella rearranged her shawl. "I like to think we have long been in the position of speaking freely to one another."

"Aye." If Will's cheeks had been red before, now they were the color of over-ripe plums. "It gladdens my heart to hear you say as much." The young man ground to a halt.

Isabella stepped closer, wanting to offer reassurance but instead rearing backward at the strong smell of liquor on his breath.

"Have you been drinking, Will?"

"Aye, milady." The youth's voice trembled more than his hands. "For courage."

Isabella raised her eyebrows, but she felt something in her stomach plummet with foreknowledge of what was about to happen.

"Will," she said quietly.

"I know I'm no one and nothing," he said, his words tumbling over each other in their haste. "All I have is my skills with words and rhythms and rhymes. But you have always seen the beauty in poetry and music, milady. And I would ne'er forgive myself if I watched you walk away without telling you what is in my heart."

Isabella sank down into her chair. She opened her mouth to speak but he held up an anxious hand.

"I have been dreaming of and dreading this moment for days, months. Years, even." He squared his shoulders, unaware how the winter sunlight, shining through the windows, framed his fair-colored hair like a halo. "Lady Isabella." He bit down on his lip until she worried it might start to bleed. "Isabella, if I may?" He waited for her nod. "You are about to leave your home. If you wish, you might find a new home with me."

Isabella's eyes flew to his, but her quick retort died on her lips when she saw the sincerity shining from his narrow face.

"'Tis a kind offer, Will," she said instead, as gently as she could manage.

"'Tis a bold one," he countered, making her lips curl into a surprised smile. "But I dare to believe I could make you happy." He paused, awkwardly, scuffing his feet into the deep pile of the rug. "We have been happy, together. Have we not?"

"Aye, we have." Isabella could not deny it. She smiled again, recalling both the lively dances and soothing melodies he had played—and all for her pleasure. "You are a fine man and a wonderful musician. You shall make some woman very happy, of that I have no doubt. But my future lies elsewhere."

With Lord Gaunt.

No sooner had the voice spoken in her mind, than Isabella was moved to reconsider. Will was kind, honest and caring. He loved her. Or at least he *thought* he loved her. The truth of that was radiating from every muscle in his trembling body.

Her eyes flickered to the fireplace as her thoughts struck out on a novel new path.

Mayhap I could find contentment as the wife of a travelling bard.

Why not? Others married beneath them and seemed happy enough with the consequences. Her own sister had wedded a mere warrior. Was it not better to be married to a decent man who valued her happiness, than a man whose eyes had raked over her with cold disinterest?

But when Isabella looked back at Will's anxious face, she found her answer.

Esme had fallen in love with her warrior, whilst Isabella could only ever see this young musician as a friend.

Love was the crux of it. That important, elusive elixir which had never yet beaten a path to her heart.

All Isabella knew was the value of a title, lands, and a grand home. And she was not ready to give any of that up.

"I'm sorry," she added with sincerity.

Will smiled ruefully, a familiar light returning to his blue eyes. "You have naught to apologize for, milady. 'Twas impertinent of me to e'en imagine you might care for a man like me."

"Do not say that." She resisted the urge to reach out to him. "Your presence at Westchester Hall has been a great comfort to me." She nodded for emphasis. "I will miss you." Her voice wobbled as she found this was true.

Will I ever find such a friend in Greenock?

Will looked more comfortable now that he had said his piece and bowed again. "I will take my leave."

He had grown into a handsome man, she realized, and a little kernel of regret formed in her breast at the knowledge that she could not simply take his hand and walk into the future by his side.

But she had to make her family proud.

More than that, she had to make *herself* proud.

"Here, take this." She fished for her coin purse and brought out a silver coin that shone brightly against the dark silk of her glove.

"I cannot." Will flushed.

"You must," Isabella insisted. "'Tis less than you deserve, but in truth I have naught else to offer." She laughed, half with hated self-pity and half with genuine amusement. "Unless you would like a trimmed gown or a fine piece of jewelry. I have plenty of those."

For now, she added silently. Until Lady Catherine saw fit to search her trunks and reclaim aught she decreed should belong to the Westchester estate.

But Lady Catherine would have a fight on her plump hands if she tried to lay claim to Isabella's rings or emerald necklace, for she cherished these jewels above all else.

"Isabella. I will not take your last coin."

"But there are coins aplenty where I am headed." She stood up, took a firm hold of his hand and pressed the coin into it, closing his fingers into a fist and giving him one final squeeze.

"I wish you well, Will."

"And I you." He smiled down at her in a way no one had for many a year.

Once again, Isabella felt the sharp pull of temptation.

Shaking her head, she stepped back to put some distance between them. "Mayhap our paths will cross again."

"I would like that very much."

Walking briskly toward the window, as if she had some business there, Isabella threw a final smile over her shoulder. It was a gesture of dismissal and Will, to his credit, took the hint and bowed his way out of the chamber.

Leaving her alone. *Again.*

Loneliness was a state she had grown well used to. Over the years, she'd developed a hard façade which shielded her from the pain of it. 'Twas not unlike her brother, Tristan, donning a suit of armor before a battle. Though Isabella's armor was comprised of her straight shoulders and the practiced lines of her smile, which deflected both pity and gossip from the visitors she continued to graciously entertain, even as her status of countess became more precarious with every passing year.

Precarious or not, her title had provided her with gravitas and grandeur. And soon she would have a new title. The Lady of Greenock.

Isabella closed her eyes at a sudden wave of nausea. When she opened them again, she cursed aloud in a most unladylike manner as she spied a familiar figure walking with brisk determination through the rose garden to the tower doorway.

Her sister, Frida.

Frida had travelled down to Westchester as soon as she heard of Charles's passing. Being of a kind and practical disposition, Frida's help in arranging the funeral and packing her belongings had been invaluable. Isabella knew she owed a debt of gratitude to her eldest sibling.

But 'twas not a debt she wanted to repay just yet.

Ye Gods. If only someone could enact a spell to take them all back in time. To when Isabella shone the brightest of all the de Neville daughters, and a glittering future was predicted for her.

Instead, she was the only one with naught to show for her time on this earth. Seven and twenty years of time, to be exact.

As a child, Isabella recalled a lot of chatter around Frida having some kind of second sight. If only she had deployed that to some good. She could have saved Isabella the embarrassment of a barren marriage and instead pointed her toward some more vigorous husband. Plenty of men had once lined up for her hand.

Unlike now.

Frida's regular footsteps sounded up the spiral staircase. By the time her silver-blonde head appeared, Isabella had donned her armor and was able to welcome her with a bright smile.

"You have found me, sister."

Four summers Isabella's senior, with four children safely birthed and raised, Frida's natural grace and energy were undimmed. She stood tall and slim, dressed in a well-cut gown which was trimmed with fur at the neck and cuffs. The only discernible difference between the woman of today and the girl who had once hunted for healing herbs in the woods behind Wolvesley Castle was her long silvery hair.

Frida's golden crown had lost almost all of its color, following a near-fatal fall from her horse many years earlier. Remembering how close they had come to losing her, Isabella shifted uncomfortably at her cavalier thoughts around Frida's second sight.

"Aye, well, I recall you always had a fondness for heights." Frida put her hands on her hips as she caught her breath. "Unlike Lady Catherine, who tells me she intends to close up this tower." Catching Isabella's stricken expression, Frida added, "I told her that would be a mighty loss to Westchester."

Isabella grasped for her dignity, hiding her distress by examining her sapphire ring. "What did she say to that?"

"I do not believe she was fully listening."

The sisters shared a small smile.

"She has already told my chief musician that she does not require his services." Isabella fixed her gaze on the distant trees, pretending that this news had not cut her to the core.

Frida came to stand beside her at the window, bringing a scent of fresh air and lavender. "You are no longer mistress here, Bella. Whatever mistakes are made, you must accept them and move on."

Anger sliced through her. "You can spare me your lecture,

Frida. 'Tis clear enough that I am indeed moving on. Not that I had a choice in the matter." The spiky branches waved in the wind. "Edward and Catherine made no pretense of wanting me to remain at Westchester."

"You could not tolerate remaining here and watching Catherine take charge of what had once been yours," Frida replied, her voice calm and reasonable.

I cannot deny it.

Frida touched her arm. "Don't fight with me, Bella. I am on your side."

Of all things, Isabella could not countenance sympathy. "There are no sides." She smoothed her silken skirts, taking familiar pleasure in the feel of the supple material beneath her slender fingers. "Only tasks. And I am so grateful for your assistance."

She had an urge to link arms with her sister, as she might once have done. But her armor was too unyielding for such a gesture.

Frida stood quietly and gazed at the view, but Isabella could tell her sister's attention was far from the neat lawns. There was something she wanted to say.

And Isabella didn't want to hear it.

"You don't have to do this, you know."

There it is.

"Do what?" Isabella raised her eyebrows.

"Marry Lord Gaunt. Move to Scotland." Frida folded her arms and met Isabella's gaze without flinching. She had never been one to back down from a challenge.

Isabella feigned nonchalance. "You moved to Scotland and seem to like it well enough."

"But I did not marry a man I did not love."

"And how fortunate you are in that." Isabella walked away from her sister, fighting back sudden tears. "You and Esme, both. And Mirrie and Tris, of course. Oft-times, it seems I am the only one of us siblings who lives in the real world."

Frida stayed still, but followed her across the room with her all-seeing blue eyes.

Eyes that seemed to read the secrets of her soul.

"What do you mean by that?" she asked softly.

"I mean that most people marry for land or coin or title. Preferably all three." Isabella made a show of straightening a tapestry, aware of Frida's gaze burning into her back. She spun around and almost winced at the pity shining from her sister's face. "Let us not discuss this. You will not understand."

How could Frida hope to understand? Not one member of her family did. Isabella was near trembling with frustration. It took all her practiced poise to appear calm and in control, when deep down she had a strong desire to rip the tapestries from the wall and wail.

"You could return to Wolvesley. Wait a while. There is no need for you to remarry so quickly."

Isabella answered with a short laugh. "Until my child-bearing years are done, you mean? Or until my looks have faded?"

Frida shook her head sadly. "You cannot force love."

"I do not attempt to." Isabella felt as if she was explaining something simple to a child. "I am happy for your good fortune, Frida. But I do not seek something so grand as love. I only wish to be a wife and mother."

Something that came so easily to others.

Frida's face creased with regret. "I see I will be unable to convince you."

"Quite so." Isabella nodded.

"In that case, why not ride with me to Greenock? 'Tis not far from our home at Kielder. We are set to depart at noon, but can wait until the morrow if you are not yet ready to leave." Frida dredged up a smile that did not quite banish the sympathy in her eyes.

Isabella could not countenance several days of such pity.

"Nay. 'Tis kind of you, Frida. But a detour to Greenock would only slow your journey and I know how you long to be back with Callum and the children." The words fell smoothly from her lips.

Frida inclined her head with a small smile. "I cannot deny that I have missed them all."

Envy tugged at Isabella's heart. "Anyway, 'tis all arranged. I am to meet an escort party from Greenock at Ember Hall. Our brother, Jonah, is expecting me."

"Of course," Frida shook her head in wonderment. "'Tis strange to think that Jonah is now the man of the house. He only ever came as a guest, but somehow he never left."

Isabella rubbed at her arms and looked away. "Aye, well, with Esme and Adam so oft at Wolvesley."

"So Mother can help with the twins," Frida interrupted, smiling fondly.

"Of course." Isabella smiled in return, though her smile was rather fixed. "I believe that Jonah has the house half closed up. He has only kept a skeleton staff."

A thoughtful expression crossed Frida's blue eyes. "I do not like to think of you journeying so far, with only our intractable brother and a skeleton staff to greet you."

"What do you imagine could go amiss?" Isabella asked lightly.

Frida opened her arms. "Who knows, as far as Jonah is concerned?"

"All shall be well, I am certain." Isabella grew weary of the conversation. With so much of her future unsettled and unknown, the prospect of breaking her journey at Ember Hall was the very last thing she wished to debate.

"I must give you a key." Frida nodded emphatically. "That will make me easier in my mind."

"Sister, there is no need." Isabella shook her head, laughter on her lips.

But Frida was not to be reasoned with. "I always carry one, though Ember Hall has not been my home for some years now. You must take it. Put it in your luggage if not on your person."

"My luggage is being sent on ahead," Isabella protested. "I

will only take what few things I require for the journey in some saddlebags."

"Then put it in your saddlebags. I will give it to your maid to pack. Please, Bella, do this one thing for me."

"If you insist." Isabella forced herself to smile through her mounting frustration.

"I do." Frida walked lightly across the room and took Isabella's hands in hers. "Though the fact remains, I am sorry to leave you, sister."

The warmth in her touch and in her eyes was enough to move Isabella to tears once again. Instead, she leaned forward, pecked her sister on the cheek and hastily withdrew, tightening her shawl. "Mayhap we will visit one another in Scotland."

"I will make certain of it." Frida paused. "Will Edward spare a suitable escort to see you safely to Ember Hall?"

"Of course," Isabella replied airily, though in truth she doubted Edward would spare her many of his men. "Do not worry about me, Frida. I will be perfectly fine."

She would have to be, for she had no other choice.

CHAPTER THREE

THE WINTER SUN was low and bright, making Hamish squint as he kept his silent vigil atop the fortified wall. This was farming country and acres of pasture stretched before him. Some miles ahead, undulating green fields met with a dark line of ancient woodland in the dip of a shallow valley. If Hamish's suspicions were correct—which they nearly always were—this was the point at which his quarry would emerge.

A gust of wind stirred the folds of his heavy cloak. Beside him, Aleric swore.

"What is it?" Hamish did not lift his gaze from the bare trees.

"Something sharp flew into my eye." Alaric threw back his hood and rubbed at his face. "'Tis an unholy place we have come to."

Hamish grunted. 'Twas true, they had crossed over the border into England. But somehow these rolling hills and vast skies put him in mind of home. Even now, with his body braced for battle, part of him was conscious of the silvery song of a ruddock drifting over from the house's gardens.

A nice house it was, standing four square and strong with mullioned windows and neatly tended lawns. He had not allowed his men to cross the threshold but he guessed, if the situation were different, therein they would find comfortable furnishings and a warm welcome. Mayhap a smiling serving maid offering warmed wine and a hearty broth.

And there the fantasy faltered. Pleasing as his surroundings may be, he could not pretend that any warm welcome would be extended to their party. No Scottish raiders would be welcome in the home of an English lord. Especially not raiders who had so bloodily dispatched a small band of men whilst they slept.

Siegfried was right.

We should not have done it.

Hamish glanced sideways at his long-trusted companion, who stood so still he might have been hewn from granite. Only his long grey hair moved in the brisk breeze. His breathing was steady and calm, but his pale blue eyes still held a glint of steely disapproval.

"Cursed, we shall be," Siegfried had muttered, when the rising sun illuminated their massacre two days prior.

"Well fed we shall be," Alaric loudly corrected Siegfried. "And our path forward will be cleared of difficulty. Ye mark my words, old man." He had been heating what remained of their enemies' pottage on the spluttering embers of their campfire.

Relations between the two of them were now strained so tight that Hamish could almost see the bands of tension shimmering between the young warrior and the loyal Seneschal. He stood between them, head held high, inhabiting the role of peacemaker.

But Alaric's prophecy had indeed come to pass. Their slaughter of Lord Gaunt's men had set in motion a chain of events that saw the three of them situated within the grounds of Ember Hall itself. Within hours, the future Lady of Greenock would pass through this very gate.

Into his hands.

"There they are." Siegfried extended his hand toward the distant line of trees.

"Three riders," declared Alaric.

"Three?" Hamish's eyebrows shot up. "What Lady travels about such troubled lands with an escort of just two guards?" He sniffed in derision. "I begin to think you were misinformed, Alaric. This is no prized bride we are about to capture. She is hardly worth the bloodshed."

Alaric looked unconcerned. "Ye will see the truth for yerself in nay time at all."

"And we will have nay more bloodshed." Siegfried's voice was firm. He planted his hands on the low wall and leaned his weight upon it.

"We will do what needs to be done," Alaric spoke before Hamish could reply.

Siegfried spun around, his eyes blazing. Hamish quickly put both arms out to his sides, keeping his comrades apart. "To be sure, Siegfried, I am nay dressed like a lavvy heid just for the fun of it." He indicated the red and gold crest blazing from the borrowed cloak that hung inches from the ground. Hamish was a tall man, most likely standing a full head higher than the former owner of his current attire.

Siegfried's mouth quirked. He and Alaric were still dressed normally, in the faded tunics and well-worn cloaks that had seen them through these last weeks. After the massacre, they had only been able to salvage enough clothing for one of their party. The rest had been either torn to shreds or soaked with blood. But Hamish said it would be enough for him alone to appear in Gaunt's livery.

Enough to cause momentary confusion, at least.

"We introduce ourselves as the Lady's onward escort," he said firmly. "The exchange will be peaceful. Why should she doubt the tale?"

Alaric inclined his head. "Ye dinna look like a man who serves the English aristocracy."

"I can be humble and mild when the occasion demands it." Hamish gave a little bow to demonstrate, his untamed hair tumbling forward over his powerful shoulders.

"But the place is deserted." Siegfried looked behind him, into the empty courtyard. "If she has but half her wits, she will suspect something is amiss."

"And if she raises the alarm and her guards mount an attack, we will deal with it." Hamish held his gaze steadily. "But if not, there is nay cause for bloodshed."

"There was nay cause for it on the moors." Siegfried shot a look of daggers at Alaric. "Those men were sleeping. We could have set their horses free and let the men live. Beaten and bruised, mayhap. But alive."

"To run back to Gaunt and swell their ranks?" Alaric spat on the stone slabs. "Ye have gone soft, old man."

Hamish cleared his throat. "'Tis true, this mission has not gone to plan. But ye canna deny, Siegfried, that 'twas unexpected good luck to find no family in residence here."

"'Twas not luck. 'Twas news spreading of what we had done." Alaric crossed his arms and widened his stance.

"The violence of it." Siegfried spoke slowly, his disapproval evident.

"Which proved a point. Which sent yon English lord scrambling back to his parents' castle." Alaric curled his lip, half in disgust and half in amusement.

Upon finding Ember Hall empty and unguarded, Hamish had wasted no time. He immediately set off riding south, fast and hard. In less than a day, he intercepted a messenger boy carrying an important message to the Dowager Countess of Felsham. It was a letter of warning, telling the future Lady of Greenock to steer clear of the borderlands. To join her family and take shelter at Wolvesley Castle until the danger passed. It was a letter penned from a brother to a sister, and this was enough to give Hamish pause.

For a moment.

But if Hamish did not stand against Gaunt, the man would harm *his* sister. Elena. The only sister he had left. Gaunt would strike her down with no more feeling than a man carving up a chicken.

Hamish knew this, like he knew his own name.

The Laird of Greenock.

As he would be until his dying day.

"She is coming," Alaric breathed.

Something in his voice made Hamish look at him askance. Alaric's dark eyes glittered in his unwashed face as he beheld the approaching Lady. She was close enough for them to make out the shimmer of golden hair across her slender shoulders.

"Come, pretty lady," Alaric mocked.

"She is not for ye." Hamish nudged him with his elbow, making his voice light.

"The spoils of war?" Alaric raised one eyebrow before clapping him on the shoulder. "I am jesting, man. Fear not. I ken ye havena had a woman for some time now. This one is all for ye. If ye want her."

Hamish's eyes travelled back to the approaching party. The woman was mounted on a chestnut destrier. Her seat and hands were light. Was it his fancy, or did the set of her shoulders indicate some inner determination, a glint of steel that was borne out by the upward tilt of her chin? He dampened his lips with his tongue, unsure why it had become momentarily hard to breathe.

He was about to say that he did not want this woman, nor any other woman for that matter. But neither did he want Alaric laying claim to any man's sister. Hamish grunted instead. "'Tis not the first thing on my mind, right now."

"Nay?" Alaric snorted. "'Tis most always the first thing on mine."

Siegfried glowered at them both. "They are almost upon us."

Hamish waved his hand. "Go down and stand before the gates. Allow them through. I will greet them in the courtyard. Close the gates behind them so we can better deal with any trouble."

"Pen them in, ye mean?" Alaric was pleased with the picture.

"'Tis only a precaution." Hamish checked his sword belt, conscious of the short-hanging cloak flapping about his calves as he descended the stone steps. The grounds of the hall had seemed peaceful before, but now there was something menacing about the unnatural stillness. Not so much as a wisp of straw blew about the cobbles. The barns were barred and bolted, though they had managed to gain access to the stables for their three horses. Hamish could hear Luar pawing at the stone floor. Was she trying to warn him?

Girlish laughter filled his ears.

"That's a mighty poetic notion, brother mine."

Hamish could see Brianne, clear as day, standing between Siegried and Alaric as they bowed a stiff welcome to the approaching riders. The woman came first, her blue cloak billowing over the horse's hindquarters. The two riders following her both slouched in the saddle and hardly spared a glance toward their surroundings. Brianne shook her head in disgust while Siegfried and Alaric struggled with the hinges of the gate. It seemingly had not been closed in some time, which might explain why it had been standing open when they themselves arrived.

Hamish snapped his attention away from his men and back to the woman, who rode toward him like a queen approaching a subject. She reined in her horse as he bowed low.

"Welcome, milady."

There was no point in trying to disguise his Scots brogue. In any case, she was the future Lady of Greenock; headed to the highlands. She had better get used to it.

"You are here to escort me to Greenock?"

Her voice was rich and sweet, with an edge of aristocratic entitlement that made his hackles rise.

"That is to be our honor," he answered, keeping his voice free of emotion.

She sniffed in displeasure, but sat easily in the saddle as her destrier wheeled around with agitation. Her blue gaze clashed with his and for a moment, Hamish felt as if she was reading the secrets of his soul.

"There are few of you."

The steely challenge in her voice was undisguised. Hamish inclined his head.

"Even fewer of you."

Had she rumbled them? By the grim set of her pink lips, he fancied she might have. This Lady of Greenock was no simpleton. But was she wise enough to judge the strength of her men against his? Or would she cry out in protest and force them to draw out their weapons?

He put a hand to the hilt of his sword in readiness, knowing that her sky-blue eyes were watching his every move. Behind them, Siegfried and Alaric closed in behind the saddle-weary escort.

"Is all well, milady?" The querulous query came from the first rider. A slight man who would give them little trouble.

His companion scratched his stubbled face and yawned. He was broad across the shoulders and might put up a fair fight, if he could summon the interest. "Our orders are to leave you here."

The lady sat still as a statue atop her chestnut horse. Hamish fancied he could see the workings of her mind. She assessed her guard. Then she assessed Siegfried's steady stance and Alaric's wide grin. Both of them had followed his lead and stood ready to unsheathe their swords.

Her guards were mounted, reasoned Hamish. She might think that would give them an advantage. And she would be correct. But his men were seasoned warriors. They would unseat these riders within moments. The Lady would be his to deal with. He might choose to pull her from her horse and hold her tightly against him, only so she could not run away. Or he might spring up behind her and take control of the destrier.

Mayhap his thoughts showed too easily on his face, for a look of alarm crossed her delicate features.

He must calm the situation, whilst it was still in his power to do so.

"Lord Gaunt has sent us to escort the Lady on to Greenock," he proclaimed, throwing back his shoulders and daring the two English weaklings to question his authority.

Happily, they looked minded to deposit their charge and be on their way. One jumped from his horse and began unclipping saddle bags.

"But where is my brother?" The Lady looked about her, confused or impatient, he was not sure which.

Hamish said nothing. Would Gaunt's men have been furnished with the details of the Lady's family circumstances? 'Twas impossible to know.

But once again he found himself caught in the spell of her penetrating blue gaze. "Can you not answer my question?" Her voice held the slightest tremor, or was it only the effects of a chill wind and an uneasy horse?

Her golden hair was the color of ripe corn in the fields of Greenock. Inexplicably, he found himself wanting to please her.

"The house was deserted, milady, when we arrived. All locked up bar the main gates. I canna explain why." He shrugged expansively, wishing she was off the horse and less likely to flee. "Mayhap we had best be on our way north. These are dangerous lands and it does not do to linger."

He half hoped to frighten her. He did not expect her to break into laughter.

"What nonsense. I have known these lands all my life. Though never have I known Ember Hall to be so quiet. Some incident must have befallen my brother. And I do not intend to go anywhere until I have discovered what it is."

As if picking up on the growing tension, her destrier shied to one side, flinging its head up and down.

Alaric stepped forward menacingly. Hamish stopped him with a sharp look.

"The door is locked, milady."

"That is a problem I can easily solve."

She solved the problem of the flighty horse easily enough, sitting deep in the saddle and bringing the creature back under control seemingly by effort of will alone.

Were it not for the broad-shouldered guard bringing forth four bulbous leather saddlebags, Hamish might have momentarily forgotten that anyone else was in the courtyard with them.

When the Lady looked directly into his eyes, his consciousness of everything else began to fade. He breathed deeply to silence the humming in his ears and nodded to the guard, who had dumped the saddlebags on the cobbles by his feet.

He had to keep the ruse going just a little while longer. Once the guards had left and the Lady was undefended, the battle would be all but won.

He would send word ahead of them to Gaunt and set out his stall.

A bride for a sister.

And his castle.

But the younger guard was now looking at Alaric with a frown of confusion.

"Why does he reach for his sword?" he demanded of his companion.

"Because he is a young fool," answered Siegfried, projecting both weariness and wisdom across the bleak courtyard. "We are all on the same side here, lad," he enunciated, as if speaking to a half-wit.

Hamish thought for a wild and terrible moment that Alaric would retaliate against his own ally. He exhaled with relief when reason returned to the warrior's angry face.

"I am charged with the safety of the Lady of Greenock. I believe ye canna be too careful with such a beautiful charge." Alaric winked.

The older guard smirked as he sprang back into the saddle. "I shall carry word of your dedication back to the Earl of Felsham. I am certain he will be well pleased."

"I am certain he will not care in the slightest," the Lady murmured so quietly that only Hamish could hear her.

He hastily disguised his surprise. Victory was within reach and he must say and do nothing that would deter these men from leaving.

"Open the gates," he ordered his men, waiting until the guards had trotted after them before reaching for the reins of the chestnut destrier. Triumph swelled in his breast as his hands closed around the supple leather.

She is mine now.

The Lady reacted quickly, snatching the reins back and plunging her heels into the horse's sides so that it reared in retaliation. Hamish ducked away from the animal's plunging hooves, regretting his impulsive move but unable to help admiring the way she steadied the creature in mere seconds.

"Do not presume to touch anything of mine until I give you permission," she stated, her voice icy cold. Her horse lowered its head, its sides heaving.

Hamish bowed to hide his scowl of displeasure.

She should not talk to me that way.

But then again, he'd always admired a display of courage in a woman.

"We have much to discuss, *milady*." He put mocking emphasis on the word. No Lady could be Lady of Greenock without his say so.

Once again, those vivid blue eyes locked with his. She gave him a tight-lipped smile, which tightened all the more when Alaric shot back the bolts of the gate after the departing riders.

"It seems we do." She sighed, more with resignation than regret, and gracefully jumped down from her destrier. She was a tall woman, he noted, but much too thin. Her pale riding habit was well cut and trimmed with fur at the neck and the sleeves. She patted her horse's neck and spoke to it gently, despite her obvious awareness that all was not as it should be. "Perchance we should first introduce ourselves. I am Isabella, dowager Countess of Felsham, recently betrothed to the Laird of Greenock."

Hamish took a calming breath and put his hands on his hips, meeting the challenge.

"I am Hamish."

"And do you serve the Laird of Greenock?" The aristocratic edge had returned to her voice. Her eyes showed a glimmer of desperate hope that the answer might be yes.

Hamish smiled grimly. "Nay, milady. Gaunt is my sworn enemy. I *am* the Laird of Greenock."

CHAPTER FOUR

G OD'S BLOOD, WHAT *a predicament.*

The red-haired highlander held her gaze, as if daring her to scream or fuss. But Isabella knew better than to risk his ire. She'd calculated the scene as soon as they rode through the gates, realizing that something was amiss the moment she saw the shuttered house. Not so much as a chicken was about, and the only sound was the gusting wind which groaned eerily through the deserted courtyard.

This was not the Ember Hall she knew, busy with family and children and laughter.

And these men did not serve Lord Gaunt.

She had been confused by the livery of the tallest man for a while, as no doubt he intended. But the cloak did not fit him. Moreover, he did not stand like a guard or soldier.

He stood like a leader. Authority shone in the set of his shoulders and the straightness of his back.

Conviction shone in the pale blue eyes which never left her face.

I am in danger.

Yet somehow, she knew that this man would not physically hurt her.

"The Laird of Greenock, you say." She pretended to frown, shielding her eyes from the low winter sun. "It seems we are at cross purposes. You are not the Laird that I know."

"Indeed, I am not." His voice was calm and steady, though foreign to her because of the Scottish brogue. He looked over her shoulder and called out. "Take the Lady's horse to the stable."

Her destrier was the last link with the past, and most likely her last chance of escape. She half thought to spring back into the saddle and gallop for freedom. But the gates were closed, and the dark-haired warrior striding toward her looked like he would relish the chance to grapple her back to the ground.

She would not give him the opportunity.

Instead, she handed over the reins, repressing her shudder when he stood so close their shoulders brushed. His breath was sour as he looked down at her with a smirk.

"Thank ye kindly, *milady*."

She stood tall, masking the fear which threatened to make her knees tremble.

"Thank ye, Alaric." Hamish's voice carried a warning, and the man turned away, leading her horse toward the barn.

Her instinctive fear lessened, but Isabella knew she must keep her wits about her. She glanced at the hall, which appeared both familiar and strange. Frida had always kept the shutters open to invite sunlight into her home. On Isabella's infrequent visits, Ember Hall had exuded a warm welcome, like her mother's embrace at Wolvesley. Now it seemed cold and forbidding. She shivered in another gust of wind and in that moment, knew what she must do.

"I have no intention of conducting this discussion out here." She moved toward the saddlebags but then paused, unwilling to close the distance between herself and the well-muscled high-lander.

"We can talk in the stables, if ye wish it."

She shook her head, aware that her hair had come loose from its pins some time ago. She had thought she would go inside and beg the ministrations of a housemaid to re-secure it. But her disheveled appearance was no longer of such consequence.

She put back her shoulders and looked him square in the face.

"We will talk in the house, like people, not animals."

"It is locked," he explained, as if she were simple.

"And I have a key." She nodded toward the saddlebags. "Somewhere in there."

A beat passed. The man scratched at his head, half frowning and half smiling in puzzlement. "Do ye ken what is happening here, Isabella? I am not yer friend. We are nay here for a tea party."

"I believe I have grasped that much," she made her voice equally condescending. "And I still say that we should talk indoors, like civilized people." She lifted her chin. "Though that begs a question, highlander. Are you civilized people?"

For a moment, she thought she had pushed him too far. Some strong emotion flickered in his pale blue eyes, but then he guffawed. "Occasionally so."

"Well then." There was nothing for it but to squat awkwardly on the cobbles whilst her trembling fingers worked the stiff buckles. Alas, she had not paid attention to where her maid stowed Frida's key. She had not thought it was important.

Had Frida foreseen this would happen?

Isabella paused, one hand rummaging through the soft linens inside.

Nay, surely she would have warned her if that were the case.

She fought a swell of dizziness as she reached for the second bag. She had not eaten since breaking her fast at Westchester at dawn. How long ago that seemed.

A heavy hand rested on her shoulder. "Are ye well?"

Her vision broke up into dots and then reformed. Isabella took a breath. "I am fine."

"Will ye allow me?"

It was not a question. The highlander took the saddlebag from her and made short work of the buckles while Isabella summoned her strength and rose to her feet, ignoring the urge to steady herself by reaching for the man's arm.

He is my enemy, she reminded herself.

It made no sense at all that he exuded such an air of calm.

"I have it." He brandished the long iron key, seemingly waiting for her to take it from him.

Isabella was more accustomed to giving than receiving instruction. She folded her hands in front of her and nodded imperiously. "You may proceed."

His voice rippled with surprise. "I may proceed?" His bushy eyebrows disappeared beneath his thatch of hair.

She nodded again, thinking hard. "But only you. Not your men. They must stay out here."

She could not stand to be near the man with dark hair and shifty eyes.

Hamish rocked back on his heels, pursing his lips thoughtfully. "And why do ye think ye are in any position to make such demands?"

She met his gaze calmly. "Because you told me you were civilized and moreover, I sense this about you. Of course, you can do with me what you will. There is no one here to stop you. But I choose to believe that highlanders can also be men of honor. My brother, Tristan, has always insisted upon it." She raised her eyebrows sharply. "Is he correct?"

Please God, let him be correct.

A smile tugged at the corner of his mouth. "Again I say, occasionally so."

"Then let us hope that this is one such occasion." Isabella's voice was arch; the voice of a lady who expected to be listened to. Though she warned herself not to overstep the mark as she followed the highlander's long strides down the well-worn path to the arched front door.

But where is the mark?

Isabella had never before been in a situation with such ill-defined social rules.

She rested her hand briefly on the iron door handle. How many times had Frida, Esme, or Mirrie rushed out of this very same door to wrap her in a welcoming embrace?

Too many to count.

Oh, how she wished that one of them was here now. Her sisters formed the backdrop to her life; in thought and memory, if not in person, now that they were all grown and scattered. She took strength from the knowledge they had all lived and loved within these walls. The scent of lavender greeted her as Hamish pushed open the heavy panel and she stifled a swell of longing for her family.

I must find the strength to do this on my own.

Hamish stood back to allow her to pass through the door ahead of him, and Isabella walked steadily down the stone-flagged hallway into the feasting hall. Here, she half hoped to find her brother-in-law, Callum, slouching in a tapestried chair by the fire. Or Jonah, hobbling through from the solar and scowling at the interruption. But the house was silent and defiantly empty. The long trestle table, which had hosted so many family dinners, was pushed up against the far wall. For the first time that Isabella could remember, there were no slumbering hounds to raise their heads or thump their tails in greeting.

Isabella paused before the unlit fireplace, uncomfortable in the shadows and already regretting her decision to come inside. There was no warmth. No welcome. Nothing to be gained by this charade of confidence.

But what else do I have?

She folded her arms about her and nodded toward the log basket. "You can make up the fire."

Mayhap with warmth and light she could think more clearly.

He stood beside her and she flinched at the proximity. Hamish had seemed a large, forbidding man outside in the courtyard. But inside, amongst the trappings of gentility, she was even more aware of the breadth of his shoulders and the watchful intelligence in his gaze.

He is not a man to cross.

"If you wish," she added, glancing up at the smoke-blackened rafters as if they held particular interest.

"It was not part of my plan."

His voice was loud in the pressing silence; his breath plumed in the chilly air. Isabella resisted the urge to shuffle away.

"What is your plan?" she asked instead.

Hamish walked over to the fireplace and rested a hand against the mantle. His expression, when he turned to face her, was neutral.

"Lord Gaunt has taken something that is mine."

Her heart began to beat heavily in her chest. "Your castle?" she guessed.

"That is one thing, aye."

"So in turn, you have taken something that is his?" She waited a moment. "Me?"

"Ye have it right." He watched her carefully. "'Tis naught personal, ye understand."

"I understand." Her heart picked up speed as her thoughts raced ahead. She stalled for a moment by playing with the fur trim on her sleeve, but the words that had formed in her mind were determined to be heard. She lifted her chin. "Though I fear you do not."

If her words shocked him, he didn't let it show. "Explain yerself."

"You seek to use me to bargain for the return of your lands?" Isabella folded her hands together to stop them from shaking. She wished she had thought to take a seat before beginning to talk. To sit down now would show a weakness she would prefer to keep hidden.

"I do." Hamish regarded her steadily.

She gave her head a little shake. "But Lord Gaunt cares little for me. For certain, he will not relinquish an entire estate for my sake."

It was the truth, though she felt far from certain that declaring it was wise. But she could not travel all the way to Scotland with these men, only to have Lord Gaunt refuse their conditions at the end of a long and painful journey. She winced at the very idea of it.

Better to face facts now than after an arduous ride north. However hard and unpleasant those facts may be.

Hamish blinked, as if he did not fully understand. Then he sighed deeply and dragged a hand through his long, russet-colored hair, making his braids jump and dance. "I suspected as much when I saw you approach with just two guards. Two," he emphasized, glaring at her as if this was some personal failing.

His voice echoed around the cavernous room. Isabella buried her growing fear, drew her cloak about her and eyed a nearby armchair. Her back ached even more than her head.

"I was told that you were called the Rose of England," he continued.

Isabella gave up and crossed over to the tapestried chair, sinking into it as gracefully as she could. She crossed her legs at the ankle and looked unflinchingly up at him. "What of it?"

He folded his arms across his broad chest. "'Tis bold of ye, Isabella, to tell me that ye are a woman who would not be missed."

She grasped the arms of the chair and leaned forward, her aches and pains forgotten. "I said no such thing. I am Isabella de Neville. The *Rose of England*. And if any harm befalls me, Hamish, you will be made to suffer the consequences." She articulated her words clearly, so they fell like hoofbeats on cobbled ground.

He looked bewildered. "But ye just said that Gaunt cared little for ye."

She tossed back her hair. "And I care little for Gaunt. He plays no part in this. Does my name mean so little to you, highlander? Angus, my father, is the Earl of Wolvesley. My brother is Tristan—"

"—de Neville," he finished for her, his eyes wide as if he had just come to this realization.

"That's right." She took a breath. "You know him?"

"I know of him." Hamish stared past her, his gaze loose and unfocused.

Isabella allowed a beat to fall, grateful for the chance to calm herself. But when several seconds passed with no further comment from her captor, she grew uncomfortable. The cold of the hall was seeping into her bones. If only she'd chosen her warmer riding habit made of wool rather than this one with the elegant trim. She pulled her cloak further over her shoulders and tried to find some warmth in its folds.

What is he thinking now?

She attempted to look at Hamish without him noticing, but as soon as her eyes swung toward him, his gaze clashed with hers.

Her lips parted as a frisson traveled through her.

What is this strange effect he has on me?

"You are the sister of Tristan de Neville," he repeated. "The knight who negotiated for peace between England and Scotland?"

Isabella sat up straighter, ignoring her fluttering pulse and thinking instead of her family. "The very same. My brother-in-law, Callum, is Laird of Kielder."

She hoped to increase the common ground between them, but Hamish appeared unmoved by her Scottish connections. "I have a sister," he said, his words thick and slightly slurred. "I had two sisters, but one died."

"I'm sorry to hear that." She pressed her hands beneath her legs, hoping to warm her chilled fingers. Her breath plumed in front of her, hanging in the frigid air.

Hamish's gaze refocused as he noticed her discomfort. For a long moment, they looked at one another. "I will make up the fire."

She watched him lay the logs and spark the tinder, noticing how the grace of his movements was at odds with his height and brawn. When the first flame caught, he sat back on his haunches and gazed at the orange glow as if he had forgotten she was there.

The front door slammed and footsteps sounded across the flags in the hall. Isabella stiffened with fear, but the man, when he appeared, had grey hair and a grey beard.

He was not the dark-haired warrior for whom she had such an instinctive aversion.

"I have brought your things," he said without preamble, sliding a pack across the wooden floor toward Hamish.

"Thank ye, Siegfried." Hamish glanced toward Isabella. "I'll join ye outside momentarily."

"Alaric is impatient to be off," Siegfried stated calmly. "He is right. We should try to cross the border before night falls."

Hamish made a dismissive gesture. "We will not travel this day."

Siegfried raised his bushy eyebrows but only gave a short bow in response. "Very well. I shall await further instruction."

"Outside," clarified Hamish.

But Siegfried had already left, his booted footsteps sounding heavily down the hall.

Isabella cleared her throat. "He could have stayed. It's the other one I don't want inside."

Why am I trusting him with this?

Isabella could not explain it. She trusted Hamish as instinctively as she trusted her father and brothers.

Alaric?" Hamish gave her a considering glance. "Siegfried doesn't like him either."

The fire had fully taken hold and Isabella longed to hold her chilled hands out to the blaze. "Then why do you travel with him?"

"He is a skilled warrior." He stood up wearily and indicated that she should also stand. "Here, *milady*." His voice was still mocking, but kindlier. "Let me move your chair closer to the fire."

His chivalry was only partially surprising. The dynamic between them was fluctuating and uncertain, with Hamish sometimes her captor and sometimes her subject. But she could not forget that he had a sword at his hip, whilst all she had was her wits.

Isabella took her seat once again, and her muscles began to unclench in the newfound warmth of the blaze. "Thank you," she said sincerely.

He inclined his head.

"What are you thinking?" she asked, daring to press her temporary advantage.

Hamish gave a tight smile. "I am thinking that, after all, I have a bigger prize than I anticipated."

"*I* am the prize?" Isabella was a little affronted. It was as if the years had melted away and she was once again a bright and sparkling object to be scrutinized and valued by the men bidding for her hand in marriage.

"A rare beauty. And a wise man's sister." Hamish rubbed at the stubble on his chin. "The situation requires more thought. 'Tis not as I expected, but perchance it is better."

All my life I have been a pawn of men, Isabella thought. *This is no different.*

"I am glad to have the warmth of the fire whilst you do all this thinking," she replied tartly.

He tugged the cloak from his shoulders, the suddenness of his movements making her rear back in the chair. He glanced down at the length of material for a moment before throwing it on the flames. The acrid smell of burning made Isabella wrinkle her nose.

"Ne'er again will I wear another man's standard," Hamish muttered.

He looked better without the cloak, Isabella decided. The defined lines of his muscles were more visible beneath his tunic.

As if her silent observation had drawn his attention to her, Hanish slowly turned around. He put his hands on his hips and gazed down at her with unblinking eyes. "Are ye going to try and run away?"

She shrugged. "Where would I run to?" It was a genuine question, though she did not expect an answer.

He grunted. "Ye ken that 'twould do ye no good to put up a fight?"

"I ken."

Mayhap 'twas neither wise nor polite to parody the highlander's brogue, but Isabella had little idea how to handle this spiraling situation. All she was certain of was this—her earlier show of strength had resulted in a warm fire and a comfortable chair.

"I am not so foolish as to attempt combat with an armed man." She nodded toward the helm of his sword, which gleamed at his hip. "I grew up with two brothers and learned that lesson at an early age."

He blanched as she mentioned her brothers and she recalled how his voice had changed when he spoke of his sisters.

A family man.

Perchance this was another tool she could use against him.

For Isabella had no intention of putting up a fight. But neither was she prepared to accept her lot as a sacrificial victim. As Hamish stomped toward the front door, she leaned her head back in the chair and closed her eyes.

How would Tristan get out of this, she mused.

She had been raised as a Lady. But now she must think like a knight.

CHAPTER FIVE

H AMISH WOULD HAVE liked some time alone to mull over this turn of events, but he knew it was not to be. As soon as the front door closed behind him, he sensed the wall of Alaric's displeasure.

The dark-haired warrior was waiting for him at the bottom of the wide stone steps, his arms folded and his eyes flickering dangerously.

"Does Siegfried speak the truth?" he demanded, before Hamish had fully descended the steps.

It had been cold all day, but mayhap Hamish had grown overly used to the warmth of the fire inside, for now the freezing air wrapped around him like a vice.

I dinna have a cloak, he realized belatedly. He had flung Gaunt's livery onto the flames, then grown distracted by the golden-haired beauty sitting beside him when he meant to reach into his pack and fetch out his own cloak.

The cloak of the Laird of Greenock. It had seemed pressing important to remind himself—as well as the lady—who he rightfully was. For Isabella de Neville made him feel like a peasant with her haughty ways and sharp gaze. With her calm demeanor and air of assurance, which had not faltered even when she realized the gravity of her situation.

She took his breath away.

"Well?" Alaric barked.

Hamish would not allow one of his own men to rile him. "Well what?" He reached the bottom step and came to stand quite deliberately in front of the younger man.

"Does Siegfried speak the truth?" Alaric repeated.

"Aye, most often he does." Hamish put his head to one side as if considering the matter.

Alaric hissed, "Ye know what I mean. Must we stay in this cursed land e'en longer?"

"This land isna cursed. I'll wager on a clear day, ye can see Scotland from yon highest part of the moors." Hamish pointed to his left, resisting the urge to wrap his arms around him to preserve what little bodily warmth he still had. "Where is Siegfried?"

"He is feeding the horses."

"Whilst ye wait here in the cold for me?"

"I want to know what ye have planned. I didna join yer ranks to live on an English farm."

"Ye dinna have to set a single foot inside the place. Let us go now and see if sleeping quarters can be found in the barn." He clapped a hand on Alaric's shoulder and forcibly turned him away from the hall.

'Twas not for want of keeping his word to Isabella. At least, 'twas not only that. Hamish had a strong urge to keep Alaric away from her.

He did not trust *him*. That was clear enough.

And he felt an overwhelming need to protect *her*.

That was an ongoing source of confusion.

Hamish shook his head, wanting to clear his thoughts. Happily, Alaric seemed willing to walk with him into the barn, which Siegfried had accessed through the stables and opened from the inside. Chickens scratched about their booted feet and the air smelled sweetly of hay.

"The horses are settled and fed. There is plenty of animal feed," Siegfried declared, looking up from a barrel and answering an unspoken question.

"Enough to last us a sennight?" Hamish gazed about at the well-swept floor and tidy shelves.

"Enough to last us till spring."

Alaric bristled with frustration. "The plan was to seize the lady and return to Greenock, where we belong."

"Plans change, laddie, as ye know well enough." Hamish kept his voice light.

"So we are ter stay?"

Hamish could not guess at Siegfried's thoughts on this. His Seneschal replaced the lid on the barrel as if this was all in a day's work.

"For the moment, aye." He sighed with cold and weariness. The barn roof was high and the wind whistled around the rafters.

"Why do we not ride for Greenock with all haste, put a knife to the lady's throat and demand the return of Scottish land to Scottish men?" Alaric kicked at a chicken who scuttled out of the way just in time, clucking and shaking its feathers.

How can I answer that?

"Dinna take out your frustrations on a dumb animal," Hamish said quietly, but he could see by Alaric's lowered brow that he would not be so easily distracted.

"Have ye a better idea?" Siegfried offered.

Hamish could have hugged him.

"I believe I might."

Alaric tutted and crossed his arms. Hamish ignored him, walking over to the row of barrels and perching atop the nearest. Once again, he cursed himself for forgetting his cloak. His tunic was tailored from the finest cloth, but it could not withstand the chill of a winter's eve in these northern lands.

"There are three of us," he began. "'Twas always going ter be a risky business, storming Greenock Castle with just three men bearing arms."

"We can recruit others along the way," Alaric argued.

Hamish could not argue with his logic. In fact, this had been his original plan. He had imagined riding into Highland villages with the so-called Lady of Greenock sitting before him on his horse. He'd cried out for support and his plea had been answered by men wielding swords, axes and pitchforks.

A grand plan that had been. But it all hinged on Gaunt's desire to save Isabella's life.

Hamish should have guessed that the English Lord did not have such humanity. 'Twas shrewd of Isabella to realize it.

Brave of her to admit it.

In the silence, Siegfried had turned toward Alaric with a resigned sigh. "Will ye show the Laird some respect? Let the man speak. Or do ye look to lead us now, Alaric?"

Hamish caught his ally's gaze and shook his head imperceptibly. He did not wish to present such possibilities to a warrior with a strong sword arm and an uncertain temper.

"Gaunt has no long-standing affection for the Lady." He nodded toward the house. "We could have guessed as much for the paltry guard he sent down."

"Then we kill her and be on our way. Think of a new plan." Alaric shrugged with such insolence that Hamish was half inclined to strike him.

"Nay more unnecessary bloodshed," Siegfried spoke through gritted teeth.

"And nay such haste!" Hamish interjected. "We were wrong about Gaunt's affections. But the Lady is of good standing. I believe we might yet use her to wield influence."

He stopped short, not wanting to articulate his full thoughts on this.

He had yet to fully articulate them, even to himself.

Alaric narrowed his eyes. When he smiled, he was a good-looking youth. But when anger showed across his angular face, he had the look of the very devil.

"How so?" he demanded.

Hamish rose from the barrel and drew himself up to his full height, widening his stance on the dirt floor. "Ye misunderstand me, Alaric. I am not asking for yer approval. I am telling ye what we are about to do." He took a breath. "Ye dinna have to stay."

In truth, now that he was no longer thinking to storm Greenock Castle, he would almost prefer it if Alaric did not stay. The man was a mighty warrior, but an untrustworthy companion.

Siegfried had been right about that. As he was right about most things.

The Seneschal had wandered over to the open door of the barn. "Methinks we might be wise to stay for a while, in any case."

Hamish strode over to him but could discern naught amiss. The empty courtyard stretched up to the grand manor house, which was still shuttered up. All was quiet save the gusting wind.

"There is snow coming," Siegfried warned.

Alaric snorted derisively. "Ye canna tell that. Not with the sky so clear."

"I can smell it," the older man stated implacably.

Hamish wanted only to stop this disagreement before another argument took hold. "Either way, 'twill be dark soon." The slanting winter sunlight which had hurt his eyes had now faded to a colorless half-light. "We must find food and lodging for ourselves."

"There are sleeping quarters above the adjacent barn," Siegfried jerked his head upward. "Pallets and blankets all laid out."

Alaric sniffed again and Hamish rounded upon him. "Are ye forgetting, lad, that we have been bedding down in a cave? Pallets and blankets are luxury indeed."

He would love to lay claim to a blanket right now.

"One of us must sleep inside and guard the Lady." Alaric wiggled his eyebrows suggestively.

"That will be me." Hamish turned away before he was again inclined to strike him.

"As it should be," Siegfried decreed.

"We must find food." Hamish was brisk. "I shall look in the kitchens."

"I can take care of it?" Siegfried offered.

Hamish did not hesitate. "Ye have done enough for one day. Rest awhile. Both of ye. I shall rustle up provisions and bring them out to ye."

He deliberately avoided Siegfried's eye, knowing his old Seneschal would sense an ulterior motive.

Hamish had never thought himself above serving the men who served him in turn. But in truth, he longed to return to the warmth of the hall. To fetch out his cloak and check the security of the building.

But most of all, he longed to return to Isabella.

DARKNESS HAD FALLEN and Hamish was busy in the well-stocked kitchen. He had already taken cheese, cold meats and ale out to his men. 'Twas more of a feast than they had enjoyed in days, not that Alaric had thanked him for it.

Now he was stirring a broth for himself and Isabella.

The Lady needed something hot. When he visited her again in the feasting hall, she had seemed frozen half to death, despite the warmth of the fire.

She is too thin, he thought, finding a blanket in a trunk and tucking it around her knees. She had smiled her thanks, but her gaze slid over him and left him disappointed.

He had enjoyed their lively and honest conversation earlier in the day, her flashing eyes and obvious spirit. Now, something of a trance had come over Isabella de Neville.

He wanted to wake her from it.

God's Blood. He was close to wanting to ask her for advice on how to proceed.

"Ye do ken ye are her captor, not her sweetheart?"

He pictured Brianne perched atop the scrubbed wooden table, mayhap munching on the end of a carrot as she had when she was younger.

"I know it," he answered steadily. *"But the lady has a brain in*

her head. And a better knowledge of the likely reactions of her brother than I could e'er have."

"Not all brothers are as loyal as ye, Hamish."

His eyes stung for a moment. *"She is close with her family. I can tell by the way she talks of them."*

"And what of it?"

He put down the ladle and forced himself to put his fanciful notions into actual words. *"Tristan de Neville is a favorite of the King. If anyone can speak for me—for the return of Greenock and the safe-keeping of Elena, 'tis he."*

Brianne tossed her curls, her expression almost as scornful as Alaric's. *"Has the pretty lady sent ye soft in yer head? Why would Tristan de Neville help the man who is holding his sister captive? Why would he not storm this place with his vast army and behead ye?"*

"Most likely he would," Hamish admitted, breathing in the meaty scent of the broth to distract himself from Brianne's relentless commonsense. *"Which is why I need more time to think things through. And there is no rush."* He brandished the ladle. *"The Lady is not expected at Greenock for several days."*

"Ye shall need a sight more than several days to think yerself outta this predicament," Brianne predicted.

The broth was ready, and Hamish deliberately pushed his sister's words to the back of his mind.

He filled two bowls and carried them out to the hall, where the fire had reduced to mere glowing embers. Isabella sat where he had left her, as still as a stone statue in the darkness.

Why has she not lit candles?

Hamish tutted, placed the bowls on the trestle table and heaped more logs onto the fire. He waited until the lick of flames appeared, before turning to the lady.

"Why are ye sitting here in the dark?"

Her heart-shaped face was in shadows, her expression un-readable.

"I do not mind the dark."

He grunted. "Will ye eat something with me?"

God's blood, he had not intended to make it sound as if he was asking a favor.

Her nostrils flared at the scent of the broth as he offered her the bowl, but still she did not move.

"I have questions for you."

Her voice was clipped and cold, her words hitting him like a splash of cold water.

Hamish blanched, poised awkwardly with a bowl extended in one hand. He recovered quickly enough and returned her serving to the trestle table.

He could nay force her to eat. Nor was he prepared to beg.

But his belly cried out for food and he had no intention of waiting any longer. He took his bowl to the second chair and sank into it with an audible groan, which he cursed himself for. Only after three hearty mouthfuls did he turn back toward her.

"Ask away."

The broth was good and had taken off the edge of his hunger. Relaxing in a comfortable chair by a roaring fire, Hamish was inclined to be good-humored—even if his companion refused to eat and they both sat in near total darkness.

"My brother Jonah should be in residence here. Where is he?"

He paused with a spoon midway to his lips. Isabella's voice betrayed no emotion, but he had already perceived how she was a master at masking her anxieties.

Does the lass think I have killed her brother?

He laid down his spoon. "I dinna ken for certain. But I imagine he is with yer parents at Wolvesley Castle."

He felt the heat of her gaze upon his face. "How do you know this?"

"I dinna for certain, as I said." He took another mouthful of broth and swallowed slowly.

Isabella made a strangled sort of sound. "How can I believe you? How can I trust that my brother is not lying somewhere, dead or worse?"

He lifted an eyebrow. "What can be worse than *dead*?"

'Twas a fool's question and she did not bother to frame an answer.

Hamish sighed and placed his bowl on the floor. There was naught for it but to tell the truth. He templed his fingers beneath his chin and gazed into the glowing fire. "Yer brother left Ember Hall of his own accord. He sent a messenger telling you not to come here, but ye did not receive it."

He heard her shift beneath her blanket. "Because of you?"

"Aye."

Why did he feel so ill at ease when he was the one with the power?

'Twas because when Isabella spoke, he did not feel like a man in control of the situation. Her golden hair fanned out over the dark wool of the blanket, and he found himself transfixed by the way that individual strands seemed to glow and dance in the light of the fire.

She leaned forward so her hair rippled over her shoulders. "What did you do?"

Enough of this.

He echoed her posture, his gaze burning into her even though he was not sure if she could properly see his face. "Why do ye ask?"

Isabella was not cowed. "I want to know what manner of man holds me hostage."

How to answer that?

He could tell her that he played the lute as well as any bard. That in days of peace, he had penned poetry and even put some of it to music.

He could tell her that, if given the choice, he would have sacrificed his life to save his sister's. That he would move heaven and earth to save his remaining sister from Gaunt's clutches.

That all of *this* was to ensure Elena's safety.

He had allowed Isabella to believe his interest was solely in the recovery of his lands and property. But by the side of Elena's wellbeing, he cared little for the ancient stones of Greenock Castle.

Was now the time to divulge the secrets of his heart?

Nay. His heart was his own affair. Moreover, if she knew the truth, she would likely think him a weakling.

If she thought him weak, mayhap she would try to leave. Consequently finding herself face to face with Alaric.

Or face down in a ditch.

Hamish flexed his fingers. "I am the man with the power to decide if ye live or die, Isabella."

A beat passed. He fancied he heard her gulp. "You have lit me a fire and brought me food. You seem disposed to let me live."

"For now," he agreed. "You may still be of use to me." His voice caught and his next words were unplanned. "Perchance we can be of use to one another."

But how could a displaced highlander be of use to one of the wealthiest women in England?

He could almost hear Brianne demanding the very same of him.

Hamish could not answer. It was a foolish notion. He only knew that he sensed some deep sadness in Isabella de Neville. A sorrow that could not be disguised by rich robes or fine words.

A sorrow I long to remedy.

Ye Gods, was Brianne right? Had the pretty lady sent him soft in the head?

He dampened his lips with his tongue, searching for words that might re-establish his dominance of the situation, if not of the lady herself.

He was her captor. She was his only viable means of negotiation for the return of all that he loved. He must maintain control.

Isabella rose to her feet. He heard her booted footsteps crossing the floor, followed by the slight squeak of a hinge as a cupboard door swung open. A taper flared, and he made out her golden head bent low over a candle. When she turned to him, her pale face was brightly illuminated by the flickering flame. He saw dark smudges of exhaustion beneath her blue eyes.

Eyes that held wisdom as well as weariness.

She was not a young woman. But she was still the most beautiful woman he had ever beheld. Her beauty was in her poise and grace, as well as her smooth skin and delicate features.

He closed his mouth, embarrassed to have stared for so long.

"I cannot guess what you mean. Perchance you abide by different rules up in Scotland, but allow me to make one thing clear. You are my enemy, Hamish. You hold me captive, against my will, threatening me with death one minute and then proffering help the next. It is clear to me that you have no plan. No clear idea what to do with me. And therefore I am as likely to be put to death as I am to go free. We cannot possibly be of use to one another whilst you treat me so ill."

"What do ye mean, treat ye ill? I have brought ye food and bade ye eat it," he spluttered.

Isabella lifted her chin. "I shall retire for the night. Do not attempt to follow me." Her voice had acquired an edge of steel.

Where is she going?

Before he could ask, Isabella scooped up her blanket and walked quickly into the shadows at the back of the hall. He saw the flickering flame of her candle rise higher as she mounted the stairs.

Stairs which must lead to the family's bedchambers.

"It will be as cold as the grave up there," he spoke aloud.

Isabella did not respond. Seconds later, the light of her candle disappeared around the corner.

Hamish widened his eyes but stayed seated in his chair. If Isabella wanted to play lady of the manor, then so be it.

Perchance it was wise to put distance between them, for his thoughts were running amok. Mayhap a few hours' sleep would lessen this spell that Isabella de Neville had put him under.

Mayhap come the morn, everything would be clearer.

CHAPTER SIX

ISABELLA WAS NUMB to the winter cold of the long gallery. She strode across the wooden floorboards, sheltering her candle flame from draughts but oblivious to the steam of breath pluming ahead of her.

Adrenaline pumped through her veins, whilst her mind hummed with nervous energy. She had been driven from the feasting hall by impulse alone, like a horse bolting from one too many surprises. Almost companionable they had been, sitting by the fire like two people that—

Here, Isabella's internal dialogue failed her.

How had they been together? Like friends? Nay, for no friend she had ever known had made her pulse flutter so.

Like lovers, her mind sneakily suggested.

Isabella's candle flame flickered in her quick exhale of breath.

How should she know? The only lover she had known was her elderly husband. Kind as he was, the Earl of Felsham had never made his young bride's heart pound in any way.

But what nonsense was this? Aye, they had conversed almost as equals. Sparring in a way Isabella had not enjoyed since youth. Her questions and accusations ricocheted from his rebuttals. His piercing blue eyes shining in the darkness.

But then he had spoken words that sent a fresh chill through her bones.

"I am the man with the power to decide if ye live or die, Isabella."

Never had a foolish woman recovered her senses so quickly.

She knew she must put distance between them. Thank goodness she had the presence of mind to light a candle before she fled.

Although the highlander was right. It was as cold as the grave up here.

But that was not a comparison Isabella was minded to enjoy at the present time.

She paused by the long window, discerning the outline of the barns by the silvery light of the moon. Somewhere out there lurked the dark-haired warrior with cruel menace in his eyes. Whilst downstairs sat a highlander who talked calmly about deciding her death.

Isabella hesitated no longer. She turned toward the chamber door that had once belonged to her sister Esme, lifted the latch and sighed with relief when it opened. Once inside, she closed it firmly and shot the bolt.

I am safe.

Isabella's knees weakened and she lent her weight against the solid panel of the door, tears threatening at the corners of her eyes.

What a terrible day.

How could it have been mere hours since she left Westchester Hall, imagining no worse fate awaiting her than marriage to a disinterested man?

Isabella tucked the blanket under her arm and pushed back her hair with shaking fingers. She had only stood still for a moment, but already the cold of the chamber had seeped into her bones.

I must light a fire.

Her eyes roamed the tapestried walls until she found the fireplace with an adjacent log basket waiting only for her ministrations. She carefully set her candle down on the mantle and squatted down by the grate.

How many times had she watched the maids light a fire?

Isabella frowned. Perchance the answer was none, for she had no clear idea how to proceed.

How difficult can it be?

Pursing her lips, she reached for the largest log and settled it in the grate. Was it merely a matter of setting her candle flame to the log?

But if her candle were to go out, she would be left in total darkness.

Pleased with her foresight, Isabella walked tentatively over to the nightstand, feeling with her hands until she encountered another candle. This, she lit with the first, the tremors in her hands abating a little as a second glow of light took hold.

Now she held a flame to the log, stiff with hope and anticipation. Alas, the log only smoked a little and made her cough.

Disappointment coursed through her, leaving her limp. Isabella settled her candle holder on the wooden floor and cradled her head in her hands, rocking sideways like a child.

But no one was coming to save her. Not her maid, not one of her siblings, and certainly not Lord Gaunt. Isabella took a deep breath and stood up slowly.

I shall light more candles, she decided.

Within minutes her heart lightened. With more candles lit, she was able to identify those waiting in the wall sconces. Soon, the chamber was transformed into a blaze of light.

Light which banished the shadows.

Shadows which had long threatened her ability to think and act rationally.

Isabella did not stop until every candle in the chamber was topped with a yellow flickering flame. Then she sat on the bed and pulled her blanket over her legs, pleased with how the candlelight illuminated the familiar polished wooden furnishings and bright tapestries on the walls.

"Light and warmth," she muttered, as if to a child. "And soon will come the morn."

Her comforting words reminded her of her mother, smoothing back her hair and speaking gently after Isabella was woken by a nightmare. Neither of her sisters had ever been troubled by bad dreams, but Isabella frequently woke in her childhood bed in a twisted tangle of blankets and fright.

Mayhap it was a harbinger of what was to come—of being held captive by a band of highland warriors.

She shivered and pulled the blanket further over her body. She had imagined climbing under the rugs on the bed, but could not shake the idea that they would be chilled and damp. The room needed heating thoroughly.

Mayhap I have long underestimated the work of a housemaid.

Isabella rubbed at her temples and took deep, soothing breaths. But despite her best efforts, her pulse pounded and her mind endlessly replayed the conversation downstairs.

Should I believe Hamish about Jonah?

The prospect of harm befalling her youngest brother had set Isabella's whole body shaking and kept her prisoner in the armchair, when really she should have gone about lighting candles or stoking the fire, anything to banish the encroaching darkness.

Darkness meant night.

Night meant nightmares.

Isabella had long been afraid of the dark.

But when Hamish told her that he did not know where Jonah was—that he had not harmed him—she had perceived the gleam of truth in his blue eyes.

Aye, she believed him. Partially because she had no choice in the matter. But mostly because she fancied that, deep down, Hamish was a man of honor.

Isabella tutted in frustration. Had the events of the day turned the balance of her mind? The highlander was keeping her prisoner. On pain of death even. Yet here she was, delighting in his perceived honor and brilliant blue eyes.

She should threaten him with the retaliation of the Wolvesley army. Watch from the battlements as Tristan faced him in combat.

But this last image refused to come into focus. The two faces of her golden-haired brother and the russet-haired highlander swam before her eyes, but she could not force them to turn against one another.

'Twas a flight of fancy anyhow, for she had no way of getting word to Wolvesley. The skeleton staff that Jonah kept on at Ember Hall had seemingly been dismissed or given leave. Mayhap they had even accompanied her brother back to Wolvesley? Either way, there was no one to carry a message for her.

There was a village nearby, she dimly recalled, but she had no idea what direction it lay in. She had as much chance of getting lost on the moors as of finding sanctuary in the church. And either way, she risked being caught by the dark-haired warrior if she attempted to escape.

She had not been lying when she told Hamish that she would not attempt to flee.

Isabella settled herself back against the pillows, forcing herself to think of the glow of light against the looking glass rather than the proprietary sneer of the young warrior.

I am safe. The door is bolted. The window shutters are fastened tight.

She clenched her hands and took perverse pleasure in the pain of pressing her fingernails against the flesh of her palms.

Ye Gods, how low I have sunk.

Isabella had once been treated like a precious jewel; cosseted and sheltered and given aught she desired.

As a child, she had roamed free in the fields around Wolvesley with her siblings. But later, when the full flower of her beauty came into bloom, she came to be perceived differently to her sisters.

She became a woman defined by her looks. A woman who needed protection from nettle stings and harsh winds and mud.

How did that transformation happen? she wondered now. Surely it was not her loving parents that had imposed such restrictions upon her.

Mayhap it was her own doing. Her own desires to secure the most sparkling future, with naught but her looks to distinguish her.

And those famed looks were now fading, whilst she kept company with highland vagabonds in a freezing farmhouse.

And no one knows of my plight.

Her fingernails dug deeply into her palms as a wave of desolation swept over her.

But she was expected in Greenock within the sennight. When she did not arrive, surely Gaunt would act?

He would act, she reasoned, if only to appease her father. Search parties would be dispatched, and Ember Hall would be among their first ports of call.

Isabella flexed her feet beneath the blanket. All she had to do was stay alive until then.

Her stomach rumbled loudly, disturbing the peace of the candlelit chamber. Now that some of her fears had been put aside, hunger had taken hold.

She really should have eaten something downstairs. The broth the highlander prepared had smelled good. Come the morn, Isabella decided, she would accept whatever food he offered.

Nay, she would not accept it. She would *demand* it.

The only way through this was to remind everyone—including herself—that she was a woman of import.

THE CANDLES HAD burned low by the time Isabella awoke from uncomfortable slumber, half-sitting and half-lying atop the high bed. Shafts of pale light filtered between the gaps in the shutters, casting horizontal patterns onto the plastered wall behind her.

She pushed herself upright, groaning a little and rubbing at her sore neck. She was chilled and stiff. The chamber was no longer in the shadows, but it was still as cold as the grave.

She winced again at the comparison, swinging her legs down toward the floor and flexing her ankles experimentally.

Perchance it had not been a good idea to sleep in her leather boots. Her toes were cramped and numb. But she had not dared to remove the boots last night. Both because of the cold and a clearly-defined notion that she should remain on her guard at all times.

She stared with dismay at her crumpled riding habit. When she had donned it yesterday, she had imagined Jonah's embrace and the smiling regard of the housemaids.

"She looked beautiful," she had thought they might report, to anyone who cared to listen.

What a mistake. She would have been far wiser to dress for warmth.

Isabella considered what clothing her maid might have packed in her saddlebags. Again, it seemed unlikely that practicality would have been at the forefront of any decision-making.

Where even are my saddlebags?

They certainly had not been brought up to her chamber, her dresses hung in the closet and her combs placed on the dresser. Isabella tightened her lips as she considered the possibility that all of her belongings remained out in the courtyard, where the Felsham guards had left them.

What she wanted was warm water in which to bathe. And a maid to comb out the impossible tangles in her long hair. But there was not even cold water in the pitcher.

Stifling a swell of self-pity, Isabella walked stiffly over to the closet, opened the door and glumly regarded the contents.

"You should be grateful there is aught here at all," Frida's sensible reprimand sounded in her mind.

She rifled through faded woolen day dresses and over tunics, until she found a dated gown in blue taffeta overlain with lace. The excess of material made the dress heavy enough to chase away any chill, she thought, holding it before her and assessing the length.

Perfect.

Then her eye fell on the long row of pearl buttons snaking up the back, and she hung it back in the closet with a sigh.

Such a gown would require the ministrations of a maid.

In the end, Isabella dressed herself clumsily in woolen stockings and a shapeless dress that might once have been a shade of green. It was warm, at least, and surprisingly comfortable. She found a comb on the nightstand and dragged it through her hair, pulling several strands out in her displeasure. Once the worst of the tangles were gone, she plaited it and secured the end with a thin blue ribbon from the dresser drawer.

Esme used to love ribbons and gowns and jewels. Isabella hardly recognized this spartan wardrobe. But, she reasoned, her sister would have likely taken the brightest and most beautiful of her clothing to Wolvesley. And the shapeless gowns that remained were possibly those she had worn deep in the months of her pregnancy.

Isabella gave her head a little shake as she bunched up the extra fabric at her waist.

What irony!

All she wanted was a child of her own.

All she had was her sister's maternity clothing.

There was naught for it but to cinch a belt about her waist and drape a shawl about her shoulders. Isabella was glad the looking glass was clouded, for it could not possibly show her anything that she wished to see. The flash of rings on her fingers made her pause and reach for her emerald necklace, reassuring herself that it was still there.

Should I hide my jewels?

She could secrete them amidst the linens in the dresser. But if the highlander wished to rob her, he would hardly hesitate at ransacking a deserted bed chamber.

Besides, she would not know herself without them. Dressed

as she was, Isabella's jewels were the only proof she bore that she was the dowager Countess of Felsham.

The daughter of the Earl of Wolvesley.

The future Lady of Greenock.

She shuddered a little at the last. If Hamish considered himself the Laird of Greenock, did she still aspire to that particular title?

That is a question for another day.

Breathing deeply to quell her nerves, she stepped out into the long gallery, blanching a little at the ongoing cold and silence that greeted her. Her footsteps sounded too loud across the wooden floor, but after a moment's consideration she continued on her way, tripping with deliberate heaviness down the stairs.

How else could she announce her arrival into the great hall?

At first, she thought her efforts and anticipation were all in vain, for the vast hall was empty. Then she saw the highlander standing quietly beside one of the long windows. He had opened the shutters and was gazing out at the view of rolling fields.

Fields which had turned white.

Isabella paused at the threshold, one hand going to her throat and fastening, out of long habit, around her precious necklace.

"Snow," she said.

"Aye," Hamish agreed, without looking around. "A little at least."

Isabella crossed the hall and stood on her tiptoes so she could get a better view without coming too close to her captor. The fields were blanketed with white, but the grey granite of the meandering stone walls was visible here and there. As she watched, a clump of snow fell from the barn roof.

"'Tis already thawing," he added.

Isabella said nothing. Snow made travel difficult. It meant that her absence from Greenock would not be questioned so soon.

The thaw could not come quickly enough.

Hamish turned toward her and startled a little, a smile coming over his full lips.

'Tis my outfit, Isabella thought, but she stood taller and lifted her chin.

"I half thought we wouldna see ye this day, Lady Isabella. I ken how the English like their slumber, but 'tis near noon."

Again, she stayed quiet, determined not to tell of a night spent clenched with fear. She had drifted into sleep as the first rays of dawn broke through the shutters.

Hamish had also changed his clothes since yesterday. Now he was dressed in breeches and a blue shirt, with a dark padded jacket which further emphasized the breadth of his shoulders. His hair had been combed and hung just above those powerful shoulders. His eyes fixed upon hers.

"Were ye perchance waiting for a maid to waken ye? 'Tis a pity if so. It seems there are none to be found in these parts."

Isabella wrenched her eyes away from him. He was taunting her, but she would not give him the satisfaction of a response.

"I am hungry," she said instead. "I wish to break my fast."

He gave her a low bow. "Whate'er the lady wishes." He waved his hand toward the trestle table, which had been pulled from the far wall and laid with foodstuffs.

Much as she wished to show disinterest, Isabella could not prevent her legs from carrying her over to the dais; nor her hands from reaching out for a hunk of bread and pushing it into her mouth.

The bread was hard, but she chewed and swallowed with the beginnings of relief.

"Where is the wine?" she asked.

Hamish gave a little shrug, his eyes glinting. "Mayhap in the cellar. There is a jug of ale, milady."

Isabella had never relished the taste of ale. But thirst drove her to pour some of the brown liquid into a nearby tankard.

Has he deliberately brought up the meanest fare and cheapest crockery?

Isabella scanned the table and concluded that yes, he probably had.

But the ale tasted surprisingly good and she refilled the tankard and drank again. Then she spread a hunk of bread with butter and ate it quickly. Only after she had swallowed the last crumb did she realize that she was still standing beside the table.

And the highlander was watching her every move.

Isabella pulled out a chair and sank into it, crossing her legs at the ankle and attempting to recover her dignity.

"Are there no berries? No cheese?" She motioned toward the table, which was set with only bread, butter, and some unidentifiable cold meat. She shuddered at the smell of it.

Hamish came to stand at the opposite end of the table. He sloshed some ale into a fresh tankard and drained it in one gulp.

"Ye ken where the kitchen is located?"

Not since squabbling with her siblings in the schoolroom had anyone spoken to her so bluntly.

She met the challenge in his eyes with one of her own. "Not really."

His lips quirked as if hiding a smile. "'Tis back there." He motioned behind him.

Isabella sat back in her wooden chair and twisted a ring about her finger, affecting a bewildered nonchalance. "What of it?"

"I do not have ye held in chains. Ye can go yerself and look for whatever it is ye fancy."

He is baiting me again.

Isabella did not allow herself to dwell on the idea of being held in chains. Surely he would not dare!

"I am asking *you* to fetch the berries and the cheese," she said instead, slowly and clearly. "And whatever else you can find. Surely more than this." She wrinkled her nose with displeasure.

Surprise blanketed his features for a moment. Then came an expression that Isabella could not properly place.

"Mayhap ye would like to take charge, milady?

It was amusement that glinted across his eyes, Isabella realized. Hamish was enjoying this.

And so am I.

Isabella splayed her fingers onto the edge of the table, allowing the winter sunlight to illuminate her jewels.

"I have never worked in a kitchen," she confessed.

Yet it was not entirely true. She had stood beside her sisters and learned to bake at an early age, impatient to eat the honey cakes from the moment they came out of the big ovens. Her mother had insisted they all knew the workings of a house and kitchen. But then she had married young and moved to Westchester Hall, where everything ran smoothly without any intervention from her.

Isabella could not recall the last time she had set foot in any kitchen.

My purpose is purely decorative, she thought dryly.

She looked quickly at Hamish, half inclined to vocalize this conclusion and wondering if he might laugh in appreciation.

He had folded his arms across his chest and was gazing back at her with his head tilted to the side.

"Would ye like me to teach ye?"

He sounded genuine, but Isabella could not decide if he was still baiting her.

"Teach me?" she echoed.

"Aye." He nodded slowly. "We could begin with something easy."

Despite herself, she was caught up in the narrative. "Such as?" She raised her eyebrows with all the haughtiness she could summon.

He pursed his lips. "Vegetable broth."

Isabella felt her lips twitching into a smile. "And then move onto something more complex?"

"Such as good manners," he finished for her, leaning over the back of a chair as if truly interested in her response.

Isabella could not help it. A chortle escaped her and she looked about for a napkin with which to cover her mouth.

Of course, there were no napkins in sight.

She reached for her tankard and drank until her emotions

were back under control.

"That is an interesting proposition," she said. "That a highland thief could educate an English lady in the ways of good manners."

He reached for his own tankard. "I speak as find," he declared. "And I am no thief."

Once again, Isabella found that she could not help herself. "What can you mean? You speak as you find."

Hamish regarded her steadily. So steadily, she began to blush.

"I was raised to eat what food was prepared for me," he said eventually. "And also to show thanks to those that prepared it."

A rebuke!

Isabella dabbed her lips with the back of her hand and took a breath.

"Forgive my rudeness," she said as prettily as she could manage. "Thank you kindly, sir, for the lavish spread you have prepared for me." She lowered her eyes and considered again the offerings on the table. "In particular the bread, which I imagine can be no less than a sennight old. 'Tis a wonder indeed that there is no mold growing upon it."

He winked at her. "Milady, I had the foresight to scrape away what mold I found."

She laughed out loud before she could stop herself. "Such chivalry," she managed from behind her hand.

"I spoke the truth when I claimed to be civilized." Hamish too was entertained; she could tell by the slight trembling of his shoulders as well as the humor in his blue eyes.

He is a man who likes to laugh, she thought suddenly, picturing him in a different setting, surrounded by family and friends.

This would never do.

Before much more time passed, Isabella imagined she might find herself fawning over his every word.

And he, the man who was keeping her prisoner in her own brother's house.

She rose abruptly from the table.

"Have you come to any conclusion with regard to my future?" She relished how he flinched from the question and added icily, "I mean, whether I am to live or die?"

Hamish recovered quickly, grasping the back of the chair with his large hands and allowing his gaze to meet with hers.

"I still say this situation we find ourselves in would resolve itself more easily if we were to help one another."

'Twas a simple statement. And one she was almost moved to consider.

Almost.

"And I still say that I do not negotiate with those who seek to threaten me." Isabella gripped her own chair, taking strength from the memory that Frida had likely once stood here. And not just Frida, but Esme and Mirrie and Jonah.

And Tristan.

"And I remind you of my family connections. And the wrath you will face when all of this is discovered." She threw back her head defiantly.

"Ye dinna need to remind me of yer family connections. They are the reason we are still here. Ye ken?"

Isabella was breathing hard as a strange mixture of anger and adrenaline surged through her limbs. It took a moment for her to make sense of his words. But as his meaning became clear, she felt colder than she had in the depths of last night.

In all the time she had spent with the highlander, she had imagined a sort of connection existed between them. A meeting of minds. A feeling of kindness.

Mayhap more than kindness.

But this morn and last night, he had been thinking only of her family connections.

Of Tristan, no doubt, and how he might help further his cause.

When Hamish considered whether she should live or die, 'twas Tristan who came into his mind, not her, however much he gazed at her golden hair.

Isabella had long known the power she wielded over men. It had been part of her, like her long fingers and narrow feet. But clearly, her powers were fading.

Perchance her purpose was no longer even decorative. She was merely the sister of one powerful man. The daughter of another.

No one's wife. No one's mother.

She backed away from the table, glad after all that she had not partaken of cheese and berries as nausea churned in her belly.

The highlander still might kill her. He still carried his sword at his hip. He stood like a man braced for action.

"I am willing to talk, whene'er ye are willing to listen," he said.

Isabella shook her head, still backing away from the table. "I will never be willing," she whispered, afraid that her voice might shake.

"I am a patient man," he countered.

Isabella looked him in the eye with the last of her courage. "You will have to be." She took a breath. "This house belongs to my family. You are an imposter here. Again I say, do not follow me."

Until she had reached the top of the stairs and was confident he had obeyed her desperate command, Isabella held her breath. Then she clung onto the banister as a wave of dizziness broke her vision into countless dancing dots.

God's blood, how could she ever hope to manage this?

Isabella straightened her legs and breathed deeply until the grooved lines of the floorboards came back into focus.

She would stay alive the only way she knew how.

Behind a locked door.

CHAPTER SEVEN

L UAR TOSSED HER glossy black mane and pawed at the stone floor of the stable. Hamish reached up to stroke her neck, crooning words of comfort, but his charger was not so easily soothed. She snorted with impatience and pranced to one side, jerking her head up and down as if to tell him that enough was enough.

"I ken ye dinna want ter be here," he murmured.

Luar was not alone. If Alaric had a mane, he would be tossing it as well. Hamish's small band of horses and men had endured more than enough of these hostile lands, but even if Hamish wished it, they could not return to Scotland yet.

"The ground is frozen underfoot and treacherous," he said to Luar, as if she understood every word. "'Tis not safe for ye to leave this barn. Believe me. I would take ye out if I could. A gallop o'er the moors would do us both a power of good."

He thought of the wind in his hair and the sense of perspective he would gain both through physical exertion and in putting distance between himself and Isabella. Alas, the snow that had begun to thaw two days prior had since frozen hard. And with the temperature showing no signs of lifting, it could be many days more before it was safe to contemplate leaving Ember Hall.

Hamish ran a hand over Luar's withers and sighed. 'Twas one thing to choose to stay here. Quite another to have no choice in the matter.

Luar flinched as a side door banged open and a dark shape shuffled through. Alaric was obliged to bend almost double to pass through the low door from the haybarn, but that was far preferable to risking his step on the slippery ice outside. He dragged a sack of hay behind him, which he wordlessly emptied into the horses' empty racks. Soon, the sound of munching filled the stables. Hamish had ordered that Isabella's destrier be kept fed and watered. Along with an old grey pony they had discovered in the paddocks.

"Thank ye, Alaric." Hamish attempted to keep the mood between them light.

The warrior merely grunted.

"Has Siegfried returned from the well?"

Alaric gave a minute shake of his head, his expression settling into a scowl. Hamish lifted his palms in a gesture of peace.

"I shall go," he said.

They both knew that Alaric had an easy job with the hay. Filling the pails with water and ensuring none slopped on the ground—to freeze overnight—was a much more challenging task.

Hamish crossed to the big arched doorway and looked out into the courtyard. The cobbles were fringed with white but other than that, appeared innocuous. However, each was coated with a sheer layer of ice, meaning that any movement across the yard cost supreme effort. Opposite stood the hall, shutters and doors all fastened tight to retain what little heat remained inside the thick stone walls. Hamish allowed his gaze to rest briefly on the first-floor windows, but there was no sign of any life therein.

His heart beat hollowly in his chest. Isabella had refused to leave her chamber for two whole days now.

What is she doing up there?

And more importantly, *is she well?*

Siegfried appeared around the corner of the barn and paused to rest, placing two large buckets down beside him. His lined face was flushed with exertion and Hamish silently berated himself.

The old Seneschal had insisted upon undertaking this task himself. But 'twas one that a younger man would struggle with. Hamish should not have allowed him to attempt it alone.

He struck out across the courtyard, keeping as close to the barn wall as possible and using his arms for balance.

"Is the well still frozen?" he asked somewhat breathlessly as he reached his comrade's side.

Siegfried's mouth set into a grim line. "'Tis frozen solid and I could not break it," he said tensely. He clenched his hands together and blew over them.

Hamish noticed with alarm that Siegfried's fingers were white and bloodless. Puzzled, he looked into the buckets and saw that they were not filled with water, but with ice.

"From the river," Siegfried explained.

"God's bones, ye must be half frozen yerself."

The Seneschal gave a slight shake of his head. "I will warm up soon enough." But he swayed on his feet as if dizzy.

"Nay, ye need to get in front of a fire. And quickly." Hamish put a hand on the man's shoulders, further alarmed to feel a tremor passing through his body. "Leave the buckets here." He guided Siegfried toward the hall and sent up a silent prayer that neither of them would slip and fall.

They had a brazier in the barn, which they moved to their sleeping quarters at night, but Hamish wanted to ensure that Siegfried was thoroughly warmed. He had known younger men die after prolonged exposure to below freezing conditions.

They had survived sieges and family betrayal, but this black ice may be the death of them.

Siegfried's leather boots scrambled for purchase on the treacherous cobbles. Hamish braced himself and supported him as best he could. Aging he may be, but Siegfried was still muscular and broad. Both were breathing hard by the time they reached the arched front door of the hall.

Hamish mopped his brow and positioned his arm more firmly about his comrade's shoulder.

"Almost there," he declared.

"Aye."

Siegfried had accepted his help with little complaint and this, more than anything, caused alarm to prickle down Hamish's spine. He half hoped to meet Isabella coming out of the kitchen—he nursed a fancy that she fed herself quite sensibly in his absence—but all was still and quiet inside. They stumbled around the corner into the feasting hall and Hamish breathed a deep sigh of relief that the fire still flickered in the grate.

He had built the fire at first light; more in hope than expectation that Isabella would come down and avail herself of the warmth and cheer. It would not take much to get a good blaze going again. But first, he settled Siegfried into an armchair and heaped him high with blankets from the trunk.

"Ye dinna have to wait on me, lad," he protested weakly.

"Happen I'll be needing your sword arm for many years yet," Hamish retorted. "Father always taught me to take care of aught I shall depend upon in battle."

Siegfried shook his head, but a spark had returned to his watery blue eyes.

Hamish banked up the fire and then fetched a pitcher of wine from the kitchen. He poured some for Siegfried and held it out. "Drink this," he ordered.

"Ye have made yerself quite at home," Siegfried remarked mildly.

"I have found what needs to be found." Hamish was calm. "Is feeling returning to yer limbs?"

"Like a hundred ants crawling upon me. Each one dragging a blade." Siegfried drained the goblet.

Hamish grinned. "Then I reckon ye shall live."

Siegfried rested his head on the back of the chair and gazed into the flames. "I am counting upon it. When I breathe my last, it shall be in Scotland."

"In Greenock Castle," Hamish confirmed. "In yer own bed. In yer own chamber. I swear upon it."

Siegfried reached out and clasped his forearm with a grip of iron. "I dinna ask ye to swear to it."

"I do anyway." Hamish poured some wine for himself and drank with relish. Until now, some murkily defined code of honor had prevented him from breaking into the family's wine store.

But Siegfried needed something stronger than ale.

Hamish put down his goblet and folded his arms across his chest. The hall was growing too warm for his heavy cloak, but he did not want to make himself comfortable whilst there was still work to be done outside.

"I am sorry for how this has turned out," he said.

"Ye have naught to be sorry for." Siegfried's reply was instantaneous.

"I didna expect us to have to stay so long across the border. In another man's house." Hamish gazed bleakly into the fire, which had begun to smoke.

"None of us know what the good Lord has planned. But methinks 'tis a blessing we remained here."

Hamish's eyebrows shot up beneath his hair. "How so?"

"The roads are not fit to travel upon. 'Tis near certain we would have perished if we slept out in the open."

Hamish inclined his head. "Mayhap ye are right."

For certain, Isabella could not have withstood such freezing temperatures. He glanced up toward the smoke-blackened rafters. She was somewhere above them, though he had never ventured up the winding wooden staircase—heeding her warning not to follow. He had left food at the foot of the stairs, but it had not been touched.

What did I say to offend her so?

And how long will she persevere with this?

As if reading his thoughts, Siegfried asked, "Where is the Lady?"

Hamish snorted. "She has taken refuge in the family bedchambers above and forbidden me from following."

"And you accept her orders?"

"My father was quite insistent that I should ne'er follow a lady to her bedchamber if she expressly told me not to."

Siegfried spluttered into his wine. "Wise words indeed."

"Aye." Hanish eyed the wine pitcher, but common sense stayed his hand. "But they do not help me ascertain the lady's health, especially in these cold conditions. If she becomes sick, 'twill be my doing."

Siegfried waved away a plume of smoke from the fire. "The lady has not forbidden me from venturing upstairs."

It took a moment for Hamish to make sense of the Seneschal's words. His instincts were to defend Isabella's honor, then understanding prevailed. "You could check on her? Perchance light a fire?"

"She doesna have a fire?"

Hamish opened his arms, feeling the claustrophobic heat of his heavy cloak. "Not unless she has made it herself."

"The lass will be perished."

"Aye." Hamish took a few paces away from the flames, glad of the cooler air. Fresh worry pricked at him. "But ye should rest, Siegfried."

"Dinna fuss. I am much recovered." He pushed away his blankets and prepared to stand, but Hamish came forward and clamped a heavy hand on his shoulder. "Stay awhile longer by the fire. That is not a request. 'Tis an order."

The older man sank down again, resting his gnarled hand atop Hamish's for a moment. "It gladdens my heart to hear ye mention yer father so oft," he said quietly. "He was taken afore his time, but he lives on in ye."

"Many of our kin were taken afore their time." Hamish searched for Brianne, but she did not appear. He made an effort to shake off a swell of grief. "Will ye manage things here if I go on out ter the barn?"

The horses needed water, no matter that the well was frozen. And Hamish did not like to leave Alaric so long unattended. Not when dislike of the English permeated his every thought.

"Will ye make up yer mind? Ye just told me ter sit by the fire."

Hamish was glad to see a flash of mirth cross over Siegfried's familiar features. As much as he longed for news of Isabella, he could not risk his old comrade's health.

"Ye are ter sit here until that log has burned low." He pointed to the smoldering log in the grate. "Is that clear, old man?"

"Get outta here." Siegfried flapped his hands and Hamish nimbly dodged out of the way.

"I shall be back," he called over his shoulder.

Outside, a brisk wind blew his cloak around him, causing a shiver to run the length of his body. The cold air stung his eyes and when his feet slipped from under him on the ice, Hamish found himself cursing the English and the ill-conceived plan that brought them here.

Most of all, Lord Gaunt, he reminded himself, rubbing his back and pushing himself onto his knees. Hamish had never longed to run any man through with his sword, but he would gladly end the life of the man who had laid claim to both his lands and his sister.

"Dinna allow anger into yer heart."

The piping voice spoke directly into his ear.

"That is what Mother always said," Brianne added, kneeling beside him on the cobbles.

"Aye." Hamish heaved himself upright. "I was wondering when ye might show yerself."

"Well, ye have been so busy with herself in there." Brianne jerked her head toward the hall, her chestnut curls almost flattened by the hostile wind.

"I have not seen her for two days," he corrected her.

"But ye have thought of little else," Brianne said, stretching out her legs as if she sat on some grassy knoll on a warm summer's day. *"And when ye are thinking of her, ye dinna think of me."*

He put a hand to his forehead. "I shall always think of ye."

God's blood. No one could ever take Brianne's place in his

heart and mind.

The sister I should have protected.

Another gust of wind made him gather his cloak about him. Hanish set off again for the barn, before he froze to death in this very spot.

Had it ever been so cold and bleak in the highlands?

Most likely it had. 'Twas only that this land was unfamiliar. Moreover, for the first time in his life, Hamish was not surrounded by friends and family—whose laughter and smiles could warm the coldest of places. He had only Siegfried.

And Alaric. A man he did not trust.

And Isabella. A woman who would not speak to him.

'Tis a grim setup," he told himself, speaking out loud in an attempt to assert some dominance, if only over his own limbs.

At last, he reached the barn, where the liquid eyes of the horses and the scent of the hay made things feel more normal.

He patted Luar, noting with a surge of pleasure that Alaric had melted the ice fetched by Siegfried and filled with water buckets of their three horses.

But Isabella's destrier and the old grey mare had no water within reach.

Hamish swallowed his curse and moved into the anteroom used as a store, where he found an axe and a fresh bucket. He tightened the strings of his cloak and set off again, headed for the small stream running to the side of the paddocks.

It was easy to see where Siegfried had cut the ice earlier. Hamish got straight to work, digging down with the axe until he was able to lift a big block of ice into the waiting bucket.

Ye Gods, it was cold work. His hands were red and stinging. But better that than white and bloodless. He reminded himself that Siegfried had first gone to the well, and spent fruitless minutes attempting to draw water there.

By the time he had successfully secured a second block of ice, Hamish could no longer feel the cold in his fingers. He contemplated sitting down to rest, but dimly recognized that he needed to get inside, and quickly. The walk back to the barn was a blur, but he stumbled toward the brazier and held his hands over the warmth. Just in time, he recalled that it was dangerous to apply heat too quickly. He took a step backward and rotated his shoulders to get his body moving again.

'Twas too easy for a man to come to harm in these conditions. Easier still for a lady who, for reasons he did not entirely understand, was refusing food and warmth.

Hamish stamped his feet and blew over his painful fingers. The situation with Isabella could not be allowed to continue. Mayhap Siegfried would achieve what he had not. Mayhap he would return to the hall to find both of them sitting afore the fire, toasting bread and warming wine.

A fine sight that would be. But it didna answer the question of what he would do the next day. Or the day after that. If Isabella would not talk to him about her brother, how could he proceed?

A wicker from the horses' stable brought him back to the present. He must melt the ice and top up the water buckets. There would be time enough afterwards to contemplate the hopelessness of his situation.

The winter sun was beginning its downward descent by the time he had finished. Hamish stood for a moment in the shelter of the barn door, admiring the pale golden light which formed a halo effect about the rooftop and mullioned windows of the hall.

He had been wrong before. These lands were not bleak. They had a wild beauty that was not dissimilar to his beloved highlands. He looked to his right, to where a path wound past the paddocks and out onto the moors. The snow was still crisp upon the moors. If only he could get Luar safely across the cobbles, she would be sure-footed and certain as soon as she reached the crisp snow. He and Isabella could ride away to safety.

His lips curled into a grimace at this, for where would he be safe?

What place could ever be safe for a man without a home?

Hamish bowed his head, feeling the weight of responsibility

press upon him. He must make a decision soon. The longer they lingered here, the greater the risk of discovery. Of retaliation even, by Isabella's family or Gaunt's army.

Though no army would advance in weather such as this.

Hamish heaved out a sigh and began the tentative process of crossing back to the hall, but an elaborately carved door set into an adjacent wall caught his eye.

Grand carvings for an outbuilding, he mused.

He pushed at the door and it opened with a faint groan of protest. It was not until he had walked inside that Hamish realized he had stumbled across a modest chapel.

Modest in size, at least. It was smaller than their family chapel at Greenock. But 'twas far from modest in appearance. Painted glass cast rainbow-hued patterns onto plastered walls which were adorned with frescoes so intricate that Hamish could not resist examining them; his worries temporarily forgotten as he made out a glorious pattern of intertwined stems and leaves twisting about the mullioned windows.

Hamish sank onto the nearest pew and rested his elbows on his knees. Golden light shone around him, almost like a blessing. He wondered how many years it was since he sat inside a house of God and concluded it was several. The glorious hills and valleys of Greenock were where he went to worship. But his mother had been a spiritual woman. For her sake, he placed his hands together and prayed to the Almighty for guidance.

Show me how to proceed, he begged silently.

He longed to be back in Greenock. To be recognized as the rightful Laird of Greenock. Not for the grandeur or riches involved—the good Lord knew there was little enough in the castle coffers. But simply because that was who he was and where he belonged.

He cared for the people of Greenock. For the families he had known all his life.

Would Gaunt spare a thought for the wellbeing of the young or old when he raised his tithes?

Nay. For certain he would not.

Hamish willed his instinctive flash of anger away and forced himself to think of Elena. His kind-hearted, loving little sister who was held prisoner by his sworn enemy.

Hamish's chest tightened and his breathing became fast and short as panic clamped iron arms about his ribs. For this reason, he tried to avoid thinking too oft of Elena's plight. Fear for her safety would overwhelm him.

What am I doing so far away, when I should be staging a rescue?

A feeling of hopelessness overtook him. If he died here, perchance at the hands of Isabella's brother, then Elena would have no one to rescue her.

Why will Isabella not help me?

She was a kind, decent woman, he was sure of it. Moreover, wit and intelligence shone from her eyes. Why would she not attempt to come to terms with him?

The wintry sunlight shining through the painted glass intensified, until Hamish was obliged to shield his eyes from the glare.

And then he knew.

His mother had always told him—told all three of them—that naught was more important than truth.

But I have not been truthful with Isabella.

He sat straighter in the wooden pew as he realized the implications of this. He had allowed her to think of him as a villain. A ruffian.

I am the man with the power to decide if ye live or die, Isabella.

God's bones, why had he said that?

At the time, he was trying to assert his control in any way he could. To stop her fleeing from the hall and coming into danger. To impress upon her that she needed to abide by his rules. Her beauty and poise had over-awed him, leaving him fumbling and bewildered. 'Twould have been better to simply tell the truth.

That he never intended her harm.

That he longed for the safe return of his younger sister.

That he was a man of some honor, despite appearances to the

contrary.

Hamish smiled to himself. At last, he had found his path forward. These problems were easy enough to remedy.

He stretched his arms above his head and rotated his head and neck, slowly becoming aware of shouting coming from outside.

Hamish snapped into action, striding to the chapel doorway and stepping out onto the cobbles. He made out the tall figure of Siegfried, his cloak billowing about him, standing at the bottom of the hall steps.

"What is it?" he hollered back, scrambling for purchase on the ice.

"Come quickly." Siegfried's words were half snatched by the wind. "'Tis Alaric. He is breaking into the Lady's chamber."

Hamish did not spare another thought for the ice. He began to run.

CHAPTER EIGHT

S OMETIME EARLIER, ISABELLA had stood quietly at the end of the long gallery and watched as Hamish made halting progress toward the river. She knew that the younger man with dark eyes—the one she so disliked—had long since climbed the stone steps to their sleeping quarters.

Does this mean the course is clear?

Her stomach growled with hunger and she decided she would have to take the chance. The older man, Siegfried had not yet come into view but of the three, she considered him the lesser threat.

He did not make her heart pound with fear. Nor her pulse pound with—something else.

She walked quietly to the end of the gallery and paused at the top of the staircase. All was still and silent, save the distant crackling of logs. Hamish must have made up the fire in the feasting hall, which meant she could thaw her chilled limbs. Even though Isabella had found Frida's winter woolens and a whole chest of warm shawls, the seeping cold of her bedchamber had taken root inside her very bones. When she looked outside at the endless expanse of white covering fields, walls and buildings, she thought she might never be warm again.

The stairs creaked as she descended, but there was naught she could do about that. Yesterday, she had withdrawn at every creak, her trembling feet tentatively seeking silent purchase, but

Ember Hall was an old house. She could not creep about the place without making some degree of noise.

I should not have to creep about.

Isabella straightened her sister's shawl as a hot flush of indignity travelled through her. Nay, she should not have to tiptoe like a common thief, always looking over her shoulder. But this was the only way she could feed her belly and avoid a confrontation with Hamish.

It was the best solution she had, for now.

She reached the bottom of the stairs and turned into the feasting hall. She was over halfway there. In another minute, she'd be within reach of the kitchens. Her stomach rumbled louder at the prospect of bread and cheese. But then she froze.

The feasting hall was not empty.

The older man, Siegfried, sat before the fire, his hands calmly folded above a heavy rug pulled over his knees. His blue eyes blinked in surprise before he nodded a greeting.

"Lady Isabella."

Should I flee?

Uncertainty coursed through her veins.

Siegfried did not move, but his voice was kind when he said, "Why not come and warm yourself by the fire?"

Why not indeed? This was her brother's house, after all.

She lifted her chin and stepped forward, as if she were entering the tower room at Westchester. It seemed a long way from the foot of the stairs to the fireplace, and Siegfried's eyes never once left her face. Isabella kept her head held high and her back straight, ignoring the fact of her shapeless shawl and audibly rumbling stomach. The warmth of the fire was like a caress and she all but whimpered with relief.

"Sit down," Siegfried invited, indicating the nearby chair.

But Isabella had no intention of moving backward from the blaze. She sank down on her knees, grateful for the softness of the hearthrug, and held out her hands.

"Drink this." He held out a goblet of wine.

Wine. Not ale.

Isabella hesitated only for a moment, before taking the goblet and drinking deeply. The wine brought a rush of feeling to her limbs, so she felt young and alive once again. She drained the goblet and placed it down beside her.

Unperturbed by her silence, Siegfried went on. "I am glad to see you down here, Lady Isabella. Hamish is most concerned for your wellbeing."

She snorted in a most unladylike way. "I doubt that."

They were the first words she had spoken to anyone in two days, but her voice came out as level and strong as ever, and she was grateful for it.

Siegfried was sitting to her left. From the corner of her eye, she saw him put his head to one side and regard her thoughtfully.

"You should not doubt his concern, milady. Hamish is a man of wisdom and compassion."

She was not inclined to hear such praises. "He is a man without a plan." She fixed her gaze on the flickering flames and tried not to recall their last conversation—or the spark of connection she had imagined between them. A log cracked in the grate and smoke drifted toward her, making her cough and inch backward as the acrid taste filled her lungs. A single noise came from the back of the hall, but Isabella was busy clearing her throat and wafting away smoke. She did not pay it any heed.

Siegfried rested his elbows on his knees. "Perchance I am speaking out of turn. But I believe his plan depends upon ye."

"Then there is no plan." Her eyes still watered. Isabella eyed the second chair, but did not want to prove the older man right.

"He could have killed ye when he discovered ye have nay currency with Gaunt," he said calmly.

He might still, her mind supplied.

Oblivious to this, Siegfried continued. "But he wants to work *with* ye, not against ye."

A second coughing fit seized Isabella, leaving her dizzy and a little nauseous. Too late, she realized she should not have drunk so much wine on an empty stomach.

"I will never work with a Scot," she declared, stumbling to her feet. "If that is his only plan, then Hamish will have to kill me after all." She clenched her hands into fists, partially in defiance and partially in an effort to steady herself.

Siegfried got to his feet and the rug tumbled to the floor. He held out his hand. "Let me help ye."

"I do not need your help." Her vision was dissolving into dots. She shook her head to try and clear them. "I do not need anything from you. Any of you. You should return to Scotland."

"We will not return until you come to an agreement with Hamish." Siegfried's voice was calm, but his logic was relentless.

"Then you will never return," Isabella cried out, knowing her manner was undignified but unable to remedy it. "You will stay here until my brother arrives with his army and they will cut you into pieces and I will watch." Even as the words left her mouth, she regretted them. "Or until you kill me."

Siegfried did not so much as flinch. "Hamish will not harm ye."

"But I will."

The voice came from the back of the feasting hall. Siegfried startled backward but a cold rush of fear robbed Isabella of the ability to move.

It was the dark-eyed warrior. He had been crouching in the shadows, watching and listening.

"Alaric," Siegfried began in warning.

But the younger man strode forward and held out a hand to silence him. "Dinna speak to me. Dinna try and stop me. This ends now. Ye heard the lady. She will ne'er come to any agreement. 'Tis her life or ours. And I ken which I choose."

The length of his speech gave Isabella the time she needed to regain her senses. This man meant her harm and although Siegfried looked ready to defend her, he would be no match against a warrior so much younger and stronger.

She could run outside, but he would catch her easily. Her

only hope was to flee to her chamber and lock the door.

Isabella did not waste another moment. Whilst the two Scots glared at one another, she picked up her skirts and ran.

Never had she ascended the stairs so quickly. She stumbled briefly on the long gallery, but the sound of footsteps behind her urged her on. She recalled how she had long been able to out-run her brother Tristan, despite his height and breadth. She may be slight, but she was fleet-footed. Like a charger, her mother had once laughed, not a warhorse.

She over-shot her chamber door, but quickly recovered. In moments, she had wrenched it open, flung herself safely through and shot home the bolt.

Safe.

Isabella took a ragged breath, aware that her shawl had slipped from her shoulders at some point. No matter. Her blood pumped around her body and chased away any remnants of cold with a mixture of exertion and adrenaline.

Then a crash sounded against the fastened door, sending her reeling backward. She stood helplessly in the center of the bedchamber as the crashing noise sounded again. A loud, resounding thump reverberated across the wooden floor and settled somewhere beneath her ribs.

The iron bolts across the heavy wooden door were holding fast for now, but for how much longer would they keep her safe?

She could hardly believe that the narrow-eyed warrior had turned upon her with such ferocity. And that no one was coming to protect her.

Not even Hamish.

Isabella stifled a sob.

Thump.

She jumped backwards as the door jolted in its hinges, and looked about in desperation for something she could use to defend herself. Esme had taken the majority of her belongings to Wolvesley, leaving only an old comb on the polished dresser and some faded ribbons in a drawer. Isabella shook her head, her loose hair swinging over her shoulders. There was naught suitable.

Then she spied something long and thin, propped in a sewing basket and leaning against the plastered wall by the large closet. Her eyes widened as she realized what she was looking at. Some years past, Esme had urged the man employed as her personal guard—now her beloved husband—to teach her how to wield a sword. Adam had whittled her a wooden sword for training.

And there it was!

Isabella rushed over and grasped it by the hilt. The sword was light in her hand and may not yield much damage. But it was a darn sight better than nothing.

Thump!

The man, Alaric, must be hurling himself at her door, determined to break in and…

Here, Isabella's inner monologue became silent. What exactly would he do when he had broken down the door? Ravish her? Beat her? Kill her?

She gulped and gripped the sword tighter, thinking of Alaric's height and battle-honed strength. The looking glass over the dresser showed her a slight woman with disheveled hair, wearing a rose-pink woolen gown and holding the sword ahead of her like a fire poker.

She looked like her niece, Mary, playing at pirates.

She was foolish to think she could hold her own against a warrior. She'd been foolish to ever leave this chamber and engage in honest conversation with the older man she instinctively trusted. If she hadn't sat beside him by the fire, disarmed by his kindly smile and the rich wine he poured for her, she would never have uttered the words that so angered his companion.

Foolish words, spoken by a foolish woman who should have known better.

Thump.

Still gripping the sword, Isabella dived beneath the large bed and scrambled to tuck her long skirts beneath her. 'Twas far from the best hiding place, but it may buy her some time. She put a hand over her mouth as the door finally broke from its hinges and crashed to the floor. Alaric strode into the chamber, a cruel smile playing about his thin lips. He paused and looked from right to left, and in the brief silence, Isabella heard footsteps pounding up the staircase.

Hamish?

Please God, let it be Hamish.

She had thought him her enemy, but in comparison to the devil striding over to the closet and flinging open the door, Hamish was kindness personified.

"Are ye in here, *Lady Isabella?*" Alaric taunted, rooting through Esme's gowns.

Isabella made her breathing as shallow and quiet as possible, daring to place hope in the possibility of rescue.

But as she watched, Alaric's gaze moved over to the looking glass, which must have shown him a flash of pink beneath the bed.

I should have tugged down the rugs, Isabella realized, a moment too late.

He turned slowly and ducked down, so their eyes were on the same level.

"What are ye doin' down there?" he crooned.

Without waiting for an answer, he grasped a fistful of hair and dragged her out, making Isabella's eyes water in pain. Through the blur of unshed tears, she saw him leering over her, his breeches stained and his tunic torn. His stance was entirely relaxed; clearly he was not expecting her to put up any defense.

This was her moment.

She swung the sword upward, striking him full in the belly with all the strength she could muster. Alaric grunted and doubled over in pain, but he recovered in seconds.

"Ye want it rough, do ye?"

Isabella tried to scramble away, but her skirts had no purchase on the wooden floor. He dropped to his knees so he straddled her, and before she could make sense of what was happening, his fist flew toward her.

His fist landed and her face exploded with pain.

"I'll teach ye to have more respect fer the Scots." Alaric's cheeks were the color of over-ripe plums. His eyes, always mean, had narrowed to slits. He leaned forward so she could smell the sourness of his breath, and his hands fastened around the neckline of her gown.

Isabella could not breathe.

He was going to tear the garment, top to toe. She could see the intention writ large across his angular face. His knees pressed against her ribs, holding her still and ensuring her gaze fell upon the front of his breeches.

She flinched away, desperately seeking a means of escape but already sensing the probability of defeat.

He was too strong. Too powerful. And too angry.

But even an angry man cannot force wool to tear without extreme effort. Alaric's contortions bought her some time. She inched her hand toward the blade of the wooden sword, which had clattered to the ground just inches beyond easy reach.

With a howl of rage, Alaric pinned her wrist to the floor.

"Dinna try owt more, milady. Else ye will regret it."

Leering down at her, he pulled the neckline of her gown toward his face and fastened his teeth about it. Isabella tensed with terror as the material began to give. She closed her eyes, unable to bear what was about to happen.

At first, she felt the release of pressure about her ribs. Then came a muffled sound and her wrist was freed. Slowly, Isabella opened her eyes to see Hamish hauling Alaric to his feet; one hand wrapped about his mouth and the other holding him firmly about the waist—trapping his arms by his side. Alaric struggled, swinging violently from left to right, but Hamish merely tightened his grip.

"Enough!" he commanded, a slight break in his voice the only outward sign of any exertion.

Alaric's eyes shot daggers at Isabella, still laying on the floor. Hamish swiveled the man around, so he faced the door, in time to see Siegfried stride through it holding a length of rope. Hamish nodded and the older man moved toward the bed.

Alaric spluttered something that was intelligible beneath Hanish's hand.

"We have nay interest in aught ye have to say," Hamish told him. He gave his prisoner a firm shove so he lay face down on the bed, then pinned him down with a knee placed on his back while he quickly bound his hands behind him.

"Thank ye, Siegfried," he said mildly.

"I'll kill ye both," Alaric raged, lifting his head from the covers. His eyes swung to Isabella and fixed her with a glare so dreadful that she shuffled backward until she hit the wall. "But as fer ye, killing is too good fer ye. I'll keep ye until yer begging fer death."

She didn't see Hamish swing back his fist. She only heard his fist connect with Alaric's head and saw the younger man slump back down.

A fleeting smile flickered across Siegfried's steady features. "He's had that coming fer a while."

Hamish merely grunted as he divested Alaric of his sword and flung it across the room to land with a clatter. "I should not have allowed him access ter the house."

"Ye didna." Siegfried's voice was calm. "Ye expressly forbade it."

Isabella found her eyes drawn to Hamish's and as soon as their gazes met, she began to feel safe again.

"I'm sorry," he said.

She shook her head. "'Twas not your fault."

A voice spoke in her mind in protest; pointing out that if Hamish were not holding her prisoner here, none of this would be happening. Isabella pursed her lips and silenced it.

For two days, she had stayed away from him. Now, she only wanted to drink him in. His broad shoulders, his blue eyes, his wide stance. Control and compassion radiated from him.

She wanted to put her arms around him and give him a kiss.

"Ye have taken a blow ter the head." Hamish looked at her with concern as he manhandled Alaric back onto his feet. "Are ye feeling okay?"

Isabella nodded, even as her cheeks grew warm. Mayhap she was not thinking clearly after all.

"I'll see ter the fire." Siegfried gave her a small smile.

"Aye." Hamish nodded toward Alaric. "Is there somewhere I can put him? Some place with a door that will lock?"

Isabella rubbed at her arms, alarmed that her whole body had begun to shake. She dampened her lips with her tongue and reached for her customary composure.

"The bakehouse," she declared. "The old bakehouse. 'Tis past the barn." She recalled that, years earlier, Tristan had ordered that Callum be locked up in the bakehouse. That was when everyone believed Callum to be a spy for Robert the Bruce and an enemy of the de Nevilles. What none of them realized was that his love for Frida eclipsed all else. In turn, Frida risked everything by setting the man she adored free, infuriating her brother in the process. For a while, it had seemed as if Tristan would never forgive her for it.

But all had turned out well in the end.

She twisted her neck to gaze into the empty fireplace and avoid Alaric's cruel eyes.

For certain, she would not be staging any rescue of this particular prisoner. He could stay there and rot, for all she cared.

Isabella put a hand to her head, wincing as her fingers came away sticky with blood. Her thoughts were running along strange and vengeful paths.

Hamish wrestled Alaric toward the door. "I shall find my way. Stay warm, my lady." He threw a glance at Siegfried. "Bring her wine and then stay with her."

"Ye havna seen the last a me, *milady*," Alaric taunted.

Isabella put her head in her hands, unable to bear the tension and hostility for a moment longer. She heard the thump of footsteps descending the stairs, then the spark as a flame caught against kindling in the grate. Cautiously, she looked through a crack in her fingers as Siegfried built up the fire, sitting back on his haunches until satisfied.

"There we are," he said.

The flames flickered merrily with the promise of warmth and comfort. Isabella sniffed and shuffled closer to the blaze.

"Thank you," she said shakily.

Siegfried regarded her steadily. "Neither Hamish nor I ever wanted ye to sit and freeze."

Her fingers were white with cold and red with blood. What had she been hoping to achieve by hiding out in a chilled bedchamber? Isabella could hardly remember. These last days had become a blur. Her stomach rumbled and she recalled that on her last foray to the kitchens, she had encountered Siegfried sitting calmly in the feasting hall.

"Or starve," he added.

She inclined her head. "I would be grateful for something small to eat." She abandoned any attempt at superiority, knowing she had naught to gain by it.

"I shall fetch something for ye."

When the old warrior had left the room, Isabella allowed her hot tears to slide down her face.

If Hamish had not arrived when he did—

Nay, she would not allow herself to think such thoughts. Alaric was bound behind a locked door. He could not hurt her, even though his parting threat still rang in her ears.

Isabella linked her fingers together and took several deep breaths. She must get a tighter control of her emotions, else both Siegfried and Hamish would see her with puffy eyes and a running nose.

They had almost seen far worse.

She should not have spoken so carelessly downstairs. Sometimes it was wise to show power and strength; but sometimes humility was a better friend.

She fished in her pocket for a handkerchief and dabbed at her eyes, careful to avoid her injury, which throbbed with pain.

It seemed she had no further choice but to put her trust in Hamish.

CHAPTER NINE

HAMISH FOUND THE bakehouse easily enough. 'Twas a four-square building with stone walls and a heavy oak door which locked from the outside with an iron key. The floor was earth, but the interior was dry.

He pushed Alaric inside, deaf to his threats and protests, and turned the key. Only then did he allow his emotions to surface.

God's blood, Alaric had been within moments of inflicting grievous harm to the lady. Hamish did not wish to ruminate on what form that harm might have taken. It was enough that he had seen the blood on Isabella's face, and Alaric's hands on the neckline of her gown.

Such a swell of rage overtook him that he swung his fist into the stone wall of the bakehouse, taking grim satisfaction in the sharp pain as his knuckles slammed against the granite. Perhaps aware of the blow, Alaric began to shout once again from inside.

"Silence," Hamish roared, all dignity abandoned. "Unless ye want my blade against yer throat."

That quieted the prisoner, although Hamish's blood still pounded in his ears.

I would ne'er forgive myself if harm came to Isabella de Neville.

He put his back to the wall and leaned his weight against it, gazing out across the white fields that glinted silver in the last of the day's light. His breath plumed ahead of him, hanging in the cold air like some kind of ethereal spirit.

His failure to protect Brianne had led to her death.

His failure to protect Elena had led to her being taken captive.

And now I have failed to protect Isabella.

Not failed, he corrected himself. Forsooth, her attacker was behind this locked door. But he had come dangerously close to failure.

For certs, he had not been vigilant enough.

The memory of Isabella's anguished blue eyes caused a pain to lodge somewhere under his ribs. He would give any amount of coin to never see such an expression on her beautiful face again. He wanted only to keep her safe.

Hamish dragged a hand through his unkempt hair and forced himself to acknowledge the truth of the matter.

I am falling for the lady.

He could not remember feeling this way about anyone. Certainly not Belinda, the sweet-natured clanswoman he had reached an understanding with in those long-gone, carefree days before Uncle Donald's betrayal. Hamish and Belinda would have wed, were it not for the family feud that had splintered the peace of Greenock. Instead, Belinda and her sisters had fled to the islands. And Hamish could not blame them for it.

But were it Isabella that had run off in the night, he would have likely run after her.

He inspected his aching knuckles, unsurprised to find them dripping with blood.

"Ye are a fool, Hamish McIvor."

He spoke the words loudly into the darkening sky, but his only response was the distant hooting of an owl. Behind the stone walls of the bakehouse, Alaric had grown quiet. Mayhap he was planning an escape. For certain, he would be plotting revenge. But for now, he was contained and could cause no further harm to anyone.

The problem of what to do with Alaric could wait for the morn. With a deep sigh, Hamish began walking back toward the house. He was now so accustomed to feeling his way across the ice that he hardly noticed his feet sliding across the cobbles. Nor the numbing cold that had laid claim to his extremities. It was only when he entered the feasting hall and stood before the fire there, that he began to tremble.

"Ye need ter drink this." Siegfried appeared beside him and thrust a finely-wrought goblet into his hand. "I warmed some wine for the lady."

The wine was fragrant with spices. Hamish did not protest, but drank deeply, twitching as feeling returned to his hands and feet.

"This cold will defeat us all, faster than any enemy," declared Siegfried.

"It will nay last much longer," Hamish replied with more confidence than he felt. Then he remembered his resolution to speak only the truth. "At least, that is what I tell myself." He threw his comrade a small smile.

"The lady says ye have no plan. And that ye shall have to kill her afore she will work with ye."

"I will ne'er harm her." Hamish fixed his gaze into the red and orange flames which burned with the same intensity as his newly acknowledged feelings for Isabella.

"That is what I told her." Siegfried folded his arms beneath the folds of his faded cloak. "Which is when Alaric decided to take matters into his own hands."

"I see." Hamish had wondered what first sparked the incident. Though with a man like Alaric, any small thing might do it. He turned to his father's loyal friend. "Ye were right about him. I shouldna brought him here."

"It gives me no pleasure." Siegfried lifted his face to the smoke-blackened rafters as if seeking guidance from above. "But Alaric was also right. We do need a plan, Hamish. We canna stay here indefinitely. If the lady willna work with ye, we need to move on."

"I know it." Hamish drained the goblet and placed it down on a low side table. The warmth of the fire, the comfort of the wine, and the steadiness of Siegfried had all combined to make him sleepy and slow. He would like to sit in this overstuffed chair, drink more wine and talk long into the night with his old ally.

Nay, if he were being truthful, he would like to talk long into the night with Isabella.

As if conscious of his thoughts, Siegfried said, "I laid her fire, as ye asked. And she ate some bread and cheese. I was about to take up water to clean her wound when I heard ye come in."

"Ye are a good friend." Hamish clapped him on the shoulder. "I ken ye didna wish for any of this."

"No more did ye," Siegfried interjected. "We all must live the lives we are given."

"And none of us know what the Good Lord has in store fer us," Hamish finished for him. They both smiled into the fire, remembering how Hamish's mother would offer such words of comfort to her children and men-at-arms alike.

"What will ye do?" Siegfried asked softly.

"I shall go ter her. Tend ter her wound." Hamish shrugged. "I shall make one final bid for her aid. If she refuses me again, then we must leave this place."

"Without her?" Siegfried's bushy eyebrows inched up his lined forehead.

"Aye." Hamish inclined his head toward the shuttered windows. "As soon as the thaw comes, that is. Until then, we must muddle along as best we can."

"And Alaric."

Hamish laughed and grasped the man's arm. "I pray, friend, dinna ask for more of me right now. I dinna have the answers ye seek."

"The answers will reveal themselves," Siegfried prophesied.

"Aye. Things are always brighter come the morn," Hamish quoted another of his mother's favorite sayings.

Siegfried nodded toward the back of the hall. "There is a pitcher of water and some linen cloths back there."

"Thank ye."

What Hamish wanted more than anything was a warm bath. Failing that, a comb for his tangled hair and the time for a shave. It seemed many moons since he rose that morn. He glanced down at his crumpled tunic and wondered if any suitor had ever appeared before Isabella de Neville in such disarray. At least the snow kept his boots free of dust and his breeches free of mud.

In any case, he was not appearing before the lady as a suitor. His new alliance with truth-telling did not extend to making a damn fool of himself. But he knew that the strange push-and-pull conversational games that he and Isabella had been engaged in ever since they arrived here must now come to an end.

This is the end of the line.

He could no longer issue threats and expect them to be believed. If he could not enlist Isabella's support, he must count his losses and leave Ember Hall without her.

Hamish shook his head as he wearily climbed the stairs. What that meant for Elena, he could not allow himself to consider.

Then he paused at the entrance to her chamber, brought up short by the sight of the fallen door. He had been determined to enter whether she gave her blessing or not, but the fact that she had no choice in the matter made him uncomfortable. He raised his eyes beyond the door, to see that Siegfried had indeed set a fire. The flames licked around a bank of logs, smoking only slightly. Isabella was sitting on the hearth rug, her elbows on her knees and her head in her hands.

Her eyes were closed, although surely the lady could not sleep in such an unstable position?

Still, his heart began to beat faster at the sight of her lovely face in repose. The usual lines of watchfulness were smoothed away, giving her a look of youth and innocence.

How old is she, wondered Hamish.

Younger than he, he would wager.

She was so poised, so alert, so quick-thinking, that she oft gave the impression of having lived through many summers.

So distrusting of men, his inner voice added. *With a wisdom that speaks of experience.*

Hamish realized with a jolt that Isabella had opened her eyes and was looking straight at him. He offered a short bow.

"My lady."

She winced. "Must we attend to such formalities? I have not the energy to leap to my feet and curtsy."

His lips twitched. "On this occasion, we may put them to one side." He stepped over the door and placed the pitcher of warmed water on the nightstand. Candles flickered from sconces around the chamber; their warm glow of light reflected in the looking glass.

Were it not for the broken door and splattering of blood on the wooden floor, this could be a heartwarming domestic scene.

Hamish cleared his throat. "I have come to tend to yer wound."

Isabella's eyes slid from his. "'Tis kind of you to bring water, but I can see to myself well enough."

Hamish had cleaned many a wound in the aftermath of battle, and he was well-accustomed to the self-reliance that made usually sensible men shun the ministrations of those looking to help them. He stepped closer and squatted beside her, placing firm fingers on her chin and tilting her head so he could better examine the cut on her cheek.

"'Tis deep," he remarked.

Isabella gulped. "I do not understand it. He only hit me."

"*Only* hit you?" The remnants of his earlier rage still rippled through his voice. Her breath caught and Hamish forced himself to simmer down. He released her chin and stretched out his long legs upon the hearth rug, affecting nonchalance when in truth, every inch of him bristled with awareness of her proximity.

Another truth he would be keeping to himself.

Isabella folded her hands in her lap. "I mean, how did he break the skin? There is so much blood." She looked askance at the smeared stains on the floor. They tracked a path along the grooved floorboards from under the bed to where she now sat.

Hamish grimaced, keeping his surging temper under wraps. "He wears a ring." He indicated his right hand.

"Ah." Understanding dawned across her delicate features.

"He will not hurt ye again. I will make sure of it."

She did not ask how he would do this. And he was grateful, for he had no proper explanation. All he knew was that he would go to his grave protecting this woman. How he longed to put an arm about her shoulders and coax her head onto his chest. He could inhale the citrusy fragrance of her golden hair and all would be well in his world.

Hamish rose abruptly to his feet and fetched over the pitcher. "Dinna move," he instructed her. "I will be as quick as I can."

He dropped to his knees, dampened a linen cloth and dabbed gently at the wound, cleaning away the blood that had encrusted on her cheek. Isabella closed her eyes, so he had full view of her curling eyelashes and porcelain skin. His gaze lowered to her slender neck, but he could not allow himself to go further; not after the liberties that Alaric had wreaked upon her.

His hand shook and he told himself to concentrate on the task at hand, rinsing the cloth and applying minimal pressure until the cut was finally cleaned.

Hamish prayed it would not leave a scar. He could not bear for Isabella's pure beauty to be marred by his neglect of her safety.

He sank down onto his knees and dropped the cloth into the pitcher. "I am finished."

Still, she did not open her eyes. "Thank you, Hamish."

"Are you in pain?" The thought troubled him.

"Only a little," she replied hesitantly.

"Then why do ye not open yer eyes?" He wanted to look into their blue depths; to see the thoughts racing across her quick mind. Some said that the eyes were the window to the soul, and if that was the case, Isabella had shuttered her soul away from him.

She gave her head a little shake, her long hair rippling over her shoulders like a waterfall over rocks. "I cannot tell you."

Purely on impulse, Hamish gently placed his hand on top of hers. "Please."

Her breathing came faster, but she opened her eyes and he was immediately a prisoner of her transfixing gaze. "You will think me touched in the head."

He could not help it. He reached out and touched her face, his hand slipping into her golden tresses. She leaned into his palm and he closed his eyes, unable to countenance his good fortune.

"Stay like that," she whispered. "'Tis easier to speak if you are not looking at me."

With his eyes closed, Hamish was near defenseless. She could reach for his sword or strike him over the head without his foreknowledge. But somehow, he trusted her.

"Speak then," he whispered back.

She leaned closer, so her clean citrus scent almost overwhelmed him. "I was enjoying having you near me. I wanted to prolong it."

Shivers of anticipation ran down his spine. "I was enjoying it, too."

He should say something more profound. Words had always come easily to him, but now he floundered for them. He tried again. "I always enjoy being with ye, Isabella."

He smelled smoke from the fire and heard the raggedness of her breathing. He dared not open his eyes lest he scare away whatever this magical thing was that was happening between them.

He felt the moment she moved away and severed the connection between them. Full of regret, he opened his eyes to find her staring blankly into the flames.

He sensed her next words before she said them. "You enjoy threatening me?"

"Nay. Never that." His knees ached, but not more than his knuckles. Hamish swung his legs from under him and tentatively stretched them out. Now he was more on a level with Isabella.

Now, he fancied, they might have the honest conversation he

had planned.

She pursed her lips, not knowing how much he wanted to kiss them. "Then why?"

"Because I am a fool." He answered quickly. "I was a fool. I thought to scare ye into submission. In part because I was frightened for ye. If ye ran from here, ye might find yerself in worse danger. But also because I wanted yer help."

"To reclaim your lands," she said flatly.

"Is that not a good reason?" he demanded, a flair of temper taking precedence over finer thought. "Greenock Castle has been in my family fer hundreds of years. The lands are the lands of my forefathers. The farmers that toil those lands look to me fer safekeeping." He opened his arms. "Ye speak as if I shouldna fight to reclaim my home."

"I do not think that." She massaged her temples and pushed back her hair, as if deciding what she did think. "I can guess how I would feel if some imposter laid claim to my family estate of Wolvesley."

"Aye." He nodded firmly. "Ye would want yer family to take it back." He propped himself back on his elbows, but Isabella's silence made him look at her. "Well?"

"Yes." She sighed. "I suppose."

"Ye suppose?" Bewilderment chased away his temper.

Isabella met his gaze. "'Tis just that I cannot imagine any army strong enough to overpower us." She shrugged.

Hamish sat up. "'Tis a strong failing of mine that I allowed yer English King to conquer Scotland," he said sarcastically.

She hugged her knees and looked into the fire. Shadows flickered at the far corners of the wall, like dark spirits threatening to descend.

Hamish scowled at his feverish imagination. Then he scowled again, for allowing this ignorant English woman such power over him.

It is time to leave this place.

And this woman.

"'Tis a terrible thing that has happened in Scotland," she said, stopping him as he was about to rise up from the rug. "Especially when we had reached an agreement of peace. My family celebrated that peace."

He nodded, unable to articulate a response.

Isabella gave him a quick, assessing glance. "I have led a cosseted life, I know it. But that does not mean that I have never known hardship or pain. Or that I have ne'er longed for something I simply cannot have." She balled her crumpled gown in her slender hands. "Something that is not meant for me."

Hamish noticed the break in her voice but was still too riled to offer comfort.

"What I am trying to say is this." She took a breath. "Are people not more important than property?"

He was caught by surprise. "I believe so, aye."

"And any attempt to reclaim your lands will lead to lives being lost."

"I cannot deny it."

She nodded slowly, as if her point was proven. "Well then."

He was not inclined to debate the ethics of war with a woman who had never stepped onto a battlefield. But he was not made so stupid with residual anger that he could not seize the opening she had unwittingly handed to him.

"My family has always been the most important thing to me. My mother, my father, my two sisters." He paused. "They are all gone now." He spoke on, over her sharp intake of breath. "All dead, apart from my younger sister, Elena." Grief swiped him with sharp claws, but he pushed it away. "Elena has been taken prisoner by yer Lord Gaunt."

There, he had said it.

Isabella's big blue eyes swung to his face. "Gaunt has taken your sister captive?"

He nodded.

"As you have taken me captive?"

He shook his head. "I doubt he has built her a fire or bathed any wounds she has."

Please God, let her not be injured or afraid.

Isabella considered this. "He is not a kind man," she agreed. "Nor is he *my* Lord Gaunt." She twisted her fingers together. "I do not even like the man."

"Ye are about to wed him," he pointed out, dryly.

She sighed deeply, her eyes unreadable. "If I marry him, I may be able to set your sister free."

Nay, that was not what he wanted. Though the idea had sound logic behind it. Hamish scratched at his growth of beard. He had yearned for the lady's help, and she had offered it, freely, as soon as she heard of his sister's plight.

But the notion of her marrying Lord Gaunt made him itch with anger all over again.

"I canna ask ye to wed such a man for my sake," he said carefully. "I had hoped we might find another way forward."

"You want to involve my brother, Tristan."

In her refined English voice, the idea sounded preposterous. But Hamish had come too far to give up now.

"Aye," he said simply.

"He is a family man, with a wife and two children. Innocent children," she stressed.

"There are innocent children in Greenock whose lives are in the hands of Lord Gaunt." The shadows in the corners reared up again as a candle sputtered its last. "The livelihoods of their parents now depend on Gaunt and whether he proves generous or self-serving." He tried to keep his voice even. "On whether he is knowledgeable with the land and the crops, or whether he allows the harvest to fail."

When Isabella said nothing, he pressed on. "What do ye think? Is he a generous man? Does he care to keep up with farming practices?"

She shook her head. "I cannot imagine it."

Hamish had said all he had to say. He got to his feet, feeling again the pain in his knuckles and the lingering regret of his own foolishness.

He had tried and failed. He would not persevere with false hope.

"I shall see yer door is properly mended come the morn," he said. "And we shall leave ye here just as soon as the thaw begins." He gestured toward the shuttered window.

Isabella also scrambled to her feet, a frown chasing across her brow. "You are leaving?"

"We shall return to Scotland, where we belong."

She shook her head. "No. I meant are you leaving me now?"

He could not allow himself to look at her. Instead, he busied himself with picking up the water pitcher. "I have seen with my own eyes that ye shall have no lasting injuries."

"And that is the only reason you came up here?" Her voice grew louder.

"I decided I would tell you the truth about my sister. So you knew I was no villain." He grimaced. "And to ask one last time for the help of your brother." Warm water slopped over his hand as he gestured too violently with the pitcher.

"But you do not stay to hear my answer?" Isabella raised her chin defiantly, daring him to look her in the eye.

As soon as he did so, he felt himself once again in her power.

"What is your answer?" he asked helplessly.

Candlelight haloed her golden hair. She was like a Goddess from the old religion which still had roots in the hills and valleys of the highlands.

"I will speak to my brother on your behalf."

Relief made him weak. He placed the pitcher on the nightstand before he dropped it.

"Thank ye," he began.

Isabella held up a hand to stop him. "I cannot promise his assistance."

"I understand."

Her eyes flashed. "And I ask for something from you in return."

"Anything." He meant it.

Isabella took a step closer and tilted her face up to his. "I want you to kiss me."

CHAPTER TEN

Perchance the blow to her head had muddled her thinking, but in that moment, Isabella felt she had never been more certain of anything in her life.

She was using what power she had, whilst she still had it.

Minutes earlier, sitting on the hearth rug with her eyes closed, it had occurred to her that she had never once been kissed by a young, vigorous and healthy man.

And never had she wanted such a kiss as much as she did now. There was something about the raw combination of roughness and sensitivity in Hamish that she found impossible to resist. It was in the wildness of his half-braided hair and the calm intelligence of his blue gaze; the hard muscle of his arms and shoulders, along with the compassion that oft showed in his voice.

But his voice held no compassion now. "You want me to kiss you?" he repeated.

At first, she thought him angry. Then she realized that it was desire that brought such a throaty edge to the question.

Desire which answered that same emotion thrumming inside her very core.

"Aye." She held his gaze unflinchingly.

"Is this a trick?" Uncertainty flickered in his blue eyes, but he wanted her. She had known it as soon as he put his hand over hers by the fire. His touch was gentle, but it still sent rivers of warmth surging up her arm.

She stepped closer, tilting her face so her breath mingled with his. "'Tis no trick. Does the notion of kissing me seem so strange?"

A pulse flickered in his strong jaw. Isabella resisted the urge to reach up and touch his stubbled chin. He was a bear of a man, who could overpower her in an instant.

"Ye must ken ye are a beautiful woman, Isabella. Ye must ken that I would willingly kiss ye." His gaze lowered to her lips, which she instinctively parted. But still he hesitated.

"I know naught of this, when I ask for something so small but you deny me," she breathed.

His eyes fluttered closed and for a moment she admired the upward sweep of his thick eyelashes, but the next moment his lips pressed against hers, and Isabella forgot all else. His mouth was soft and firm at the same time. His hands rested lightly on her waist and drew her closer, so her slight body came against his vast wall of muscle. Nerves jangled in her arms and legs, not with fear but with excitement.

And then he pulled away.

"One kiss," he whispered. "As requested."

But Isabella wanted more, like a child standing before a tray of cakes recently drawn from the oven. Why stop at one?

"'Twas a very small kiss," she whispered back.

His lips quivered. Those same lips that had recently been pressed against hers. "As you stipulated, my lady."

She shook her head. "I knew not what I asked."

"Ah." Hamish slowly returned his hands to her waist and very gently caressed her. "But now you know better?"

"A little better." She tipped back her head and smiled. Was she flirting? Was this wise? She hardly knew and certainly did not care. Her husband, bless his soul, had never ignited such fires inside her. Had never made her long for the feel of his hands upon her flesh.

Ye Gods. She wanted so much more than just a kiss from

Hamish.

As if conscious of her thoughts, he ran his fingers lightly along her spine so she arched her back with pleasure. His hand travelled back down again and settled about her hips. His blue eyes gazed into hers, seemingly looking straight into her soul.

"Tell me what it is you do want," he said throatily.

She had no words for what she wanted. And if she found them, no doubt they would make her blush. Instead, Isabella rose onto her tiptoes and brushed her lips against his. Hamish stood unmoving, allowing her kiss but not responding to it. Emboldened, she linked her hands about his neck and kissed him again, full on the mouth.

With a groan of longing, he crushed her toward him, slanting his lips over hers to deepen what she had so willingly started. When his tongue touched hers, she gasped at the physical intimacy of it. And at the jolt of desire that shot through her core. His hands stroked her face and hair, careful always to avoid the painful cut on her cheek, and in turn, her hands began to explore his muscular chest, tentatively travelling beneath the heavy wool of his cloak. When she reached his waist, he caught her hands in his.

"Isabella," he said. He was breathing hard, and his eyes had grown dark with passion.

She understood his meaning. They should stop now, while it was still safe.

But she didn't want safe.

All her married life, relations between herself and her husband had been safe and polite.

And woefully unsatisfactory.

Now she wanted excitement and the unknown.

She wanted Hamish.

Is he about to deny me?

For as long as Isabella could remember, men had followed her with their gaze, wanting her, desiring her. She had been a worthy prize, bestowed upon the man with the deepest coin chests. But now, she finally understood what people meant when they spoke of passion. She was more than a doll with a pretty face, dressed in fine silk.

She was a woman.

She stood in the circle of his arms and met his gaze, as her breathing slowed to match the pace of his.

"Ye dinna want this. Come the morn, ye will regret it," he rasped.

"How do you claim to know the workings of my mind?"

She wondered if she should push her hands beneath his shirt and feel the warmth of his flesh. It would take but a moment. And she dared to believe there may come a point where Hamish no longer exerted such willful control of his actions.

Should I take him to that point?

Isabella trembled with growing desire and mounting indecision.

"I dinna claim ter know e'en the workings of my *own* mind where ye are concerned," Hamish said simply. "Ye take me from human compassion to frustration and back again, all in the space of a dunnock's song."

She reached up and touched those russet-colored curls that had her so transfixed. His hair was coarser than hers, but just as thick. She ran her fingers through it and fancied she caught the scent of fresh air and moorland.

"Is that all?" she asked. She was no longer flirting. She simply wanted to know.

"Nay, 'tis not all." His eyes darkened again, and a frisson of excitement travelled through her. "I have wanted ye from the first moment I saw ye, Lady Isabella."

As if they had minds of their own, her hands ran down his arms, tracing the smooth curves of muscle. His body was so different to hers; large and broad and strong. The wildest wind could not topple him.

Whereas Isabella was like a Will-o'-the-wisp, faltering this way and that, always at the whim and mercy of happenstance.

She sagged in his arms and rested her forehead against his chest. He cradled her head in his large hands.

"I didna mean to upset ye," he whispered.

She wrapped her arms around his waist, anchoring herself to his warmth and solidity. "I don't know why I am upset."

The adrenaline and excitement that had chased around her body with such fervor had drained away, leaving her limp.

"I shouldna have embraced ye so."

Sheltered in his arms, she shook her head, her face still pressed against the soft folds of his shirt. "I am no pure maid, Hamish. I am a woman of nigh on thirty summers. A widow. I knew well enough what I was doing when I asked you to kiss me."

He gave a low chuckle. "I am mighty glad ter hear it."

His laughter stirred the remnants of desire and she shifted a little, placing her palms against the angular planes of his shoulders. "'Tis just the events of the day. So much has happened."

So much is happening.

"I am no longer yer captor, Isabella. Ye ken so, aye? All of that is behind us."

She reached up to touch his face, enjoying how he responded to the brush of her fingers against his stubbled cheek. She had never stood so close to such a force of raw, masculine energy. But neither had she ever felt so safe and protected in a man's embrace.

"We are allies," she said. "Friends perchance."

An unreadable expression passed through his eyes. "It would be my honor to be yer friend, Isabella. Even if parts of me might be longing for something more than friendship."

He pursed his lips and she smothered a smile. She could feel that part of him pressing against her hip. Desire flickered again inside her, like a pulse which thrummed slowly and steadily.

"Parts of me want more as well," she whispered.

"But we shouldna." His voice was uncertain. His hands moved in her hair. "Ye have suffered a blow to yer head. We have only just reached a truce between us."

She arched her back, deliberately pressing the softness of her curves into the unyielding hardness of his chest. "And it is so very cold."

"The kind of cold that addles a man's thinking," he agreed, stroking her spine.

"'Tis sensible, mayhap, to stay close together for warmth." She cocked an eyebrow and met his darkening gaze.

"Yer a wise woman, Isabella de Neville. I have always thought as much."

His hands moved slowly up her sides and brushed gently against her breasts. Isabella felt as if she had been set alight. She gasped and leaned into his touch until he lowered his lips to her collarbone and nibbled her gently. At that point, she lost both strength in her limbs and direction in her thoughts. There was no more planning or intention; only a delicious pleasure growing inside her as he kissed her neck and caressed her body. The golden glow of candlelight shimmered at the edge of her field of vision, so that Hamish appeared touched by the Divine. She was his, in a way she had never been anyone's before.

"I want to lay ye down on the bed," he said, his voice rough with desire.

"I want that, too."

He scooped her into his arms and laid her reverently atop the covers.

"Ye are the most beautiful woman I have ever seen."

She gripped his shoulders, holding him in place. "Is that all I am to you?"

A frown flickered at his brow. She felt the tremor of restraint rippling through him. "I dinna ken yer meaning."

Isabella gulped. Why was she asking such questions when she could simply close her eyes and submit to the wonderful sensations he had kindled within her?

But this is important.

"I have heard that phrase so oft it has ceased to have meaning to me." She tightened her hold of his shoulders, needing him to understand. "In all my years married, my husband rarely saw me as anything else."

Hamish lowered himself onto his forearms, bringing his long, lean body tantalizingly close. "Are ye asking me if I see ye as *more* than a beautiful woman?"

Her throat ached. "I am."

His breath fanned across her face as his eyes looked deep into hers. "I see all of ye, Isabella. I see yer courage, yer strength and yer love for yer family."

She was close to tears.

"I see yer intelligence," he continued. "Yer stubbornness. Yer pride."

"What's this?" Her eyes widened.

He dropped a light kiss onto her lips. "I begin to see ye have ne'er been worshipped the way ye should have been worshipped."

A buzzing sensation started in Isabella's ears as her eyes flickered closed. Hamish kissed a line across her jaw and down her neck while his hands moved gently across her body, caressing and stroking until she writhed with wanting more. She lifted her hips when he tugged at her skirts, and half sat up so he could draw the woolen gown over her head. Her shift was sheer and she guessed the candlelight showed him all the curves and valleys of her body, but she felt no embarrassment, only a burning, liquid desire.

Hamish hovered above her and she impatiently grasped at his shirt. She wanted to feel him against her, flesh next to flesh.

"Take it off," she whispered when he made no move to do so.

"Ye are certain 'tis what ye want?"

In answer, she reared up against him, sliding her palms beneath his shirt and encountering the warm planes of his flat belly. Hamish tugged off his shirt, and she wasted no time moving her hands to the next item of clothing she wished him to remove. When he was fully naked and holding her close, she knew a swell of contentment that was almost as deep as her desire.

This is where I am meant to be.

The log crackled in the gate as he stroked the length of her body, lingering in the places she wanted him most. This chamber, in which she had been so cold and lonely, was transformed into a place of golden warmth. Sparks flew before her eyes as he tugged down her shift and fastened his lips around the rosy nub of her breast. She entwined her fingers in his hair and gave herself over. She was molten when he gently removed that final garment and settled between her thighs.

"Isabella," he said.

She thought for a frenzied moment that he was about to delay. 'Twas a delay she could not countenance, for she could not bear to be apart from him any longer. But when she whimpered in protest, it quickly turned into a groan of appreciation as he entered her, and they became as one.

Never had she known anything like this.

Hamish moved slowly inside her, coaxing her into higher waves of pleasure which spiraled from her core and made every inch of her tingle and dance. She pressed her lips to his and wrapped her arms about his back, pulling him even closer, even deeper, until his hips ground against her and he called out that he could not hold on any longer.

But Isabella hardly heard his warning as her body had broken into shards and she was both breathless and senseless with the intensity of release. She floated serenely downwards, still bathing in a rosy glow of pleasure, as Hamish groaned deeply and sank against her.

They laid in a tangle of warm limbs. Isabella was not certain where her body ended and his began. No more did it matter. He rolled onto his side and gathered her against him, still breathing hard.

"I have wanted to do that since e'er I laid eyes on you. But ne'er did I think it would happen."

She opened her eyes, sensing his gaze upon her. The chamber had darkened, with several candles having sputtered their last and the logs in the fire burnt almost to ashes. She could make out the gleam of his blue eyes and the silvery outline of his broad shoulders.

Had she wanted the same?

Nay, but she had not known what it was to lay with a man she truly desired.

I am become a different person.

Hamish's hands stilled upon her. "Do ye regret it?"

"Nay." She kissed him on the lips to prove it. "But right now, I have no words to explain myself."

"Nor do ye need to." He settled himself on the pillows. "So long as ye are happy."

She rested her head on his chest and heard the rhythmic thud of his heart. A light, buoyant feeling rose in her breast.

"I am happy," she said.

It is true.

His hand stroked her hair. "Then rest. 'Tis late."

She lifted her head and met his gaze in the dim light. "Do you promise not to leave?"

"If ye want me to stay, I will stay." He paused. "I want to stay."

Isabella closed her eyes, comforted by his hand stroking her hair and the regular rise and fall of his chest. She had never fallen asleep beside a man before.

But it was the easiest thing in the world.

CHAPTER ELEVEN

H E WOKE TO the subtle fragrance of lemons and for a moment, could not make sense of it. Then he opened his eyes to find his face pressed into Isabella's thick tresses of golden hair; they had slept curled up together, like lovers.

It was not too strong a word for the heady emotions that gripped him whenever she was near.

Nor for what had passed between them last night, which was a sight more than the slaking of lust.

Hamish rolled onto his back and gazed up at the plastered ceiling. Nay, last night had been a meeting of souls.

An act of love.

Yer touched in the head, man, he told himself, gruffly.

But his feelings for Isabella de Neville were as real as the russet hairs on his brawny forearm.

He turned his head to see that the lady was still sleeping deeply, dark blonde eyelashes fluttering against her pale cheek. Perchance she dreamed.

Does she dream of me?

Hamish reprimanded himself. 'Twas more likely the lady dreamed of the fine carriage that would take her back to the life she knew; one of liveried servants and silk dresses. He must not make the mistake of hankering after something that was not meant for him.

His heart grew leaden, but Hamish was a realist, not a

dreamer. Two years living in a damp cave would do that to a man.

He must hold onto what he knew to be true. Isabella had promised to speak to her brother on his behalf. And Tristan de Neville not only supported the Scots, he also had influence with the King. The man was a worthy ally.

Today dawned with more hope than yesterday. Hamish would not ask for more than that.

But now he twitched with impatience to be up and about. Alaric was locked in the bakehouse, which was hardly a long-term solution. There were the horses to tend to and water to fetch. Please God, might the well have thawed?

Hamish stretched his legs beneath the rugs, moving slowly and carefully so as not to disturb Isabella. He baulked at leaving her, but could not be idle when so much needed to be done. He dressed quickly, guided by the milky morning light filtering in from the shutters. His clothes were stiff and cold, for the fire had all but died and the temperature was still below freezing. His breath plumed in front of him as he crossed to the log-basket and added fuel to the fading embers in the grate. When Isabella awoke, the room would be warmer.

With a last, lingering look at the sleeping beauty on the bed, Hamish stepped over the broken door and out into the long gallery. Mentally, he added mending the door to his long list of jobs.

Isabella deserved her privacy.

He picked up his pace, heading toward the stairs and blowing on his bruised knuckles for warmth. His cloak billowed behind him as he strode across the wooden floor and Hamish felt renewed with purpose for the first time since King Edward's troops had successfully seized Greenock Castle.

But he would not darken this bright new day by dwelling on that particular memory.

He tripped down the wide staircase and barreled into the feasting hall, where he encountered Siegfried standing before an uncertain fire.

"Good morn," he hailed his old ally.

But when he turned around, Siegfried's face was grim. "Alaric has escaped," he announced, by way of a greeting.

A cold feeling slid into Hamish's belly. He halted at the far side of the feasting hall, as if he might yet run after the young warrior. "When?"

"I dinna ken for certain." Siegfried shrugged beneath the heavy folds of his cloak. "I took him some food at first light but found the door wide open."

Hanish cursed loudly, glad that Isabella was out of earshot. "The bakehouse must not have been secure." He rubbed at his forehead, thinking hard. "I should have checked it more thoroughly."

"Mayhap. But what's done is done." The lines of worry etched across Siegfried's face belied his apparent calm.

Hamish's joviality had entirely drained away. He shook his head. "He was an angry man."

Alaric's threat hummed in his ears. *"I'll kill ye both,"* he'd said to Hamish and Siegfried. But worse was his warning to Isabella.

Hamish could not bear to think of it.

"We must find him." He put a hand to the hilt of his sword, reassured by its presence. Thank all that was holy that he'd had the foresight to divest Alaric of his weapon last night. "Though first we must check the sleeping barn." He thought of the stash of knives and blades that they had brought with them from across the border.

Siegfried nodded toward the sideboard. "I already recovered our weapons."

An untidy pile of metal shone brightly in the growing light of the fire. Hamish checked them over, relieved to find all were present. "Yer a great man, Siegfried."

His Seneschal inclined his head. "'Twas the first place I went when I discovered him gone."

Hamish folded his arms beneath his cloak, warming his hands

and ordering his thoughts. "His horse?"

"Still in the stables."

"So he is on foot and unarmed." Hamish paced before the fire, which had now taken hold and was burning brightly. He reflected that this high stone fireplace had borne witness to much of this soul-searching since they arrived at Ember Hall.

Siegfried stepped nimbly out of his way. "And the weather is set to stay foul for another day at least."

Hamish did not waste time asking Siegfried how he knew this. The man was born and raised in the highlands and could read the signs of nature better than anyone.

"Then the odds are against young Alaric." He tried to take comfort from this, but could not forget the menace of the warrior's final warning. "But we must still take heed."

"He has taken against the Lady Isabella." Siegfried put into words what Hamish struggled to articulate.

Words which turned his chill of foreboding into ice.

"Exactly so," he managed.

Siegfried lifted his greying head and fixed Hamish with an unflinching stare. "And what of the Lady Isabella herself?"

Hamish turned away so that Siegfried could not read the truth in his eyes. The question made him feel like a green youth. He could only answer by ignoring the layers of meaning Siegfried had laced into it.

"She is sleeping."

He walked briskly to the nearby shutters and opened them enough to allow a shaft of winter sunlight into the hall. *This room needs light and warmth and gaiety*, he thought. *All we have brought in is darkness and doubt.*

"Will she help us?" Siegfried demanded. "Or are we to leave?"

"Both." Hamish put his hands on his hips and swiveled back around to face his ally. Dust motes danced in the sunlight. With a swell of unease, he noticed how the feasting hall stretched about them, vast and empty. Some months prior, he had been Laird of Greenock and commanded an army. Men-at-arms, many of whom he had trained himself, had awaited his every command. Until that dreadful day when he commanded them to leave him.

Now, he had but one loyal follower from his homelands.

"The lady will speak to her brother. He has influence with the King." At Siegfried's look of skepticism, Hamish opened his arms. "He is the best chance we have."

The only chance we have.

Siegfried considered this. "You will go with her to Wolvesley Castle?"

"Ye and I both will." Hamish was firm. "We will take a proper leave of this place, just as soon as the thaw sets in." He knew that Siegfried would sooner return to Scotland. Neither of them had planned to spend so long south of the border. But with a vengeful Alaric on the loose and no telling how long negotiations in Wolvesley would take, Hamish did not wish to risk anyone's safety.

Siegfried stood still, his face impassive, but Hamish knew by his silence that the older man was thinking hard.

"Ye ken that I will serve ye until my dying day?" he said.

Hamish swallowed his instinctive qualms. "Ye have said it so oft 'tis all but engraved across my mind." He softened his words with a smile. "And right grateful I am."

"I dinna wish to travel to Wolvesley," Siegfried said simply. "I canna explain the misgivings I have. But I ken my place is in the highlands."

"As is mine." Hamish fought to keep his voice even.

"Aye, ye are the right and proper Laird of Greenock. I will go to my grave swearing it. But I dinna wish for that grave to be on English soil. I canna travel south from here."

Hamish reeled. Never before had Siegfried shown fear such as this.

Aye. *Fear.*

He baulked at labelling it cowardice.

To give himself time, he walked to the window at the other side of the fireplace and slowly opened the shutters until he was obliged to shield his eyes from the incoming burst of winter sunlight.

Sunlight which illuminated the weary slope of Siegfried's shoulders and the shadows around his eyes. In Hamish's mind's eye, Siegfried was a mighty warrior, with a steady stance and a sword-arm made of steel. But in this vision, Hamish was but a wee lad, and Siegfried some twenty summers younger than in real life.

He sighed, forcing himself to let go of bitterness and regret. "I willna ask aught of ye that ye dinna give willingly."

"I will return to the highlands and seek out those loyal to the McIvor clan in the valleys and villages around Greenock."

Hamish could not hide his surprise. He pursed his lips. "Ye expect me to return, aye?"

Siegfried strode over and clasped his arm. "I dinna expect it. I am counting upon it."

Then he does not doubt me.

Hamish looked beyond his friend to the shadowy hall beyond, hoping for a glimpse of chestnut curls and Brianne's knowing smile. But the room stayed defiantly empty.

"Ye are yer father's son," Siegfried continued. "The same man that led us to victory against the traitor, Donald. Even though those odds were stacked against ye."

It was the battle he never allowed himself to relive. When he had to choose between fighting beside his father or his sister. His father was an old man by then, plagued by weakness after two years residing in a cave. His sister was young and strong; one of their most valiant warriors.

Brianne had fallen at the last. Their father had survived the battle, but died of a fever some months later, soon followed by their mother.

Hamish and Elena were all that remained of the once mighty McIvor clan.

Hamish brought himself back from the past and clasped Siegfried's arm in return. For a moment they stood together, bonded and bathed in sunlight. Hamish said, "We will raise a toast together, ye and I, in the old keep at Greenock."

"Looking out over yer mother's gardens," Siegfried nodded. "We will, lad." His expression tightened as he dropped his arm. "So long as ye dinna allow yerself to be distracted."

"Distracted?" Hamish was taken aback, but he stayed calm and raised his eyebrows enquiringly. "How so?"

"I am speaking outta turn. I ken so. But I believe ye have taken a liking to the Lady." Siegfried jerked his head toward the upper floor. "Mayhap more than a liking, aye?"

Hamish's ready denial died on his lips.

Why should I lie?

"'Tis nay distraction, Siegfried. We need the Lady's help."

"But ye dinna need to share her bed." Siegfried spoke plainly. "And ye dinna need to invite her into yer heart."

Siegfried flattened his palm against Hamish's chest, leaving the younger man too surprised to respond.

Are my feelings for her so obvious?

He did not query how Siegfried had discerned the events of last night. His old ally knew Hamish to be a man of flesh and blood.

But the rest...

"Ye speak of love, Siegfried," he said, once he could manage it. "'Tis a bold claim."

"I speak as I find." The Seneschal poked at the fire and avoided looking in his direction.

"I am not so foolish as to believe I have aught to offer the likes of Isabella de Neville."

And nor do I wish to examine this further.

Hamish pulled his cloak over his shoulders and traced the grooves in the floor with his boot.

"Ye are the Laird of Greenock." Siegfried laid down the poker and stood up slowly, rubbing at his lower back and wincing.

Hamish's mind raced. He needed to persuade himself as much as Siegfried that he was not headed down this particular path.

"Greenock is a cold and draughty keep e'en in high summer. Made more so, I'll wager, after the last siege." Hamish attempted a smile, closing his mind to vivid memories of loud and ruinous warfare on the battlements. "And if I return to Greenock as Laird, 'twill be thanks to the Lady's brother." He rubbed his hands together as if that settled the matter. "Ye do ken, Siegfried, how I hate to be in anyone's debt?"

Siegfried nodded, but still looked unconvinced.

"Ye dinna have to worry," Hamish said bleakly. "I willna go near the Lady again. Except to escort her to Wolvesley."

"In a right and proper fashion?" Siegfried folded his arms.

"Of course." Hamish felt the distant walls of the hall beginning to close in on him. There was too much for him to digest and try to make sense of. He stood tall with assumed purpose. "Let us discuss this later, Siegfried. I must tend to the horses. Luar is whinnying fer me."

It was a lie.

But 'twas rooted in fact. Luar was a creature of routine, and Hamish usually filled her bucket with oats at sunrise. Perchance she was whinnying and the stone walls were too thick for him to hear her.

Siegfried looked at him askance. "Ye have not yet broken yer fast."

"I am not hungry." The truth, at last. "Ye should eat something though, my friend. Take yer time. I can see to everything outside."

Outside, where the air was fresh and clean and he could breathe more easily.

Hamish strode out of the front door and did not look back.

CHAPTER TWELVE

WHERE IS HE?

Isabella knew a wave of keen disappointment when she woke and discovered herself alone.

The bed beside her was still warm, where Hamish had lain. She herself was still warm from the imprint of his body pressed against hers. But the highlander had gone.

She lay back on the pillows and allowed a swell of frustration to ripple through her. Last night had been magical. There was no other word to describe it. Finally, she knew the thrill of a man's touch. Her sisters had not been exaggerating all these years.

But she had hoped for more kisses this morn.

Her eyes traveled over to the bright shafts of sunlight filtering through the shutters.

Is it still morn?

After a lifetime of troubled sleep, in these last hours, she had slept deeper than a babe. No demons woke her, no fits of fear seized her. Hamish had been the balm she needed to soothe her turbulent mind.

But did that mean she had slept too long?

Isabella sat up in a tangle of covers, perplexed to find the chamber pleasantly warm. Then she saw the fire flickering in the grate, and realized that Hamish must have built it up for her before he left.

'Twas kind and practical, just like him.

Happy again, she stretched her arms above her head and rotated her head. What bliss to not be cramped with cold and doubt.

I will go and find him.

She dressed quickly—and daringly—in a woolen tunic and braccae which she found in Esme's closet. 'Twas a far cry from the taffeta gowns in shimmering silk which she wore in Westchester, but more fitting for the current climate and circumstance.

'Tis more important to be warm than elegant, Isabella told herself.

Besides, a mischievous voice spoke in her ear, Hamish has seen you dressed in nothing at all.

Heat rose to her cheeks, but she did not allow herself to feel any lingering guilt or shame. Last night, she had done what she *wanted* to do, rather than what she knew she *ought* to do. 'Twas the first time in her life that she had followed her impulses—or her heart—rather than the dictates of others. And it had brought her a deeper pleasure than she'd known was possible.

Whatever happened next, she did not intend to regret her decision.

She flinched at the chill of the long gallery after the warmth of her bedchamber. Stepping over the fallen door reminded her of Alaric, and the paralyzing terror that had imprisoned her in the moments before Hamish appeared.

Together, she and Hamish had turned fear into joy.

It was strange to walk across the long gallery without the swish of skirts about her calves. Strange, but also liberating. The woolen braccae were snug, not allowing the merest hint of a draught.

Mayhap I will dress this way more often.

As soon as the thought occurred to her, she pushed it away, lest her imaginings take her to the cold stare of Lord Gaunt. 'Twas unsettling to think of the future and what it may or may not hold. Better to stay rooted in the present. She turned the corner in the feasting hall and stopped in surprise.

Siegfried was sitting before the fire, fast asleep and snoring lightly.

Isabella swallowed a giggle and crept past him. Hamish must be outside, she realized. There was no telling when he might return.

No matter, I will look for him.

Galvanized into action, Isabella wandered toward the kitchen; a place she had only ever entered under the cover of darkness, fearful of every creaking floorboard in those long-since nights when she tried to evade Hamish's notice. It was pleasing to see the room flooded with light. Isabella rummaged in the well-stocked larder until she found a bucket of red apples, most likely picked from the orchard. She bit into one and closed her eyes, enjoying the sweet flavor flooding her mouth. Her eyes landed upon a number of cloaks hung by the back door and she smiled with relief.

This was what she sought.

Her own traveling cloak brought back painful memories of the day she had left Westchester. Besides, it had never been fashioned to withstand such freezing temperatures as these. She ran her hands over the heavy, coarse wool of the dark and muted cloaks hanging before her, and nodded with satisfaction. These would do very well, so long as she could find one which didn't swamp her small frame.

Finally attired in a cloak which must once have belonged to Esme, Isabella pushed open the back door and stepped out into the morning sunlight.

Warmth!

Or at least, the appearance of it.

The sun's rays had strength and purpose, and the brightness was almost too much to bear. Isabella blinked at the dazzling sunlight and its reflection in the ice which still covered swathes of the courtyard, where water had once settled. Icicles hung from the mullioned windows and snow lay thickly in the distant fields. Her breath plumed before her, but if she tilted her face toward the sun, she could believe the thaw was not far away.

Once the thaw came, they would ride to Wolvesley and she would ask for Tristan's help, as she had promised. But this was the future which she still did not wish to consider. Once they reached Wolvesley, questions would be asked about her betrothal to Gaunt.

Isabella would prefer to think of the present. Of the glorious expanse of sunshine on snow and the melodious singing coming from the barn.

She cocked her head and listened again, smiling when strains of the lilting song reached her. There was no doubt, it was Hamish.

A man motivated by love for his sister.

A man who could sing.

And a man who had made her body sing just hours earlier.

Rolling her eyes at her run of thoughts, she set off across the cobbles, picking her way around the most slippery patches of sheer ice. The singing grew louder as she neared the barn, though she did not recognize the tune. She was relieved to reach the half wooden door without incident. She leaned her weight upon it and caught her breath.

"How well do I love thee, how well do I love thee," sang Hanish.

Does he sing of me?

The eager question sprang to Isabella's mind before she could stop it.

Nay, she realized soon after. Hamish was singing of love for the glens and lochs of his native Scotland.

She breathed in the scent of hay and horses, familiar from her childhood. Their mother had insisted that all her children learn how to ride and take care of horses from a young age.

Isabella stilled, her fingers gripping the rough wood of the door, uncaring of splinters.

Ye Gods, she had not spared a thought for her destrier since handing over the reins to Alaric on the day she'd arrived.

Her breath caught in her throat. The mare was willing and kind-natured. And Isabella had all but abandoned her.

Her mother would be rigid with disappointment.

Isabella pushed open the door and stepped into the barn, blinking until her eyes adjusted to the gloom. Mayhap hearing her footsteps, Hamish ceased his singing. In the sudden silence, Isabella discerned a short row of horses, happily munching at their hay racks. The stalls were clean and well-swept. The small horse nearest to her turned liquid eyes in her direction, deemed her of little interest and returned to his hay.

Isabella stepped closer, discerning the chestnut legs of her destrier standing in the middle of the row. There were five horses in total; the small grey standing a little apart from the others. At the far end of the row stood a beautiful glossy-black beast with well-shaped legs and a blaze of white across her face.

This was the horse to which Hamish tended, a brush in each of his hands. He paused in his task, and eyed Isabella over the horse's withers.

"Have ye come here alone?" he asked abruptly.

Isabella had been hoping for a softer greeting. She tried not to worry about her shapeless clothing and undressed hair. "Siegfried is asleep," she offered, immediately regretting it. She didn't want to get the older man into trouble.

Hamish grimaced. He resumed his rhythmic grooming, although his eyes strayed toward her.

"Ye must take care, Isabella. Alaric has escaped."

She put a hand to her heart. "From the bakehouse?"

He nodded. "Aye. The door is clean off its hinges."

"'Tis my fault for suggesting it." She couldn't help glancing over her shoulder as if the cruel-eyed warrior might have followed her across the cobbles.

"'Tis not yer fault," he countered. "But I would prefer it if ye stayed inside with the door bolted."

A clutch of fear made her shiver. The golden light of the courtyard seemed a long way away. She shuffled her feet on the well-swept floor and nodded toward the gleaming flanks of her destrier.

"Thank you for taking care of her for me."

He nodded briefly. "She's proven useful in keeping Luar apart from that devil." He indicated a big bay-colored horse with a bad-tempered gaze. "Alaric's," he explained. "My Luar is particular about her stable mates."

Luar pressed her face into Hamish's chest and sighed, as if to agree. Hamish rubbed gently at her ears and patted her neck, talking so quietly that Isabella could not catch the words.

The man clearly loved his horse.

Her mother would approve, but Isabella felt her chest tightening with childish jealousy. Hamish showed easy affection for Luar, but none for the lady he had lain beside last night. The frisson of connection that had always existed between them had gone, like a puff of smoke from an extinguished fire.

Perchance I dreamed it.

Perchance it was no more than lust.

Isabella pushed away her disappointment. There was naught to be gained by standing in the shadows. She had not sunk so low that she would compete with a horse for a man's attention.

"I shall return to the hall," she said, "and bolt the door."

"Wait." Hamish paused, but did not move from Luar's side. "I should walk with ye."

The very idea made her anxious. Isabella waved her hand. "No need. There's a clear view from the barn door to the hall. I shall take my bearings before I step out."

"I'll watch ye then." His voice was full and almost apologetic.

He doesn't want to come near me, Isabella realized.

She lifted her chin. "As you wish."

Swallowing her pain, she crossed to the arched doorway and plunged out into the freezing air with no more than a cursory look right and left. As good as his word, Hamish came to stand at the opening, and she felt his eyes upon her as she made her way back to the hall. Agitation made her careless, and she slipped more than once on the treacherous cobbles, but thankfully she did not fall.

She could not have borne the embarrassment.

Once she reached the door, she pulled it open and stepped inside without a backward glance. She shot home the bolt and only then allowed herself to sink her head into her hands.

What now?

HAMISH STAYED OUTSIDE far longer than was necessary.

He saw to the horses, fetched ice and melted it over the brazier, fixed the door to the bakehouse and swept out what had been their sleeping quarters. Then he walked down to the outer wall, ascended the stone steps and scanned the white surroundings for any sign of Alaric.

He sighed with frustration; his breath misting the air in front of him.

Alaric had simply melted into the night. No footsteps showed in the frozen snow. No gate stood open to show which way he had headed. 'Twas as if he had been spirited away by the faerie folk. But Hamish recognized the actions of a man trained in stealth.

Would Alaric return?

The question that would no doubt keep him awake throughout the long night to come.

Shadows lengthened across the moors as the winter sun crept downward and a chill took hold of Hamish's very bones. He should go inside and sit by the fire. But that meant facing Isabella and the rush of emotion that robbed him of rational thought whenever he was near her.

She had visited him in the stables for mere minutes, but 'twas long enough for him to forget all the excellent reasons he should steer a course away from Isabella de Neville. Now he reminded himself of the difference in their status and expectations. Of her wealth and connections, and the fact he had no home to offer her.

Even if he was restored as rightful Laird of Greenock, he struggled to envisage Isabella living a busy and purposeful life within its granite walls. Any wife of his would be required to work—and hard at that. There were times to relax, with ceilidhs and feasting and laughter. But also times when food was scarce and enemies loomed close.

For certs, there was no coin to spare for fashionable dresses and grand visitors. He had difficulty picturing the daily reality of Isabella's former life as Countess of Felsham; but surely much of her time had been spent in this manner, with formal dinners and stilted conversation.

A gust of wind lifted his uncombed hair from his neck and sent shivers of cold down his back.

He must not make the mistake of hankering after something that was not meant for him. He had told himself as much at the first light of dawn. 'Twas still true at sunset.

What was more, he would freeze to death if he stood out here and contemplated the obvious for much longer.

Blowing on his chilled fingers, Hamish tramped back down the steps and made his way to the hall, where he could just discern the glow of candlelight behind the shutters. The door was bolted, as he had specified, but when he banged his fist upon the wood and shouted for entry, Siegfried soon appeared.

Hamish walked into light and warmth and the welcome scent of cooking. His stomach rumbled, and he realized he had not eaten since last night.

"Smells good." He sniffed appreciatively and clapped his comrade on the back.

But Siegfried shook his head. "'Tis not on my account. The Lady is in the kitchen."

Hamish's eyebrows climbed up his forehead and Siegfried nodded in confirmation.

"I fixed the door to her chamber, but she said she has seen enough of those four walls and wanted to put herself to use."

'Twas as if her actions answered the very questions he had ruminated upon when he stood on the wall walk.

Hamish gave himself a little shake, aware that he was as wide-eyed as a hound awaiting a feed.

"Are ye recovered fully, do ye think?" he asked of Siegfried as they rounded the corner into the feasting hall.

"As much as I will ever be." The Seneschal flexed his fingers experimentally. "'Tis ye who should sit afore the fire, Hamish. Ye have been out in the cold all day."

Hamish grunted, reluctant to explain himself. His gaze roved around the room, which somehow appeared more homely and welcoming than it had this morn. "Why is the table set only fer two? Is the Lady not eating with us?"

Siegfried buried his chin into the folds of his cloak. "I thought ter give the two of ye some time alone."

Hamish huffed. "That is the last thing we need."

A smile flickered across his friend's face. "I also thought ye were a man in control of yerself."

"Aye, well." Hamish was noncommittal. "Surely ye have said none of this to the Lady?" The lure of the armchair proved too tempting for him to deny and he sank into it with a little grunt of pleasure.

"Give an old man some credit." Siegfried stayed standing, but leaned his weight on the back of the opposite chair. "I told her that I needed ter rest. She didna protest, ye understand. In truth, she was quick ter show me ter the solar and invite me ter make good use of it." He nodded to an oak door set into the opposite wall.

"Why are ye doing this?" Hamish frowned.

"Ye need a clear head and no regrets if ye are ter take back control of Greenock."

He struggled to follow. "And ye think I will have regrets?"

"I think ye need ter be persuaded as to whether or nay yon Lady Isabella is a proper match for ye. Aye, she has a pretty face and a quick wit. But could ye sit and talk with her night after night whilst the wind howls about the keep?" Siegfried cocked his head. "Could she face the endless winters and toil?"

Hamish was momentarily lost in a daydream of he and Isabella sitting cozily by a roaring fire in his bedchamber at Greenock, whilst snow drifted outside.

"I doubt she kens the meaning of toil," he said, forcing himself back to the present.

Siegfried nodded. "Exactly so." He straightened up. "I shall take my leave."

"Are ye not eating at all?"

"I have already sampled the Lady's cooking." Siegfried's face was inscrutable. "My belly is full and I want only somewhere soft to lay my head. The thaw may come on the morrow." He bowed to Hamish and swept away through the oak door.

Hamish settled himself more comfortably in the armchair. The fire threw out a good deal of warmth and were it not for his hunger and desire to see Isabella again, he might have dozed. When brisk footsteps sounded, he readied himself.

"I thought I heard you come in." Isabella carried a heavy tray with apparent ease. Her hair hung in a single braid down her back and her cheeks flushed becomingly.

"Ye have been busy in the kitchen." Hamish's stomach rumbled audibly as he caught the scent of cooked meat.

"I have been pleased to keep myself busy." She walked gracefully to the trestle table and began unloading her tray. "Idle hours sit heavily upon a person."

Isabella was wearing braccae. They clung to her shapely legs and made it all too easy for him to recall how those same thighs had been wrapped around him last night.

Mayhap she was aware of the direction of his thoughts, for she hurriedly sat down.

"Will you not join me?" she addressed the opposite wall.

Hamish crossed the polished floor, aware that he had not cleaned the dust from his hands. Isabella would think him a highland heathen.

Surely the Earl of Felsham would never have sat down to dinner with dirt ingrained beneath his fingernails.

'Twas too late now. And the stew smelled too heavenly to resist. He tore off a hunk of bread and dipped it into the meaty broth, closing his eyes in pleasure as the rich flavors flooded his mouth.

"'Tis good," he told her.

Her cheeks flushed again. "As I said, 'tis better to have purpose than not."

He regarded her steadily, this woman that was full of surprises.

"I would have thought ye were accustomed to servants to cook yer food and serve it as well."

At this point he noticed they had neither wine nor ale to wash down their food. Isabella had set goblets out on the table, but they were empty.

"I do not deny it."

She was avoiding his gaze and he didn't like it. "If ye were the Lady of Greenock, ye would work like this all the time. There are no hours of idleness in the highlands."

Just as he cautioned himself for his combative tone—and demanded to know what he hoped to achieve by it—her transfixing eyes flew to his. For a moment, he was robbed of breath. His spoon sat in mid-air, his food all but forgotten.

"As the wife of Lord Gaunt? Or the wife of yourself?" The question was so softly asked that Hamish had to strain to hear it.

Reality was a harsh mistress.

He chewed up his meat and longed for a mouthful of ale.

Of course, the Lady still thought of Greenock as belonging to Gaunt. *As it will*, he jeered at himself, *until her brother intervenes.*

Isabella took a ragged breath. "Perchance I would relish the chance to work and have purpose."

She was changing the subject, with all the tact and diplomacy of a countess.

He put down his spoon. "Ye would soon tire of it."

"How can you be so sure?" Isabella's fierce gaze now clashed with his. "How can you claim to know me so well?"

'Twas a mirror of the question she had asked last night.

"How do you claim to know the workings of my mind?" she had demanded as she stood in the circle of his embrace.

He could not think of that conversation—nor of what had come after it. "I ken that a lady like you was not raised to face a life of hardship," he said instead.

"We never know what hardships we will face in life."

He could not argue with that.

But what hardships had Isabella de Neville ever faced? For certain, she had not bedded down in a cave, nor wielded a sword upon the battlements.

And why would I wish such a fate upon her?

Hamish rubbed at his temples, at the beginnings of a headache.

"Ye would miss the grandeur and ease of yer old life," he tried again.

Isabella's gaze became unfocused as she toyed with her food. "I would miss the music," she said abruptly.

"The music?" His interest was snagged. Music was also a big love in his life. At least, it had been, once.

"Aye." She nodded. "Westchester was known for its evenings of music. I was fortunate in the services of a talented bard. There was naught he could not play."

It was on the tip of Hamish's tongue to tell her that he played the lute. But then he looked down at his dirty fingers and felt the words die inside him.

She would ne'er believe it.

Worse, she would think him a man of enthusiasm but little talent.

Isabella rose up from the table. "I see my tales of the past hold little interest for you."

Every fiber of his being wanted to reach out and touch her. To tell her that every word she uttered was of interest.

But she is not meant for me.

"It has been a tiring day," he said instead. "Siegfried thinks the thaw may come on the morrow. If so, there will be much to prepare."

Her face changed, but her expression was difficult to read in the candlelight.

"In that case, I had best leave you to rest."

Isabella walked hurriedly away, her light footsteps sounding up the stairs. Hamish gripped the table and silently cursed himself.

He should not have let her leave. Not without some declaration of—something on his part. God's blood, he had bedded the woman and breathed not a word on the subject.

For certain, she would think him a heathen. A villain. Uneducated and unthinking. She had cooked for him, and he had scarcely even thanked him.

Not yer finest hour, Hamish McIvor.

He closed his mind to thoughts of how his mother and sisters would scold his behavior.

Perchance 'twas all for the best. There was no future for himself and Isabella de Neville. Hadn't all that transpired this eve confirmed as much?

Hamish pushed his chair away from the table and returned to his place by the fire, fixing his gaze upon the orange flames and not allowing himself to dwell on the answer to his question.

For in truth, naught Isabella had said or done this eve made it hard for him to picture her as the Lady of Greenock.

Far from having a clear head, Hamish was more muddled than ever.

CHAPTER THIRTEEN

ISABELLA BANKED UP the fire in her chamber that Siegfried had lit earlier in the evening. If she'd learned anything during her time at Ember Hall, it was the importance of keeping a good fire blazing.

But the bright flickering flames could not dispel the darkness and doubt in her heart. Nor could the warmth lull her into a state of relaxation.

She had never been less relaxed in her life.

Instead of laying on the bed, she paced across the floorboards, kicking the rugs out of the way so they could not trip her nor slow her thinking.

What am I to do?

From the first, she'd recognized her bone-deep attraction to the highlander. Ye Gods, the man was beautiful—if someone so undeniably masculine could be described in that way. But he *was* beautiful; from the sharp curve of his cheekbones to the fiery hues in his untamable hair. She felt no shame in appreciating his good looks.

Forsooth, enough men had openly appraised her looks over the years. She had sensed the lust in their gaze when they looked at her, and she thought it was high time she experienced the same.

But now she had the terrifying notion that what she felt for Hamish was more than lust.

Ever since she came across him singing in the stables, something had shifted inside her. Mayhap it was the simple words of the song on his lips that had unleashed some yearning she'd kept long under wraps.

"How well do I love thee, how well do I love thee."

She wanted to hear him say as much to her. To see love in his gaze and feel it in the touch of his hands.

Just yesterday, she had suggested to Hamish that they might be friends.

She clutched her arms about her chest and let her weight rest against the fastened door of the closet.

What lunacy is this?

How could so much have changed with one circle of the sun?

She didn't want to be his friend. She wanted to be his lover. *His wife.*

But she'd seen the expression of distaste that passed over his face when she spoke of being the Lady of Greenock. Heard the conviction in his tone when he said she was not raised for a life of productivity and purpose.

Hamish had turned out to be another man who thought Isabella de Neville was purely decorative, like her prized emerald necklace.

She kicked again at a sheepskin rug, satisfied when it slid away across the floor. But the rug had covered blood stains which even Siegfried's dedicated ministrations had not lifted from the grooves of the wood. Isabella turned her face to the closed shutters at the window.

One thing was clear. She risked making a fool of herself if she spent more time with a man she loved, who did not love her in return.

She thought of the long ride to Wolvesley, and how uncomfortable that would be.

She thought of Tristan's all-encompassing gaze. If he saw them together, her clever brother would quickly divine her feelings for Hamish. And that would surely undermine everything they hoped to achieve.

Both the release of Hamish's sister and the return of his lands.

Isabella was not one to renege on a promise. But nor did she have any intention of being taken for a fool. Not by anyone.

She crossed over to the window and lifted the shutters, but the silvery light of the moon was blanketed by heavy clouds and she could see almost naught.

Her pulse quickened. Hamish had spoken of a thaw on the morrow. Perchance he was right.

She released the shutter and backed away from the window, as the beginnings of a plan slowly began to form in her mind.

ISABELLA DID NOT sleep a wink, but passed the night in turn sitting in the wooden desk chair and standing by her window, waiting. When the first pink rays of dawn appeared, she opened the shutters and gazed outside, listening intently.

The world was still white and cold, but above the solitary song of a nearby ruddock, she discerned a steady dripping sound.

The sound of melting icicles.

Isabella smiled to herself.

The thaw was upon them, just as Hamish had predicted. Even as she carefully closed the shutters, she heard the unmistakable *thwump* of snow falling from the roof. There was not a moment to lose.

Isabella had never undressed for bed. Still wearing the practical garb of yesterday, she noiselessly pushed open her chamber door and stepped out into the gallery. Here, she half anticipated the feeling of strong arms closing around her. A mouth pressed close to her ear, asking, "And where might you be going?"

Did she anticipate *or long* for all of this?

Either way, her journey along the gallery suffered no interruption. She crept down the stairs, knowing now which steps creaked and which did not. The faint glow of the hall fire made her pause for long enough to establish that Hamish was slumped in a nearby chair; his long arms hanging downward. She listened for his breathing, slow and heavy, and pushed down her regret at leaving him without saying goodbye.

He would not allow me to say goodbye, she reasoned.

For certain, he would not allow her to make the long ride to Wolvesley alone, especially not with a vengeful Alaric on the loose.

But there is no other way.

She would rather risk meeting Alaric—a low risk, she reasoned—than face hours, or days, of awkwardness by Hamish's side.

Quelling the tears that threatened to blur her much-needed senses, she forced herself to walk away from Hamish and into the kitchen. Her hastily concocted plan had included the packing of provisions for the journey south, but Isabella found she could not countenance such a delay. There would be food enough waiting for her at Wolvesley. She tied Esme's cloak about her shoulders and slowly drew back the bolt on the outer door.

A strong gust of wind made her clutch the handle and stagger to one side, but the biting chill of the last days had diminished. It was breezy and cold; inclement indeed. But the freeze had lifted and her leather boots splashed through softened snow and melting puddles. With no danger of slipping on the ice, Isabella strode out with more confidence.

My plan may yet succeed.

She entered the barn and spoke softly to the horses, but she had not even thought to look for a saddle when she realized she had a problem.

Her trusted destrier stood placidly between Luar and a heavily-muscled dapple-grey, both of whom flattened their ears at her approach, as if sensing she was an adversary.

Isabella took a deep breath. Her mother had taught her that horses could read fear as easily as words on a parchment. If she stayed calm, all would be well.

But Luar was not so easily fooled. She scraped at the floor with her hoof and whinnied a warning when Isabella next approached; a warning that might carry all the way back to the hall. From her brother, Isabella had learned all about the close bonds between a warrior and his warhorse.

She would not risk bringing Hamish to the barn.

But at the other side of the row, Alaric's bad-tempered bay swung his head and snapped his teeth at her.

Isabella retreated with a small wail of distress. How could she ride to Wolvesley without a mount?

Then she spied the small grey pony standing apart from the others, and her fears subsided. Though tall, Isabella hardly weighed more than a child. She found the tack neatly piled in a stable to the side of the barn, and it was not hard to identify which would fit the pony. Talking gamely to the creature, which must have belonged to one of her nieces or nephews, she tacked him up with no further difficulty.

The sun was beginning to rise in the sky by the time she led him outside. How much time had she wasted?

No more, she promised herself.

She looked for the mounting block to no avail. Then she considered the height of her mount, and pulled herself into the saddle with relative ease.

Isabella smiled. Let any man underestimate her at his peril.

She pressed her heels into her horse's sides and urged him into a canter as soon as they were off the cobbles. She would need to dismount to open the gate, but that would be easy enough. Her mother had been right all these years, 'twas far more practical to ride in braccae than any riding habit, no matter how fine the stitching.

THE LAST TIME Hamish had saddled Luar so quickly was when the battle horns were sounding before the siege of Greenock. Usually he took the time to talk gently to his sometimes-skittish mare, but this morn she seemed to sense his urgency, and she stood quietly whilst he tugged up her girth.

Hamish led her out into the courtyard, shouted a farewell to Siegfried, and sprang onto her back. Spray from the puddles of melting snow flew up around them as they galloped toward the open gate. His cloak whipped out behind him and he cursed the wind which stung his eyes and made Luar shy to one side.

But praise be, Isabella had ridden a direct course over the moors. He could see the clear imprint of hoofbeats in the softening blanket of snow. His aim was to follow them—and find her—before the thaw obscured her tracks.

Isabella had been correct when she told him that he could not guess at the workings of her mind. For never would he have predicted that she would flee in the early hours, like an escaped prisoner. Or a traitor.

Is she about to betray me?

Pain rippled through his chest, and his howl mingled with the cruel wind which whistled through the distant trees. But even if Isabella had lied to him about enlisting the help of her brother— about *everything*—then he still could not abandon her to an unknown fate at the possible hands of raiders and chancers.

And Alaric.

Foolish woman.

Did she not know how dangerous this could be?

He gritted his teeth and spurred Luar to lengthen her stride so they careered over the moors as if they were being chased by demons. No horse was faster than Luar. And surely, Isabella could not have gone far on the old grey pony. Though she had a decent head start, for Hamish had slept deeply in the chair before the fire. By the time Siegfried woke him, the sun had been high in the sky.

Perchance the Lady had drugged him.

His eyes narrowed as he crouched low over Luar's neck. She had cooked the stew and served his portion, but he could not believe that Isabella would stoop so low as that.

But do I know her at all?

Has she been playing me all along?

Even as the thought occurred to him, he grimaced with acknowledgement that he was the one to take Isabella captive. Theirs had hardly been a relationship of equals—in the beginning at least. But what had passed between them most recently had been pure and real. As real as the circle of tall granite stones he was now galloping past. As pure as the love he felt for his family and his home. But bigger and more urgent than anything he had ever known. And she had felt the same connection with him. He would go to his grave swearing as much.

He reined Luar back as they reached an ancient crossroads high on the moors. For a moment, she spun in a tight circle as his eyes scanned the four diverging paths, increasingly desperate for a clue as to which direction Isabella had taken. Then he spied the telltale hoofprints tracking a neat course up a slight incline some way apart from the main paths, and he grinned humorlessly.

Isabella was trying to throw him off.

He'd always said she was clever.

Perchance she was cleverer even than he had given her credit for. Forsooth, one woman, alone and unprotected, had bested three armed men.

Nay, he could not believe that everything they had shared was a lie. He was a man of flesh and blood, with hopes and dreams and desires, and he had responded to this and more in Isabella de Neville.

With a shake of his head, he urged Luar on once again. His charger pricked her ears and gave chase, and he sent up silent thanks for her loyalty and stamina.

But even a mighty warhorse like Luar could not run forever. When the gushing of a nearby stream reached his ears, he slowed her to a trot until they found a shallow pool where she could lower her head and drink. He dismounted and filled his own water skein, realizing that he too was thirsty. Thoughts of Isabella had crowded his mind, chasing out everything else. He patted Luar and loosened her girth and told her they could rest a while.

With his hand looped loosely through the reins, they wandered from the river and up a shallow hill, from which he fancied they would benefit from a sweeping view of all surrounding countryside.

He was not wrong. As they stood atop the summit, he spied a small copse of trees some way ahead of them. And in amongst the trees, he spied the unmistakable figure of a woman standing by a small horse.

"There she is," he said in a strangled voice.

Luar's ears flickered back and forth.

"But what is she doing?"

Hamish folded his arms and watched as Isabella tugged off her cloak and hung it from a branch. She then jumped high from the ground, wrapping her hands and feet around a much thicker branch and beginning to shimmy upwards.

"God's blood, she be climbing a tree."

Luar lost interest and began to crop at the grass. Hamish leaned against her warm flanks, relieved to have found Isabella and somewhat entertained by the display. The wind had thankfully dropped and the noonday sun had a determined strength to it, so he was no longer clenched with cold.

Who would have thought that Isabella de Neville had a habit of climbing trees?

As he watched, she swung into a more upright position and clambered to the midpoint of the tree. With her back against the trunk, she lowered herself until she sat astride a sturdy branch, where she swung her legs like a carefree child.

Hamish smiled. With the sun shining down upon her like a halo, there was no denying the beauty of the scene.

There was no denying his feelings for her.

"I am falling for ye, Isabella," he whispered to the hills and the heather and the breeze.

"Finally," said a voice to his left.

"Brianne." It seemed a long time since he had glimpsed her chestnut curls and laughing eyes. He knew there were those who would mock him for the value he placed on conversations with a woman who no longer walked this realm. There were times when he privately acknowledged that their dialogue was rooted deep inside his imagination, with treasured memories adding a shine of authenticity. But at other times, he heard and saw his sister so clearly, it was as if she had journeyed from the spirit world to counsel him.

She put her hands on her hips and fixed him with a stare. "I am pleased to hear ye own up to the feelings of yer heart."

"I have nay choice in the matter. I canna pretend otherwise." He shrugged.

"Ye should stick to the promise ye made about always telling the truth, nay matter how painful it may be."

She sounded like some wise woman of the hills, not his high-spirited sister who had seen less than two and twenty summers.

He bowed his head. "I shall try."

"But dinna drop yer guard. Ye ken? Methinks the hardest battle is still ahead of ye."

He opened his mouth to ask what she meant, inwardly pro-testing that no battle could be harder than the one which had ended with her demise. But his sister had gone. Only Luar's pricked ears told him he hadn't imagined the whole encounter.

But then he noticed that Luar was not looking at the place Brianne had stood. She was looking beyond it, to a dark figure creeping through the undergrowth toward the tree in which Isabella still sat.

Hamish dropped the reins and began to run.

CHAPTER FOURTEEN

ISABELLA HAD NOT slept since the night she spent in Hamish's arms. Exhaustion overwhelmed her, but she dared not close her eyes even for a moment.

If she fell asleep, she may well topple out of the tree.

To decrease the risk of that happening, she wedged her boot firmly between two slender branches and pressed her spine against the gnarled trunk.

She'd climbed up here with the desperate hope of glimpsing the familiar turrets of Wolvesley Castle. But alas, all she could see was an endless sweep of soggy and dispiriting moorland with a patchwork pattern of melting snow. No birds sang; the only sound was the eerie groan of the wind and the occasional snort from the grey pony below her. She had no sense of how far they had traveled, and whether the greater distance was behind or ahead of them.

I should not have left Ember Hall.

Isabella was dangerously close to tears. She rubbed at her eyes with the heel of her hand, knowing there was naught to be gained by giving into this tumult of emotion.

In fact, giving into her emotions was what had gotten her into this mess.

Her father, the Earl of Wolvesley, had told his children over and over that they should never run from their fears—they should face them.

But Isabella had run from Hamish like a frightened rabbit.

Tears clouded her vision once again at the thought of the russet-haired highlander. What would he have thought when he woke and found her gone?

The answer slid into her mind. He would have thought that she had betrayed him. Worse, he would continue to think that until Isabella could prove otherwise.

And how long would that take?

She considered, bleakly, that it might be months.

I cannot bear it.

Isabella snatched at the bare branches of the tree in frustration, but the healthy wood did not yield and she succeeded only at scratching her hands.

Shaking her head at her own stupidity, she addressed the grey pony who was looking up at her with an expression of surprise.

"I should have left him a message," she said.

The pony pricked his ears as if trying to understand.

Isabella sighed. The pony was tired. Would he even get her to Wolvesley? Or should she turn back the way she had come? It was very difficult to decide. And a nagging thirst made everything so much harder.

But she couldn't stay in a tree all day. Isabella pursed her lips. The sun was high in the sky now, but night fell quickly at this time of year. She had no more than four or five hours of daylight left to her.

I need to get moving.

She rolled her shoulders and flexed her ankles, which had grown stiff from being wedged between the branches, before climbing steadily downwards. When she was a few feet from the bottom, she found an opening and jumped.

She landed in the arms of a man.

She knew it to be a man because of the hard muscle of his chest and the iron grip of his forearms. And because of a foul, unwashed smell that made her want to gag.

"Lady Isabella," he said. "We meet again."

Alaric.

She strained against him, but he held her too tightly for her to wriggle free.

"Let go of me," she commanded.

He laughed, and she winced at the sourness of his breath.

"I'm going to teach ye a lesson."

Dread pooled in her stomach, but instead of being frozen with fear like before, this time the rush of fear galvanized her into action. Isabella elbowed him sharply in the stomach, ducked down and twisted out of his reach. She didn't waste a moment looking back. She simply started running.

But she had only run a few paces when a heavy weight brought her face down in the damp heather.

"Nice try, milady."

Isabella kicked out and made contact with something hard. She turned to her side and grasped the first thing she found, which was a handful of Alaric's long and unwashed hair. She tugged it hard, hoping to rip it from his head. But in turn, Alaric caught hold of her braid and retaliated. She gasped as a sharp pain shot through her skull, but she would not give in. Her eyes scanned the ground, looking for a stick or something she might use as a weapon.

"Let go of her."

The command came from above. Isabella could not see him, but she was weak with relief at recognizing Hamish's deep, gravelly voice.

"Yer like a faithful hound, Hamish McIvor, always runnin' ter the rescue."

"And ye are a snarling cur, Alaric. I say again, let go of her, else ye will regret it."

Isabella heard the unmistakable sound of a sword being un-sheathed.

"Now," Hamish added.

She almost sobbed when the unbearable pressure on her scalp released. Instead, she pushed down with her elbows and scrambled out of the heather until she could stand upright. She turned to see Hamish standing over Alaric, who was on his knees in a patch of snow, looking anything but repentant.

The tip of Hamish's sword pointed at Alaric's chest. His stance was wide and his cloak billowed out behind him. He glowered down at his captive before casting a glance in her direction.

"Did he hurt ye?"

Her eyes still watered from the pain, but she knew there was no lasting damage. She shook her head, pride preventing her from rubbing at the sore spot on her scalp.

"He did not."

Hamish tapped Alaric with the sword. "Lucky for ye," he murmured.

"Are ye truly goin' to kill me with that?" Alaric's eyes gleamed malevolently. "I dinna think ye have it in ye."

"Sit still, man. I have not yet decided yer fate."

Hamish grimaced and Isabella thought that she understood his predicament. They were miles from anywhere and Alaric surely could not be trusted. But could Hamish kill a man in cold blood?

From his expression, Alaric clearly did not think so. He twisted to one side and let his dark eyes rove over Isabella, making her squirm and long for the cover of the cloak she'd left hanging in the tree.

"I said, sit still," Hamish growled.

Alaric chuckled. "Dinna fret so. I am only looking at the pretty lady who has ye dancing to her tune."

Hamish shook his head. "I should kill ye and have done with it. Ye have brought me naught but grief."

"I brought ye here, did I not? 'Twas my idea to kidnap the wench." He threw another leering glance at Isabella.

Isabella looked away, not wanting to hear any more. The idea that Hamish and Alaric had once conspired together, against her, made her skin prickle uncomfortably. She felt the force of

Hamish's gaze turn upon her, but she could not bring herself to meet his eye. Instead, she looked at the grey pony who was idly cropping at the grass beneath the tree.

A sudden movement from Alaric made her turn her focus back to the two men. Alaric had taken advantage of Hamish's lapse in attention to lunge forward. Whatever he was doing caused Hamish to grunt with alarm, and as Alaric reached for something in Hamish's boot, Hamish jerked down to stop him.

The next seconds passed slowly for Isabella. She saw the glint of a blade in Alaric's hand. She saw that same blade plunge, unbelievably, into Hamish's upper arm. She saw the crimson spurt of blood and Hamish's grimace of pain and shock.

Then there was a flash as Hamish's sword flew in a graceful arc to land in Alaric's chest. Time slowed further as the young warrior swayed forward, before crumpling and laying still.

Hamish stepped away from the fallen man, dropped his sword and grasped his bleeding arm. It took a moment for Isabella's rightful senses to return, but she ran toward him as soon as she was able.

"Are you hurt?"

"'Tis naught but a scratch."

His pale face belied the claim. As did the plume of blood showing through his shirt. Isabella clasped her hands with desperation. Frida would know exactly what to do in this situation.

She narrowed her eyes.

What would Frida do?

"We must stop the blood," she gasped. "Let me see."

She didn't want to look. The sight of blood had always made her slightly queasy. But there was no one else here to do it.

Hamish shook his head and flinched from her touch, but Isabella persevered, swallowing down her shock at the jagged edges of the deep cut.

"Sliced with my own blade." Hamish raised his eyebrows in an attempt at humor.

"You had a dagger in your boot?" Isabella began to make sense of it all.

"Aye. Alaric knew all my tricks." Hamish staggered and Isabella tugged at his good arm.

"Sit down before you fall down," she ordered. She spied a huddle of rocks which stood free from melting snow and urged him toward them. Isabella's thoughts were racing. She remembered a time when they were children, when an enraged Jonah had run at his infuriating older brother with a proper sword. Not believing he would strike, Tristan had stood his ground—even inflamed the situation further with some jeering words—and Jonah had inflicted a cut on his leg that sent Esme fleeing for the physician.

Isabella clasped her hands together to stop them shaking, trying to stay with the memory even as the wind whipped through her woolen tunic and lifted her braid from her neck.

The physician had said the bleeding was not too quick and the wound was not too serious. But even so, he tied a tight bandage above the cut and told them this was the way to prevent serious blood loss.

"We need a bandage."

Hamish tilted his face toward her. "I didna think ter bring my medical supplies." His voice was cold, just like his eyes, and Isabella did not think it was all down to shock or pain. He was cross with her. And he had every reason to be. But this was not the time for her to plead for his forgiveness.

Instead, she ran the few paces back to the tree and fetched down her cloak, sparing a few words to calm the alarmed pony. Averting her eyes from the face of the dead man, she then plucked Hamish's dagger from Alaric's long fingers and returned to the highlander's side.

"What are ye about?"

She answered by spreading the cloak on a long, flat stone and tearing off a strip with the dagger. Without further ado, she wrapped it tightly around Hamish's upper arm, pulling until he winced.

"That's tight enough, lass."

"It needs to be." She stood back to survey her handiwork. 'Twas not the neatest knot in the land, but she had to hope it would do the trick. She peered closer at the wound and after a tense wait, declared the bleeding was beginning to slow.

She exhaled, only now aware that she had been holding her breath this whole time.

"I think you shall live."

"I ne'er doubted it." He raised his bushy eyebrows. "But I thank ye, all the same."

Isabella put a hand in front of her eyes. The surge of adrenaline followed by heady relief had rendered her tearful all over again.

Hamish hated her. She could hear it in his voice. And why should he not? If she had not fled from Ember Hall, he would not have become injured.

Alaric would not be dead.

"I'm sorry."

Hamish didn't answer for a long while. Then he quietly said, "What are ye sorry for?"

"For running away from Ember Hall. I realize how it appeared, what you must think of me. But I intended to honor our agreement." She risked a glance through her fingers and saw that he was listening, although his face was turned towards the trees. "I was heading for Wolvesley to seek an audience with my brother," she said with as much dignity as she could muster. She lowered her hands and folded them in front of her. "To petition for his help in the return of your lands and the release of your sister," she added when he did not respond.

Hamish took a deep breath. "I see."

"I don't think you do." Greatly daring, Isabella closed the distance between them and sat close beside him. She could feel the warmth of his body, but he made no move toward her. "I regret what I did. I should have confided in you. But I could not."

Her voice wobbled with emotion.

"Why not?" He looked at her, finally, but his eyes had not regained their usual warmth. "I thought we had an understanding, ye and I, but I begin to believe I imagined it."

"You did not imagine it." Isabella summoned reserves of courage and took hold of his nearest hand. She half expected him to pull away, and was emboldened when he did not. She looked down at his large hand, with its square nails and strong, capable fingers. She clasped both of her hands around it and tried to convey the depths of her feelings through her touch. But Hamish sat as still as the stones about them, and she realized that she could only hope for his forgiveness by confessing the truth of her heart. She took a deep breath. "I ran from Ember Hall because I was afraid."

"Afraid of me?"

"Afraid of my feelings for you."

There, she had said it.

Hamish looked at her and it was as if a warm cloak of reassurance had settled about her shoulders.

"What are ye trying ter tell me, Isabella?"

Despite the chill breeze, heat rose to her cheeks. "Have you not worked it out?"

He smiled, gently. "I dinna want to jump ter the wrong conclusion."

"I am falling in love with you," she blurted out. The admission left her vulnerable and exposed, but then he placed his remaining hand on top of hers and she was safe again.

"Just as I am falling in love with ye."

Relief and surprise made her flesh tingle. Her lips parted. "You are?"

"'Tis a condition I have struggled against," he chuckled. "But ultimately, one that I canna deny, however hard I try."

"But you said—" she floundered to recall why she had become so cross and embarrassed. "You said I was not fit to be the Lady of Greenock."

"I said no such thing." His voice rose in denial.

"You did." She shook back a loose strand of hair as she tried to remember. "You said I would tire of the work and long for *ease* and *grandeur*."

"Are ease and grandeur such terrible things?" He squeezed her hands. "Ye told me ye would miss the music. As if a granite keep in Scotland would ne'er be a place for music."

Isabella shook her head in confusion. "And *is* it a place for music?"

"I play the lute," he announced.

It was so unexpected that Isabella found her lips inching into a smile. She looked down at their cojoined hands. "Now that is something I long to see."

"Perchance ye shall." He leaned forward and pressed his lips against hers in a kiss that was sweet and gentle and left her wanting a whole lot more. "But fer now, we have more pressing matters to deal with."

"What is more pressing than love?" she whispered. Her body shivered with a mixture of cold and desire.

"The small matter of our location on the moors, far from anywhere, with darkness coming upon us in less time than it will take to reach Wolvesley Castle or return to Ember Hall." He tilted his face to the side as if thinking still. "'Tis a problem compounded by my useless arm and the fact your mount stands with his head down as if already exhausted. Ye dinna happen to know of a nearby inn or a ruined barn where we might take shelter?"

She widened her eyes and shook her head. Most often, she traveled by carriage and paid little attention to her surroundings.

"I was jesting, lass," he said softly. "Forsooth, a ruined barn would serve little purpose when the nighttime temperatures plummet. Dinna fear. I will get ye ter safety. But we need to get on our way. And ye need to cover yerself with yon cloak before ye catch yer death."

He slowly rose to his feet and Isabella immediately noticed

the absence of his warmth. She also couldn't help but see how he walked tentatively and off-balance.

Hamish was more affected by his injury than he was prepared to admit.

Wrapping her cloak over her shoulders, she chased away the kernel of fear that had been growing in her belly ever since Hamish's speech. They simply must find warmth and safety before the darkest hours of night. If they didn't, 'twould be her fault.

She walked briskly to join him at the top of a small plateau. Hamish held his bad arm with his good hand, trying not to wince with every step he took. He spared her a smile and then turned to scan the horizon.

"Your horse is not here." She was winded by the shock of it.

But Hamish only pursed his lips. "She is, somewhere."

Isabella clutched her cloak about her. All she could see was an expanse of heather and sloshy snow running all the way to the distant tree line. The only break in the nearby landscape was the tree she had climbed earlier, with the grey pony beneath it.

Ye Gods, if the horse has gone, our prospects are bleak indeed.

Hamish cupped his hands about his mouth and gave a piercing whistle which made Isabella startle in fright. The whistle was long and mournful, like a lone curlew in midsummer. He paused, looked around and whistled again, before putting his head to one side and listening intently.

"She is coming."

At first, Isabella could hear nothing, but then her ears picked up a distant thunder of hooves. The sound grew louder until it seemed the ground beneath their feet was vibrating. A black horse came into view, her tail streaming behind her as she pounded toward them.

"Luar," said Hamish, with a pleased smile.

Isabella stepped back nervously. "Will she charge us?"

"I hope not." He raised his eyebrows as if amused.

Sure enough, when she was all but upon them, Luar slowed

her pace to a trot and then came careering to a halt with her face pressed into Hamish's chest. She heaved out a sigh, almost of relief, as Hamish stroked her gently.

"Your horse loves you." Isabella wondered if she was envious of their easy bond.

"Aye. I've raised her since she was a wee foal. She's soft as butter with me. But she willna let anyone near her if she doesna like them."

She thought of the way Luar had put back her ears and stamped at the floor earlier that day.

"I don't think she likes me."

"She is usually wise with her likes and her dislikes."

Isabella took this as a blow. She folded her arms across her cloak and bowed her head.

"Come closer," urged Hamish. "Ye are used to horses, are ye not?"

"I am, of course." She was a little affronted, but how was Hamish to know of the role horses had played in her upbringing? She took a breath and walked slowly toward the tall mare, speaking gently all the while.

Luar looked at her warily, then relaxed and nudged at her stomach.

"She be wanting a treat," Hamish said with a smile.

"You and me both," Isabella told Luar, stroking her muscular shoulders. "She is beautiful."

Hamish looked pensive. "If my sister was here, she would tell ye that I have a weakness for beautiful things."

"We will rescue your sister from Gaunt, I promise." She rested her hand lightly on his good arm.

He gave himself a little shake. "If anyone can help me, 'tis you, Isabella." He looked from Luar to the grey pony. "What say we both ride Luar and lead this little one. He seems all out of puff."

It was a sensible solution and Isabella nodded her approval. But when Hamish tried to hoist her onto Luar's back, his wounded arm made it impossible. His face turned grey with effort and pain, and he leaned against his horse's flanks and breathed deeply.

"We shall try again."

"Nay." Isabella decided to take matters into her own hands. "We will lead her to the rocks. I can mount her myself from there."

The distance to the saddle seemed impossibly high, even when Isabella balanced on the highest point of the rocks. But she did not allow herself to doubt. She channeled the young woman she'd once been, the one who had raced about the grounds of Wolvesley, swam in the lake and rode every horse in the yard, and she sprang as high as she could. Her eyes watered as she landed in the saddle with a jolt, and she apologized to Luar.

"Nicely done," Hamish remarked. He was holding the reins of the pony and clearly having some internal debate about how to manage this and get into the saddle himself.

"Give those to me," Isabella commanded, holding out her hand.

"Ye are sure ye can manage?"

"I am sure I can manage."

Somewhat reluctantly, Hamish handed over the reins. Isabella gave the pony a meaningful look as Hamish mounted behind her.

Behave, she implored silently.

Moments later, Hamish's good arm closed about her waist. Isabella allowed herself to lean into his warmth and strength, but only briefly. Then she straightened up and glanced behind her.

"Are you ready?"

"I am." Hamish was either winded or surprised. Or more likely, hiding his pain.

She didn't ask for permission, she simply took Luar's reins as well and urged her forward. She would take charge of this situation and do everything in her power to get them to safety.

For she was Isabella de Neville.

And Isabella de Neville was so much more than just a pretty face.

CHAPTER FIFTEEN

WAVES OF PAIN made Hamish increasingly dizzy and at times he felt dangerously close to toppling from Luar's back. Not wanting to hold any tighter to Isabella's waist, he sat deeper in the saddle and wrapped his long legs as far as he could around his horse's warm belly. Isabella perched before him, her slight stature meaning he had an uninterrupted view of the bleak moorland they travelled through. Just a few sparse winter trees broke the monotony of hills and heather and melting snow. He had lost all sense of time and could not guess how much longer they still had to travel. But every time Luar skidded on some loose ground, or shied at a shadow, he gritted his teeth to prevent himself from crying out in agony.

It had been a blow to his pride when Isabella took the reins. But he had to admit, in the privacy of his thoughts at least, that she had been right to do so. Alaric had plunged the blade through layers of muscle as well as flesh, and in his sword arm to boot.

Hamish cursed his own foolishness. He should have stayed on his guard around Alaric. But the hot surge of anger did his balance no favors, and he was obliged to lower his head and take deep breaths until the world settled once again. Seemingly mindful of his troubles, Isabella kept Luar straight and steady over the moors. She was an accomplished horsewoman, he realized, mastering a strange and headstrong mount, and leading the pony by their side, with no trouble at all.

Isabella was a clever, talented and beautiful woman, who, if his memory served him correctly, claimed she was falling in love.

With him.

Hamish's heart began to beat faster with the sheer unanticipated wonder of it. In different times, he might have shouted his good fortune from the highest tower of Greenock. But those times were gone. He could not pretend, even to himself, that he and Isabella enjoyed much prospect of future happiness.

God's blood, with his sword arm so injured, could he even defend himself? Let alone, mount an attack on the imposters who had claimed his birthright as their own. His sword hung from his belt, as usual, but would he be able to grasp the hilt and draw it against an enemy?

A cruel wind whipped up his hair and cloak, as if giving further weight to these doubts that struck like an axe at the very foundations of the person Hamish had always believed himself to be.

A leader, *with no men to follow him.*

A warrior, *who could not even swing his own broadsword.*

Hamish gritted his teeth at the shame of it.

Isabella tilted her golden head and spoke over her shoulder.

"There is an overhang, up ahead. It should offer shelter from the wind. Would you like to stop a while?"

Irritation made him gruff. "Do ye need to rest?"

She hesitated. "I was thinking of your arm."

He would not give in to weakness. Nor to this damnable surge of self-pity. "Nay, thank ye for yer concern but the sun is already setting. We should push on."

"The lay of the land looks familiar to me now." Her voice was soft and reassuring. "I am certain that once we are over the next hill, the castle ramparts will come into view."

Isabella spoke with the casual ease of one who expected a warm welcome at their destination. And why should she not? But things were very different for Hamish. He had never envisaged coming before the de Nevilles in such a state.

He grunted in response, but regretted it when Isabella threw him an uncertain glance over her shoulder.

"I thought you would be pleased at the idea of our journey's end."

Aye, how could he not long for a comfortable chair and perchance the ministrations of a healer?

But this was an English stronghold they were riding into. And Hamish was a highlander through and through.

He cleared his throat. "Methinks 'twill be difficult to convince yer brother I am worthy to be the Laird of Greenock when I canna steer my own horse."

Her laughter was like a peal of bells, incongruous given the heaviness of Hamish's heart.

"Tristan will look beyond that, I promise."

"Ye have faith in yer brother."

"I do." Isabella was emphatic. "Oft times he can be quick to anger. But he always does what is right in the end."

Hamish breathed deeply to stem the panic that sent dots dancing around his vision. Down below him, the grey pony stepped on manfully, trotting occasionally to keep up with Luar's longer strides. Hamish would have to be like the pony; accepting of these strange twists of fate and willing to keep ploughing forward.

But the pain in his arm had become a hot band of throbbing steel that took up most, if not all, of his thoughts by the time Isabella pointed ahead of her and spoke up with evident relief.

"There it is."

Wolvesley Castle blazed with light, like a Beltane celebration. Orange flames flickered against the dark sky from hundreds of torches positioned all around the ramparts. The mighty gates, however, were closed, and the guards standing in the tower showed no sign of opening them for the ragged pair of riders slowly approaching. A shiver of misgiving rippled down his spine, but Isabella still sat easily in the saddle. They rode right up to the colossal gates, as if his companion's sheer force of will might force them open. She tilted her face up to the glowing torchlight and a shout went up.

"'Tis Lady Isabella."

The cry was picked up by other guards and soon reverberated around the ramparts. The large wooden gates creaked open and the guards let out a loud cheer which ricocheted off the high walls all around them.

After an arduous day, it was too much for Luar, who was in a strange place with unfamiliar hands on her reins. Hamish sensed the frisson of panic pass through her, but was powerless to prevent what happened next. They were barely through the gates when Luar reared onto her hindlegs then launched into a gallop, leaving both riders grimly hanging on. Isabella had the good sense to drop the pony's reins, but even with her full attention fixed on her mount, she could not bring the warhorse back under control. Hamish lurched dangerously to one side and was obliged to grip the back of the saddle with the hand of his wounded arm. A shameful moan of pain came from him, as his horse careered into the stable yard of Wolvesley Castle.

A group of armed men stood waiting for them. One of them stepped forward and grasped Luar's reins as if she was no more than a runaway pony. His horse shied and tossed back her head, but the knight was not perturbed. He raised his torch and gazed at the riders.

"Isabella?"

He did not use her title and this, together with the sheen of blond hair in the torchlight, told Hamish that he was most likely looking at the man he had come here to find, Tristan de Neville.

Tristan was tall and broad-shouldered and spoke with the voice of authority. But his voice had grown more tentative when he frowned in confusion and asked, "Is that really you, Bella?"

"Aye, and what welcome is this? Let go of the horse, Tris, else she'll never settle." Isabella sounded irritated. Her brother did as she requested, and after a little more prancing, Luar finally lowered her head, snorted deeply and came to a juddering halt.

Hamish released the breath he did not know he'd been holding, and Isabella patted the horse's neck.

"Easy girl," she murmured.

Hamish had the distinct feeling he might be sick. Only the fact he had eaten little that day went in his favor. His vision had broken into swirling lines and his arm throbbed with the rhythm of a beating drum. He knew he must gather his wits to make a good impression on the powerful English lord, but that time came sooner than he had imagined.

Tristan reached up and closed vice-like fingers around his wrist. "Get down," he ordered.

Hamish tried to speak and introduce himself, but the words refused to come. He looked stupidly down into the piercing blue eyes of Isabella's brother and heard only a great roaring in his ears.

"Now, I say." Tristan did not look like a man whose commands were ever ignored.

But Hamish could not dismount without leaning his weight onto his injured arm, and his body was stubbornly refusing to do that. He measured the distance to the ground and thought he would never make it.

"Let go of him, Tris." Isabella's voice was sharp. "He is a friend of mine, an ally. Not an enemy."

"He is a Scot. I can see from the braids in his hair and his plaid that he hails from the highlands. Methinks he is one of the party that slaughtered your escort and kept you captive in Ember Hall. Am I right?"

Isabella must have been as dumbfounded as Hamish, for she had no response to this. Shaking with effort, Hamish held up his free hand in a gesture of peace.

"Ye have the facts right, my lord, but I beg leave to explain—"

Hamish got no further, for seemingly dozens of hands closed around his waist and legs, dragging him unceremoniously from his own horse. He landed with a bump on the damp cobbles and a new pain shot up his back.

"What are you doing?" demanded Isabella, asking the question which Hamish did not have the breath to form.

Luar whinnied a warning, but Tristan held tightly to her head.

"Take him to the dungeons," Tristan ordered calmly.

"Why the dungeons? What the devil is happening?" Isabella twisted in the saddle and for a precious moment, her eyes met his.

He read confusion and mounting anger in her gaze, and wanted to tell her that she should not say or do anything to risk her own safety. Not on his account. But before he could speak a word, a gag was forced over his mouth. He winced at the tightness of it, but at least the cloth was clean had no particular smell or taste. Just as he counted his blessings, rough hands grasped his arms and legs, and he roared with pain. Fingers clamped around his injury and Hamish was unable to curb his instinctive response to lash out at his aggressor.

But this only made his captors more eager to restrain him. The more he struggled, the tighter they held onto his flailing limbs.

"Let him go." Isabella's voice was loud and imperious, carrying through the stable yard like an imperial command.

Perhaps confused by the contradictory instructions, the men-at-arms released their iron-like grip, but they still carried Hamish like a sack of straw. He was conscious of the slick stone cobbles beneath him, and half hoped they would not carry out Isabella's order.

Booted footsteps travelled closer and soon Tristan's face loomed over him. His blue eyes and angular features were reminiscent of Isabella, but the simmering anger in his expression was something Hamish had never seen in the woman he loved.

"Stay still, man," he said impatiently. "You might consider yourself fortunate I have not already run you through with my sword."

Hamish forced himself to breathe slowly, to meet the man's

gaze and communicate his peaceful intentions as best he could.

I mean no harm, he tried to convey.

Ridiculous.

How can I inflict harm on anyone just now?

Tristan de Neville's reputation was of a courageous yet fair-minded knight. But Hamish saw no flicker of fair-mindedness in this man's eyes.

"Tristan, I tell you, he is my friend." Isabella jumped down from Luar and threw the reins to a waiting stable hand. If he could have spoken, Hamish would have asked her to stay away. He had no wish for her to see him gagged and bound like a criminal.

'Twas Tristan himself who held up his hand and, glowering, demanded she keep her distance.

He turned back to Hamish. "Answer me this, and answer honestly or suffer the consequences on the morrow. Have you held my sister prisoner these last days?"

What could Hamish do but nod?

Tristan's expression became cold and disdainful. "Take him away," he said.

Hamish closed his eyes as his captors bundled him over the cobbles and down a series of stone steps, which jolted his wounded arm and made him clench his teeth around the cloth. The air grew colder and foul-smelling, and he concluded they had passed into the dungeons. As a last attempt at self-preservation, he opened his eyes to try and take notice of his surroundings, but all he saw was a dark granite wall and a floor covered in straw. The tramping of footsteps echoed the pounding in his head. A door was unlocked with a large iron key, and as Hamish craned to take a look at the cell, he noticed a small, slight figure in the corner of the large room they were passing through.

Perchance 'twas no more than his imagination, for the figure neither moved nor spoke. Hamish was dropped, with little ceremony, onto a thin and stained straw pallet. The door swung closed behind him and he heard the key turn in the lock.

Then everything went dark.

CHAPTER SIXTEEN

"Y OU'RE MAKING A mistake."

Isabella could not believe this turn of events. She had been less surprised to encounter a band of highland raiders at Ember Hall than she was to behold such stubbornness in her beloved brother.

"A terrible mistake," she added, folding her arms and tossing back her braid of hair.

Tristan seemed hardly to hear her. Even in the darkness, she could see that his face was pale and he was breathing hard. 'Twas almost as if he had been the one to grapple Hamish to the ground. But he had done no more than give the order. And wounded as he was, Hamish hadn't even put up much of a fight.

Isabella stifled a sob, along with the urge to rain her fists upon her brother's chest to make him listen.

"Have you been treated ill?" he asked, scarcely even glancing in her direction.

"Nay, not once." She pushed away memories of Alaric pinning her to the floor of her bedchamber. "But I will answer no more questions until you come to your senses and release Hamish. He is—my *friend*."

She had been about to announce that Hamish was the man she loved. But by the way Tristan had folded his arms over his fur cloak and fixed her with a piercing stare, she could tell he was in no mood for declarations of love.

"Your *friend* who has been holding you captive and starving you by the looks of it."

"I have not been starved. But our ride here was long and tiring." Her voice wobbled as she realized that she was not only chilled to the bone, she was also weak with hunger and exhaustion. The adrenaline that had carried her over the moors was all spent. But now was no time for weakness. "Did you not see how I was the one to ride the horse into our gates?" She drew herself up to her full height.

"I saw a horse out of control and you on the back of it looking like a beggar woman." Tristan screwed up his face with distaste. "Forsooth, the rings on your fingers are the only things I recognize about you."

Isabella reeled with disbelief. "You dare to criticize me because I do not come before you in a fine gown?" She abandoned her dignity and screeched across the cobbles. "I am your sister, Tristan. Or have you grown so high and mighty you only judge a woman's worth by what she is wearing? I have learned that some men look beyond such material trappings. But if appearance matters so much to you, here, you can have each and every one of my rings." In a fit of rage, she snatched her rings from her fingers and flung them across the yard where they landed at her brother's feet.

He glanced down with a small shake of his head. "Bella, what are you doing?"

"Don't you dare call me that." Tears clouded her vision. "That is the name my family uses. But you cannot be my family whilst you are so cruel and uncaring."

"Cruel and uncaring," Tristan shouted her words back at her, finally becoming the brother she knew with the loss of his steely composure. "I have been worried almost to death about you. We all have. And then you berate me for doing what any brother would. God's blood, I have every right to kill that man you describe as your friend. Mayhap I should have done."

"Nay." Isabella clenched her hands into fists. "If you harm

him in any way, I will—"

"What will you do?" he demanded, ignoring the line of men growing behind him, all of whom were looking studiously in the opposite direction. "Will you tell Father? Because he is of the same mind as I."

Isabella shook her head, unable to comprehend this turn of events. Running footsteps came from the stone archway that led from the house, and moments later, Isabella was pulled into her mother's embrace. The familiar scent of lavender was enough to make her sob all anew, as was the feel of familiar hands smoothing her hair and drying her tears.

"My child," said Morwenna, the Countess of Wolvesley. "'Tis really you."

Distantly, Isabella recognized that her mother was as pale-faced and careworn as Tristan. The countess was dressed in a plain gown of heavy brocade with only a shawl for warmth. Her long, grey-blonde hair was loose down her back.

"You were sleeping," she said.

"I have not slept for more than two nights," her mother corrected with a small smile. "But your father has slipped into a fitful slumber which I did not like to wake him from."

Isabella recalled her brother's words. "I do not wish to see him in any case."

"She is near hysterical, Mother," Tristan opined, untying his own cloak and placing it gently around his mother's shoulders.

"We have all been worried about you, Isabella," said Morwenna gravely. She caught Tristan's hand and squeezed her thanks, but Tristan's face was as closed as a book.

"She is not inclined to listen to our worries; only to plead the cause of the man who took her prisoner."

Morwenna stood between her two children and held out her hands for peace. She and Isabella were of a similar height and build, meaning that her son towered above her. "Tristan, my dear, I see a line of loyal men awaiting your further instruction. And Isabella, my darling daughter, I believe you have dropped something."

The countess bent down and gracefully retrieved Isabella's jewels, as behind them, the stablemaster cleared his throat.

"Should we stable the highlander's horse, milord?"

"For certain you should," Isabella answered before her brother was able to refuse. "And there is a pony somewhere loose in the grounds."

"We have caught him, milady." The stablemaster, who Isabella had known all her life, gave her a reassuring smile, but waited for Tristan's nod of acceptance before taking Luar's reins and leading her to the barn.

Morwenna pulled Isabella a few steps away from the men and deliberately placed the jewels in her palm, closing her fingers around them.

"Keep these safe," she murmured. "You never know when you might need them."

"What use are trinkets when a good man is lying injured in our dungeon? For no clear reason?" Isabella was half inclined to throw the jewels back onto the cobbles, but her mother's hands were still covering her own.

"These are a good deal more than trinkets, Isabella," Morwenna chided. "And the man in our dungeon is Hamish McIvor. He is responsible for the slaughter of three men in the service of Lord Gaunt. Men who were to form your escort party to Greenock. Moreover, he has been holding you captive at Ember Hall. *My* ancestral home," she added, raising her pale eyebrows when Isabella went to interrupt. "Pray tell me if I have misunderstood anything." Her mother released her hands and lifted her chin, as if daring Isabella to disagree.

"You have misunderstood *everything*."

Isabella felt as powerless as she had as a child. Her whole body trembled with a combination of cold and distress as the situation she thought she could manage spiraled further out of control.

"Explain it to me then."

Isabella rubbed at her face, trying to find the words she needed. They stood in a pool of torchlight, which emphasized the dark rings around her mother's blue eyes.

How much worse must I look?

She glanced down at her torn cloak and misshapen woolen tunic. She cut a different figure indeed to the last time she had visited her parents' home.

Slowly and deliberately, Isabella placed her rings back on her fingers, hoping the display of compliance might help her cause.

"How do you know all of this?" she asked, stalling for time.

"About Hamish McIvor?"

Isabella shrugged. "I did not even know that was his full name."

"Then you cannot know him very well."

Out of nowhere, Isabella had the urge to unburden herself. To admit to her mother that she knew Hamish better than any woman, not his wife, had any business to.

That she loved him.

Instead, she held her mother's gaze in the flickering torchlight. "How did you know?" she repeated.

Morwenna took her arm and guided her along the path toward the keep. Isabella was reluctant to move further from the dungeon, but she felt unable to resist her mother's urging.

"We have a visitor. He arrived some days since, with a claim which disturbed us all."

Isabella stopped in her tracks. "Who?"

Morwenna also paused and Tristan's cloak puddled around her feet. "Your betrothed. Lord Gaunt."

Isabella reeled as if she had been slapped. The news chilled her more than the wintry wind gusting through the courtyard.

Lord Gaunt was a guest at Wolvesley.

She had an uncouth urge to spit on the cobbles. "And you believe Gaunt's claims over mine?" Wide-eyed with incredulity, she shook her head.

"He is the man you plan to marry. What are we to do but

offer him hospitality when he arrives unannounced mere hours before a snowstorm? What can we do but believe him when he tells us you are in grave danger?" At this, Morwenna's voice wobbled, and Isabella realized how much her family must have worried for her safety.

"I understand," she whispered. "But now you see me, fit and well. And I ask you to hear me when I say that Hamish is a good man. I brought him here myself, to plead for help. Instead, he is thrown into the dungeon like a criminal."

"'Tis a twist, Isabella, which you must allow us time to understand."

"I cannot allow that." Isabella wrung her hands. "Not when he is so gravely injured. He saved my life, Mother. Twice. Without Hamish, I would have suffered the fate you most feared."

Her mother looked into her eyes and Isabella gazed honestly back.

"Please," she added.

Morwenna smiled, sadly. "What help do you seek?"

"The return of Hamish's lands. They were confiscated by the King and given to Lord Gaunt, who has done naught to deserve them." In her fervor, she adopted the analogy once used by Hamish. "Imagine, Mother, if that happened to us. How could we survive the loss of Wolvesley?"

"Ah, Isabella." Morwenna reached out to smooth back a loose strand of her daughter's hair. "It does my heart good to see you standing here before me. But I am even gladder to hear you talk with passion and certitude. In these last years, you have made yourself passive and small, but now the fire inside you burns brightly once again."

Isabella blinked in surprise. "I do not think Tristan shares your opinion."

"You must remember, this is a man's world we live in. Since your husband died, Tristan and your father hold themselves responsible for you. Both of them have been half crazed with worry. Tristan would have ridden out to Ember Hall with the first signs of thaw this morn, but young Lucan took a fever some days since and Mirrie could not bear for Tristan to leave her side."

Isabella knew a tug of guilt. She had never spared a thought for what her family might be going through in these last days. Her nephew had always been a hale and hearty child, but even the strongest boy could weaken and die in the perilous years of childhood. She pulled her cloak further over her shoulders. "How is Lucan now?"

"Praise God, the fever has broken." Morwenna gave her a small smile. "Although darling Mirrie has now taken ill, perchance with exhaustion and worry as much as anything else."

Isabella gulped. Ahead of her stood the mighty keep of Wolvesley Castle. Built on a scale to intimidate and impress, its defenses had never once been breached. Inside these walls, she had believed her family to always be safe.

"I'm sorry," Isabella whispered.

"You were not to know." Morwenna took a breath. "I cannot answer for aught else. Speak to Tristan in the morn, when you have slept and bathed and become more yourself."

Isabella's thoughts spun around in a tight circle. She hugged her arms about herself and looked down at her scuffed boots on the immaculately cleared path. "I am not the woman I was," she began.

"Aye, you have learned something new about yourself. I can see it in your eyes and hear it in your voice," Morwenna interrupted. "But you are still Isabella de Neville. Still the Rose of England. It will do no harm to remind people of that. Especially when you are petitioning for their help."

Isabella thought back to her days at Westchester, and how she would don a pretty dress as if it was a suit of armor, readying herself for battle. Back then, 'twas as if her gowns and jewels were the mainstay of her days. Now she knew there was so much more to life. But she recognized that her mother was right; there was still a sort of power to appearance.

Power which she could channel to Hamish's cause.

The prospect of a warm bed was most alluring. Up above, the bright lights of the keep beckoned her home.

Immediately, she was flooded with guilt, like a drenching from a pail of water. "I cannot go inside and rest in comfort whilst Hanish languishes in the dungeon. He is injured and had only me to tend to his wound." She closed her eyes at the memory of the deep and jagged cut up on the cold and lonely moors. "He needs a healer, Mother. As well as food and drink."

Morwenna eyed her speculatively. "And if I promise to provide all of this, you will go into the keep and do as I ask?"

Isabella wanted to protest that she should visit Hamish and personally oversee what care was provided for him. But she could see it was a battle she had no hope of winning.

"I will," she said.

"You will eat?" Morwenna raised her eyebrows.

Isabella's stomach rumbled traitorously. "If you promise to take food to Hamish."

Morwenna put a gentle hand on her shoulder. "Do not doubt me, child. You are home now. All shall be well."

With that, Morwenna turned and walked gracefully back toward the courtyard, leaving Isabella to complete the journey to the keep alone. As she climbed the wide stone steps, she thought of her mother's words, taking comfort from the knowledge that these castle walls housed the people she loved and trusted most in all the world.

She paused by a stone lion, made villainous by the flickering shadows created by torchlight overhead. The lion was cold to her touch and she stepped away, irrationally afraid. Behind her, the famous Wolvesley fountain was silent and unmoving; the deep water in the pool still half frozen. Isabella took a deep, ragged breath.

Even Wolvesley Castle was not invulnerable to change.

And on the morrow, she would have to face Lord Gaunt.

CHAPTER SEVENTEEN

Hamish snuggled further down into the blankets and turned his face from the weak shaft of sunlight that had disturbed his repose. With his eyes still closed, his sluggish brain calculated that it must be past dawn. The long hours of the night were behind him. Against all the odds, he had slept deeply and he could already tell that his aching body was much recovered.

Hamish frowned, stretched his long limbs on the comfortable straw pallet, and slowly opened his eyes.

Nay, he was not dreaming, he still lay in the cell where de Neville's men had thrown him the day before. In front of him was the iron-studded oak door, bolted from the outside, no doubt. The cell was dimly-lit by an air shaft above his head. The stone floor was bare and the granite walls ran with damp. But Hamish was warm.

Am I feverish?

He sat up and his blankets fell away. Someone had come here in the night and tucked them around him. Someone with a soft voice and ministering hands. A face snagged the edges of his memory. A woman, fair-haired, slender and strong.

Isabella?

Nay, this woman was a sight older than Isabella. She had dressed his wound and held wine to his lips. Unless his mind was playing tricks on him, she had even insisted the guards bring in a second straw pallet to sit atop the first. No wonder he had slept so well.

Hamish swung his legs to the floor, moving cautiously in case his arm put out a painful protest. All was as he remembered, from the double pallet to the flask of wine in the corner. Beside it was a cloth-covered basket. He shuffled over, squatted down and found bread.

Bread!

He tore off a chunk and crammed it in his mouth, not able to recall when he had been so grateful for such simple fare. He washed it down with the wine, which was sweet and strong.

No wonder his memories of the night were so hazy, with wine as potent as this.

Hamish rubbed at his eyes, wishing for a basin of water with which to wash. He was travel-stained from the journey, with mud splats on his breeches and dried blood encrusted on the sleeves of his tunic. But these were trivial problems, when his sword arm no longer throbbed with pain and his body was rested.

But where is my sword?

Hamish scanned the square-shaped cell, which was empty aside from the pallet, and concluded his sword had been taken from him. His fists tightened at the loss, but only a fool would send an armed man to a prison cell.

And Tristan de Neville was no fool.

Hamish breathed deeply. A display of temper would get him nowhere. He must use his wits to get out of this mess. And hope that somewhere out there, in the comfort of the keep, Isabella was pleading his cause.

Please God, let her not abandon me now.

Nay, Isabella would not abandon him in his hour of need. She would find a way through the maze they'd landed in, just as she found a way to bind up his arm whilst they were high on the moors.

He said her name, evoking the brave, beautiful woman he loved and taking comfort from the sound and feel of the syllables.

In the moments after he spoke, he heard a sharp intake of

breath from the other side of the wall, and he remembered the slight figure he had glimpsed last night.

Did another human soul languish down here with him?

Hamish cleared his throat, ready to ask who suffered alongside him, but the march of booted feet into the dungeon cleared all such thoughts from his mind. He wanted to stand tall to meet whoever was coming, but the low ceiling did not allow for that. Instead, he sat down on the pallet with a straight back and his arms folded across his chest. But despite his best efforts, the bright glare of torchlight coming through the door made him lean away and shield his eyes.

He could not see who held the torch. But the man was tall and consequently obliged to slump his shoulders in the confined space.

He spoke over his shoulder. "You can leave us now."

The voice was unmistakably that of Tristan de Neville.

Hamish held himself still and met Tristan's blue gaze squarely. The earl's son had come before him in a rippling fur cloak atop a dark tunic trimmed with gold thread. His golden hair, the same hue as Isabella's, was neatly combed to curl just above his shoulders. He exuded power and wealth, but Hamish would not be cowed.

"Good morn," Hamish offered.

Tristan snorted a little in surprise. "Is it? I would not have thought it a particularly good morn for you."

"On the contrary, yer wine is good and whoever tended to my arm is a skilled healer." He looked down at the neatly-tied white bandage appreciatively.

"I shall convey your thanks to my sister. Whatever hospitality you have enjoyed is thanks to her."

There was a challenge in Tristan's voice. Thinking quickly, Hamish decided to acknowledge but not meet it.

"I understand."

Tristan allowed a beat to pass. "I have always believed in giving a man a fair trial. 'Twas my father who taught me that. He has been the judiciary since before I was born. But I am afraid my father's leniency does not extend to any man who inflicts harm on his family."

Hamish's heart thudded inside his chest. He wanted to speak up and declare that he had never harmed Isabella, but thought it wiser to let de Neville continue.

"Nonetheless, here I am. Last night you asked for a chance to explain your actions. This is your chance."

"I ne'er inflicted harm on Isabella." Hamish's mouth had grown dry. "I swear to it."

"And you never intended it?"

"Nay." Hamish put a hand to his head. "In truth, perchance we did not rule out the prospect of force, but that was before I met her and knew her—" *And loved her.* He took a ragged breath. "She has been treated with the respect she deserves."

How to convey his feelings to Isabella's brother, when he would likely take his head from his shoulders if he learned the full truth?

"She commands that respect," he added, thinking of their first meeting at Ember Hall and how Isabella had not once shown fear or faltered in her step.

"That I know." Tristan walked fully into the small cell, which barely seemed big enough to hold both of them. He sank down beside Hamish on the pallet and stretched his long legs out in front of him.

The path was now clear between Hamish and the open door. But he knew that if he made a dash for freedom, de Neville would pounce quicker than a cat upon a mouse. Hamish reminded himself that he was unarmed and injured. Whilst Tristan glowed with good health and held one hand on the shining hilt of his sword.

"I can see you have a fondness for my sister. But that does not alter my thinking one way or the other. You will not be the last man to fall for the charms of Isabella. Nay, what I want to know is this, what hold do *you* have over *her?*"

Hamish's tongue stuck to the roof of his mouth. His answer could be pivotal to his freedom, but he could not for the life of him think what to say.

'Twas not his place to claim Isabella's heart. Not when he languished in a dungeon with naught to his name.

Tristan made an impatient sound at the back of his throat. "Answer me this then. What are you doing here, at Wolvesley Castle? It appears you rode here, on your own horse, of your own free will. In God's name, why?"

"'Twas Isabella's plan," Hamish croaked. "She learned of my misfortune, of the events that led me to take her hostage, and she wanted to help me."

Tristan raised his eyebrows and waited for him to continue.

"She is a good woman," Hamish said hurriedly.

"I am not here to debate the qualities of my sister."

Hamish looked down at the damp stone floor. This was the chance he'd sought; to petition for Tristan's help. But he had imagined such a conversation taking place in comfort, perchance with them sitting by a roaring fire. At the very least, with de Neville sitting and Hamish standing.

"Isabella thought to ask for your assistance in speaking to the King for the return of my lands in Scotland. I was—I am—the rightful Laird of Greenock."

Ye Gods, he felt less and less like a rightful Laird with every day that passed.

Tristan's eyes grew as wide as Isabella's often did. He slowly shook his golden head. "Why the devil would she think I might do that?"

Hamish took a breath. He could not afford to let this opportunity escape him, no matter how dire the setting. "Because she believes you to be a fair-minded man. That has always been your reputation, my lord, even in the highlands."

'Twas true, even if the words stuck in his throat.

But Tristan folded his arms. "If that is the extent of your argument, then we are done."

Hamish held up the palms of his hands. "Also because Lord Gaunt could ne'er prosper in the highlands. He knows naught of farming the land up there. Under his rule, my people are likely to starve."

Tristan pursed his lips, but did not appear convinced.

Hamish ploughed on, his voice growing stronger as he spoke of the lands he loved. "'Tis a harsh life, so far north. Naught comes easily, save the snow and the biting wind. I have known farmers lose a whole flock of sheep when they did not watch the skies for signs of a coming storm. Harvests can fail in a sennight of heavy rain. Ye have to work with nature. Ye have to work *hard*. Ye have to *care*." He beat his own chest for emphasis, his words echoing around the stone walls. "The glen is a place of great beauty. The lands can be fruitful. The people are loyal. But 'twill all be ruined under a laird more concerned with feasting than farming."

Tristan turned his head and gazed at Hamish. "Your family have always lived there?"

"Aye." Hamish did not allow himself to consider his Uncle Donald. "My father was the laird before me, and his father before him, and so it continues. The McIvor belong at Greenock. 'Tis a part of my soul." His fist clenched over his heart and he took a steadying breath, aware that he had shouted his final words.

"You do not believe Lord Gaunt equal to the task?"

Hamish resisted the urge to spit on the stone floor. "I dinna believe him capable or willing to keep my people safe. To protect them from raiders. Nor to feed their children." He shook his head. "I dinna believe him capable of wiping his own arse, my lord."

Tristan failed to hide his smile. "You speak of my future brother-in-law."

His words wounded Hamish, but he did not let it show. "I canna speak for that."

"Yet you speak eloquently of your love for your lands and your people. I find myself half convinced."

Hamish knew a rush of relief, but before he could voice his thanks, Tristan continued.

"In truth, I am not certain there is aught I can do to remedy this situation. But I am willing to try."

"Thank ye." Hamish had never meant those words more.

Tristan gave him a shrewd look. "I do not do this as a favor to my sister. 'Tis because I hear the passion in your voice. I know what it is to be responsible for lands and livelihoods. 'Tis a responsibility that should ne'er be shirked, nor undervalued." He rose gracefully from the pallet and extended his hand to Hamish.

After a moment of surprise, Hamish took it and stood facing him, a Scottish warrior and English knight. They shook hands, the import of the occasion slightly marred by the low ceiling and their stooping shoulders.

"Let us go and speak to Lord Gaunt."

Tristan led the way out of the cell.

CHAPTER EIGHTEEN

A HEAVY KNOCKING made Isabella wake with a start. For a terrible moment, she thought herself back in the grip of her old nightmares. Then reality took hold: she was in her girlhood bedchamber at Wolvesley; they had arrived late last night after a perilous ride over the moors. Hamish was wounded, and Tristan had thrown him into the dungeon.

It was morning now. She could tell by the milky light streaming through the shutters.

The knocking came again; so heavy 'twas almost a hammering.

Perchance something has happened to Hamish.

Legs trembling, Isabella launched herself out of the high bed and stumbled to the door. She wrenched it open, expecting to find a messenger boy or Tristan's personal manservant. But it was her sister, Esme, who barreled into the chamber and gathered Isabella into a tight embrace.

"Bella. It's really you. You're safe."

"I am safe," Isabella muttered. She was pleased to see her favorite sibling, but already irritated by her family's insistence on emphasizing the danger she had faced. In truth, Hamish had kept her safe and been her protector, but no one seemed willing to hear this.

Esme held her at arm's length and surveyed her critically. "I thought Tristan was exaggerating when he said you were dressed as a farm laborer."

"I do believe these are your clothes I'm wearing," Isabella replied airily. She had not had the energy to change last night, and had simply tumbled into bed fully clothed. The woolen tunic was now pulled even further out of shape, whilst the braccae bagged unbecomingly around her ankles.

"Aye, mayhap to till the fields," Esme giggled.

"My appearance was not my main concern when I last dressed." Isabella wrinkled her nose. When *was* that, exactly? It seemed an age since she had last bathed. The ingrained dirt in her fingernails was entirely at odds with the polished splendor of her surroundings. She avoided her reflection in the gilded looking glass above the dresser.

"Never mind all that." Esme tugged her toward the canopied bed and they sat side-by-side on the edge, as they had when they were younger. "'Tis wonderful to see you. I demand to know all that has happened."

Isabella rubbed sleep out of her eyes and wondered where she might begin. It would be a relief, of sorts, to unburden herself to Esme—who had, after all, fallen in love with a man many might deem unsuitable—but the nuance of their situations could not be more different.

Adam had arrived at Ember Hall as Esme's bodyguard; whilst Hamish had lived there as Isabella's captor. Would Esme understand?

Am I brave enough to declare my feelings for Hamish?

Isabella eyed her sister uncertainly. Esme looked every inch the earl's daughter, with her hair pinned elegantly on top of her head and her taffeta skirts trimmed with fur. 'Twas as if their usual situations were reversed. Esme had become the wise older sister, and Isabella the one in a scrape.

But of course, Esme's air of wisdom and experience was to be expected. Her little sister was not only a wife; she was a mother.

"How are the twins? And Adam?" Isabella gulped down her instinctive pang of jealousy.

"Blooming, all of them. And ne'er have I been more grateful for their good health." Esme put a hand to the pearls around her neck. "These last days have been dreadful, with all of us worried for little Lucan."

"He is well now?" Isabella wanted to be sure.

"He is much recovered. Though his cough still lingers. The physician says he is out of danger." Esme shifted on the bed as if ill-at-ease. "But Adam still fears the fever may be catching."

"He fears for your boys?"

Esme nodded. "He wishes for us to return to Ember Hall," she blurted out, folding her hands in her lap and fixing her gaze downward.

"Oh." Isabella's lips parted in surprise. Having only just found her sister, it seemed she was about to lose her again.

"I know. The timing could not be worse." Esme shook her head regretfully. "He is correct, of course, we should not leave the hall empty. Look what has already happened."

Her tone was light, but Isabella was not quite ready to laugh about her ordeal. Especially when Hamish's fate was still unknown. To give herself time, she crossed to the long window and opened the shutters. Her bedchamber looked out over the fountain, with a view all the way to the rose gardens. But today, the predominant color was grey.

Grey clouds in the sky. Grey puddles stretching across the manicured paths.

It was not an outlook to inspire hope.

She crossed her arms over her chest to ward off a chill and turned back to her sister. "What about Jonah?"

Esme rolled her eyes. "Our enigmatic brother is as puzzling as ever. After so many years playing lord and master at Ember Hall, he now wishes to remain at Wolvesley. I cannot think what is keeping him here." Esme pulled at a loose thread on the bed blankets. "Of course, he refuses to explain his decision. But it means that Adam and I really have no choice but to return. Callum left the hall in Adam's safe-keeping when he and Frida went to Scotland."

"Of course." Isabella smiled and nodded, whilst inside she wanted to beg her sister to stay. She returned to the bed and grasped Esme's hands. "I am so pleased to see you, even if it is for such a short time."

"You must visit us soon," Esme insisted. "Or we will come to see you at Greenock. Or wherever you may be," she amended, having glanced at Isabella's face.

Isabella could only nod.

Wherever I may be.

She leaned over and hugged her sister. So much was unknown, but of one thing, she was certain. She would not allow her jealousy to drive a wedge between her and Esme any longer.

"But for now, there is much you need to tell me and we do not have long left to us." Esme became brisk. "Is it true you were held prisoner by a wild highland warrior who murdered three men in cold blood?"

Isabella blanched. "Those are not the words I would use."

She looked past Esme to the patterns of light on the plastered wall, and a memory stirred of last night. Her mother had also accused Hamish of murder.

Could it be so?

She closed her eyes. It was not a thought she wished to linger on.

Esme cleared her throat to recapture her attention. "Is it correct that e'en now, Tristan is interrogating your wild Scotsman in the dungeons?"

Isabella's mouth opened and closed. "I don't know."

"Forsooth, I woke you myself. 'Twas a foolish question. But I hate to leave Wolvesley without understanding what has happened to you." Esme sat sideways and looked meaningfully into her sister's eyes. "You do have a story to tell me. I can sense it." She reached out and grasped Isabella's hands, holding them tighter when she tried to pull away. "Tell me," she commanded.

The words bubbled up inside her and she had neither the

strength nor the will to deny them. "I love him," Isabella cried out. "Heaven help me, Esme, but I love my wild highlander. He is like no man I have e'er met."

"You love him!" Esme shrieked so loudly that Isabella feared she would bring the maids running in. "I thought to hear a declaration of mere fancy. But *love* is so much better."

"It is not." Isabella shook her head soberly. "It is painful. Especially when there is so much against us. I am betrothed, and to Hamish's sworn enemy at that." Tears brimmed in her eyes and she fixed her gaze on a finely stitched tapestry hanging above the bed.

"These things are not important." Esme smiled beatifically.

Isabella smoothed back a golden curl which had escaped her sister's hair pins. "I am well aware that your love story ended well."

"With much against us," Esme interrupted.

"But that does not mean 'twill be the same for me." Isabella twitched with frustration. Unable to sit still, she jumped off the bed and began to pace about the chamber. "Hamish's lands and title have been requisitioned by the King. He has little to his name."

"Adam had naught."

Isabella flapped her hands at her sister. "Hamish has been imprisoned by our own brother."

"The same brother who came to blows with Frida's husband just days before blessing their union." Esme smiled dreamily. "Love has the power to conquer all, Bella, you'll see. Especially love that begins at Ember Hall."

SOMETIME LATER, ISABELLA had bathed and dressed in a manner more becoming of an earl's daughter. Her emerald necklace, still gleaming and beautiful despite having spent the last days tucked beneath a grubby tunic, rested atop the creamy silk of a fur-lined winter gown. Her hair, mercifully washed by her mother's maid with lavender soap and an endless supply of warm water, had been braided and pinned up and over her head. It felt strange to slide her feet into goatskin slippers, rather than the leather boots she had grown accustomed to. The cold of the stone floor was more apparent, as was every groove and bump of the wooden staircase. But she knew she must look the part she had been born to play.

The Rose of England.

Holding her head high, she walked gracefully into the vast, echoing, great hall and over to the stone fireplace, where her father waited in his throne-like carved chair. Ignoring the huddle of men-at-arms, and the smaller group which all her senses told her Hamish stood among, she curtsied deep and low, not rising until she felt her father's heavy hand on her shoulder.

"Isabella," he said simply, his voice so beloved and familiar that tears sprang to her eyes. "Welcome home."

She rose and found herself pulled into a tight embrace. Angus, the Earl of Wolvesley remained a tall, strong and formidable man, despite his advancing years. His golden hair had turned to silver, but his blue eyes were as piercing as ever. He wore his customary, green-colored fur cloak, which skimmed the floor beyond his polished boots. Green was the traditional color of Wolvesley—which was one of the reasons Isabella had such fondness for her emerald necklace. It had long-served as a reminder of home.

"I am glad to be back, Father." She blinked away her tears, noting new lines etched around the earl's eyes and mouth.

Another sign that Wolvesley Castle was not as invulnerable to change or threat as she might like to imagine.

As her father sank back into his chair, she allowed her gaze to flicker to the men standing to her right. Tristan was closest, almost a double of their father in his younger years in his height, bearing and the relentless energy which radiated from him.

Hamish stood by his side.

Isabella quickly looked away, her heart pounding. Hamish still wore his travel and blood-stained clothes of yesterday. But he stood tall, exuding a quiet charisma not unlike that of Tristan.

He is alive.

And he is here!

Whatever had transpired between Hamish and Tristan, it had resulted in Hamish being brought to the great hall, unbound and unrestrained. Isabella knew a tremor of excitement. Could their audacious plan come to pass after all?

She would not have labelled their plan audacious when they first hatched it out, isolated but cozy at Ember Hall. But now that she had returned to Wolvesley, she baulked at her own brazenness. Her family were the de Nevilles, her childhood home was England's finest fortress. And she had galloped through the gates, filthy and bloodstained. She looked at the mighty pillars and vivid frescoes, and reflected that her mother was right to insist she bathed and changed before petitioning for further assistance.

Tristan gave her a sharp nod of greeting. "'Tis good to see you rested and looking more your usual self, sister."

She ignored the barb and curtsied again, aware that all eyes were upon her, from the men-at-arms behind them, to the man she loved who stood just feet away. "I was saddened to hear of your son's illness, Tris. How does Mirrie fare this morn?"

Tristan hesitated, perchance surprised by her overture of friendship after the harsh words that had passed between them. "Much better, thank you. I dare to hope she may join us later."

"Happy news indeed."

Isabella's words were sincere. Kind-hearted Mirrie was once their father's ward and had grown up alongside them, here at Wolvesley. Isabella loved her almost like a sister.

Tristan inclined his head and gave her a little smile, half teasing and half affectionate. It reminded her of how he'd looked as a mischievous little boy, when he and Frida were the best of friends.

"We have all been waiting for you, Bella." He raised his eyebrows. "Am I allowed to call you that now?"

"You have been waiting for me?" She pressed a hand to her chest and looked from her father to her brother, not daring to pause when her gaze slid over Hamish. "I do not know whether to be honored or surprised."

Tristan pulled a face. "You should not be surprised. You are, it seems, the key to all of this."

Isabella had a dreadful premonition. They could not hope to continue this exchange without the input of a man currently missing from their party.

Sure enough, Tristan gave a short bow to their father and then shot a glance at Hamish. "I shall fetch Lord Gaunt."

Both men nodded their agreement before turning their gaze back to Isabella. She realized that if she expected her father to believe that Hamish was a friend, then she must treat him as such.

"I am more pleased to see you than I can say." She spoke clearly and without hesitation, knowing that her words carried throughout the hall, but refusing to be cowed by the shame of Hamish's incarceration.

He bowed and smiled so sweetly it illuminated his whole face.

"'Tis my pleasure to look upon ye, Lady Isabella."

She thought of how he had teased her for her fancy ways and almost made a haughty retort, but she swallowed her words just in time. She must not allow her father to discern the merest hint of impropriety between them.

Instead, she satisfied herself by meeting his steady blue gaze and smiling back. A frisson passed between them, and she looked quickly away, feeling a flush coming to her cheeks.

This would never do. Certainly not before her father's all-seeing eyes.

Isabella took a step away from the fire and made a show of fanning herself. "'Tis warm in here. Perchance I grew over-accustomed to the chill of Ember Hall." Immediately, she chided her thoughtlessness. "Hamish always ensured the fires were built," she added lamely.

"We suffered an early snowfall. The freeze e'en reached us here," Angus spoke up helpfully. "I wonder you managed to keep the animals fed and watered so far north."

Hamish cleared his throat, correctly divining that an answer was expected from him. "'Twas a daily struggle, milord. The well froze early on and we were obliged to cut ice from the river and melt it."

"Not an easy undertaking." The earl stroked his beard, his curious gaze passing from Hamish to Isabella. "And a considerable change in circumstance for you, Bella."

She affected a laugh. "I did not cut any ice, Father. I stayed safe indoors."

"But ye did cook for us," Hamish said unexpectedly.

A log cracked in the fire as Isabella wondered desperately how best to respond.

Once again, her father came to the rescue. "Your mother will be pleased to know you remembered how."

Isabella summoned a smile. "I know everyone believes me to have led a life of idleness at Westchester, but I did not forget everything I learned as a child." She was about to proclaim her proficiency in steering two horses over the moors, when she felt the touch of her father's hand on hers.

"Forgive me, child, I am only teasing. I, for one, know you to be a woman of great competence. I am certain that Hamish here agrees."

Hamish.

How would he react to being addressed without his title in the great hall of Wolvesley Castle?

But Hamish only looked at her father as if they shared some understanding.

"I agree entirely, milord," he said.

Isabella held herself very still as Tristan marched back into the hall with a small man scurrying in his wake. Lord Gaunt had not improved any during his sojourn in the highlands. His expression was still sallow, his chin pointed and his expression mean. When his dark eyes roved over Isabella, she felt an answering roll of nausea in her belly. She wanted to back away, or at the very least seek protection behind her father's large chair. But she recalled Tristan's words: *you are, it seems, key to all this.*

It was true. If she had not accepted Gaunt's proposal, none of them would be in this situation. Albeit, if she had not accepted Gaunt's proposal, she might never have met Hamish. The incongruity of it all made her head spin and she was obliged to grip the arm of her father's chair and take a deep breath. Her tightly-laced gown pinched her ribs, and she reflected, again, that there was much to be said in favor of more comfortable clothing. Perchance if she were still attired as a farm laborer, Lord Gaunt would not be looking at her with such a lascivious gleam in his small eyes.

Her father cleared his throat. "Good morn, Lord Gaunt."

"My lord Wolvesley." Gaunt made an awkward bow to the earl but completely ignored Hamish. "Lady Isabella." He bowed again and reached for her hand, which she had no choice but to offer. When he kissed the back of it, she could not help a wince of distaste.

A wince that was duly noted by Hamish and Tristan.

Hamish looked as if he might strike the man down. Tristan appeared merely contemplative. Lord Gaunt gave her hand a none-too-gentle tug, clearly wanting her to stand by his side. Isabella stood firm, wrenching her hand free and placing it, pointedly, on the back of her father's chair.

"'Twas a surprise to find you here at Wolvesley, Lord Gaunt," she said.

"Concern for your welfare brought me south, my lady. We expected you at Greenock some days since. And news reached me that my escort party had been murdered by highland savages."

His voice sent shudders down her spine. If Hamish had not

taken her captive, she may already be Gaunt's bride.

What was I thinking?

Gaunt had flickered his dark eyes toward Hamish as he spoke, leaving no one under any illusions about who he held responsible for the murder of his escort party. Isabella found her vision breaking up into a maze of dancing dots.

Angus reached up to pat Isabella's hand, as if aware of her discomfort. "As you can see, my beloved daughter is hale and hearty as ever…"

"I do see that," Gaunt interrupted.

There was a moment of surprised silence.

"Aye, well." Angus resettled his cloak about his shoulders, unaccustomed to being interrupted. "Let us move onto the business in hand. My son, Tristan, has something he wishes to ask of you."

This was the moment they had hoped for. Isabella's gaze flew to Hamish's across the stone-flagged floor. She saw that his torn and stained clothing counted for naught. In these grand surroundings, he was as much at home as any visiting noble.

He was the proper Laird of Greenock. He had been raised for the role. And he would defend his lands and inheritance with the same fierce conviction of any de Neville knight, past or present.

Isabella began to breathe more easily. All may yet be well. She switched her gaze to Tristan and waited expectantly for him to begin.

But Tristan seemed disinclined to take the lead in these negotiations. He looked instead to Hamish, saying, "This is the man who should speak."

Lord Gaunt visibly reeled with surprise, but Hamish's manner was calm. He folded his hands behind his back and looked evenly at Lord Gaunt, as if they were discussing naught more weighty than a hunting party.

"I am here to petition ye for the rightful return of my lands. Lands which my forefathers farmed and nurtured. I canna think the highlands are a hospitable place for any man accustomed to a more gentle climate."

Gaunt gave a short, barking laugh which almost sent her stumbling into the fireplace. She wished her father had positioned his chair further from the flames.

"I've no argument with that. Greenock Castle has all the welcome of a poor man's hut."

Hamish's eyes widened, but this was the only outward acknowledgement he gave of the slight to his home and birthright. "Then ye are open to negotiation."

"I will be pleased ne'er to cross the Scottish border again."

Gaunt waved peremptorily to a passing servant and demanded a chair be brought for him. In the ensuing scuffle, Isabella became aware that her younger brother, Jonah, had quietly joined the group around the fire. He nodded a greeting and she nodded back. They had never been particularly close. Jonah had been an argumentative child with a scowl most often stamped across his sensitive features. He stood a head shorter than Tristan, with a narrower set to his shoulders. But Isabella—along with the rest of her siblings—had always known that, despite his limp and club foot, Jonah should not be underestimated. He had a sharp mind and was better skilled with a sword than many unwitting adversaries of the past had imagined.

He was watching Gaunt closely, closer even than Hamish. Isabella recalled Esme's words about Jonah's inexplicable urge to remain at Wolvesley rather than retreat to the home he had created at Ember Hall, and she wondered afresh what had prompted it.

But her attention snapped back to Lord Gaunt when he sat down in his chair and fixed her with a beady-eyed stare.

"I shall, of course, expect recompense."

"I will give ye all the coin I can spare," Hamish replied. "Though as ye must ken, the keep is in sore need of repair."

"In truth, there is little left that is worthy of the name." Gaunt crossed his legs and surveyed the room. "Wolvesley is a home any man would be proud of. But Greenock is not. My horses sleep in greater comfort."

A dark red stain passed over Hamish's stubbled cheeks. "Ye have yer English King to thank fer that."

Tristan held up a placatory hand. "What recompense do you desire, Lord Gaunt?"

"Lady Isabella's dower, as it stands, is hardly equal to the loss of land and a title. Perchance, my Lord Wolvesley, you could see a way for it to be doubled."

Isabella was the only one to gasp aloud. Both of her brothers retained their inscrutable expressions and Hamish had turned away so she could not read his reaction at all. Standing behind her father's chair, she could only see the top of his silvery head, but she imagined him fixing Gaunt with a superior glare.

The de Nevilles were wealthy enough to triple Isabella's dower and not notice the loss of coin. But Gaunt could not be so brazen as to demand it in such a public place. Scarcely veiled whispering from behind them indicated that Tristan's men-at-arms were following every word of this exchange.

Isabella felt a new resolve strengthen in her belly. She spoke up before the futile conversation could persist any longer.

"I'm afraid that won't be possible, Lord Gaunt. For the simple reason that I refuse to marry you."

The great hall fell silent as every man present strained to hear what would happen next.

"That is not in your power, Lady Isabella. The betrothal contract is signed." Gaunt's voice was as smooth as silk.

"My daughter has the right to make her own decisions. 'Tis a right that I gift to her and no one can take that away, not while there is breath in my body. Do not doubt that Lady Isabella enjoys the full protection of the Wolvesley army." Angus reached over his shoulder for Isabella's hand, which she gave to him readily. As his fingers squeezed hers, she knew a great swell of love.

"Thank you, Father," she whispered.

"Then these negotiations have been in vain. I shall retain the lands at Greenock and all that goes with them." Lord Gaunt's face twisted with malice.

Hamish staggered sideways as if he had been struck. Isabella drew in a sharp breath of realization.

Gaunt still holds Hamish's sister captive.

Isabella immediately unfastened her emerald necklace and held it toward Gaunt with trembling hands. "Take this. Take every jewel I have. But please release the young woman you have taken prisoner."

Gaunt eyed the necklace speculatively. Tristan looked about to intervene, but it was Hamish who spoke first.

"Ye dinna need to do that, Isabella."

"They are only jewels." She twisted the rings from her fingers and held them out as well. "What do they count against a human life?"

Gaunt smiled. If anything, it made his expression of cruelty even more pronounced.

"Lady Isabella, you have given me the beginnings of an idea."

"Take the jewels," she said through gritted teeth. She wanted this conversation over with, and this abhorrent man gone from her life. "There are more that I will send on to you. I give you my word."

"'Tis an interesting proposition." Gaunt stroked his beard. "But there is one person whose opinion we have not taken into account." He beckoned the same servant who had brought him the chair, and his next words made dread pool inside Isabella's stomach. "Fetch Elena McIvor from the dungeon."

CHAPTER NINETEEN

H AMISH FELT AS though he could hardly breathe. *What was Gaunt planning?*

And what sickening role had he devised for Elena in all this?

Whatever the answer, at least Hamish would set eyes on his beloved sister soon. If only he had his sword at his hip, then he could rescue Elena and flee from the place. If Gaunt fell victim to the swing of his broadsword, then that would be his own foolish fault.

He gazed into the fire and wrestled for control of his spiraling thoughts. He must be realistic. Not only was he unarmed, but Tristan de Neville stood but feet away. However much the man seemed to dislike Lord Gaunt, Hamish had an idea he would not welcome bloodshed by his fireside.

And what about Isabella?

He could not walk away from her.

His rational mind protested at that, pointing out that Isabella had the protection of the Earl of Wolvesley, and not one, but two brothers.

Hamish found he did not care. There had always been something in Isabella's clear blue eyes that called to him, like a torch on a dark night guiding him home. That feeling had strengthened since their ride across the moors, when he saved her from Alaric and she, in turn, saved him from bleeding out on the rocks. They were bound to one another; with bonds he had no wish to break. Even now, he was conscious of the way she stood and the way she breathed. In different circumstances he would go to her and take her hand, to offer what comfort he could, for although Isabella did not *need* to lean on any man, he fancied she might like to, just for a moment.

He lifted his gaze and met hers. Aye, he was right about it all.

He could never leave her.

And she longed for him, just as he longed for her. He could read it all in her expression. But of all the men present by the fireplace, he was least able to go to her side.

Do not give up hope.

Was that Brianne's voice whispering in his ear? Perchance 'twas just the memory of her. The sentiment was true either way. Like a warrior outnumbered on the battlefield, Hamish must carry on with his fight.

He steeled himself as the steady tramp of footsteps announced the arrival of the guard. He could not see Elena behind the tall, muscular bodies of the liveried soldiers who marched in a straight line toward them. It took all his restraint to stand still and wait for her arrival.

She had better be fed and healthy, he thought, or God help him, he would strangle Gaunt with his own bare hands.

"Elena McIvor," the first guard announced.

Lady Elena McIvor, Hamish corrected him silently, grinding his teeth in anger.

The guards melted away, and there stood his sister.

Elena had always been a slight young woman. Where Hamish and Brianne were sturdy and strong, Elena was as slender as a willow branch. But she was the daughter—and the sister—of a laird, and she stood tall and proud, even though strands of hay clung to her long auburn hair and smudges of dirt marred the pale perfection of her cheeks. Her wary gaze found Hamish and for a long moment they looked at one another across the grandeur of the English castle which such strange twists of fate had brought them both to.

Hamish swallowed painfully. He wanted to reassure Elena, to tell her that all would be well. But what power did he have to ensure that?

She had no visible cuts or bruises, nor was she in any way shackled. For this he was grateful. But her long skirts hung in tatters and her shawl had turned from cream to grey. He glanced down at his own filthy, blood-stained clothing and was saddened by how low the McIvor clan had sunk.

Isabella was the first to break the silence. She walked toward Elena and took her hands.

"Lady Elena, I am pleased to meet you, despite these sorry circumstances." She gestured to the servants. "Fetch a chair for our guest, if you please. And wine."

Elena's eyes widened with surprise. At first, she flinched at Isabella's touch, making Hamish fear once again that she had been ill-treated by Gaunt's men. But then she relaxed and smiled.

Who could not smile at Isabella?

"I have not been publicly addressed as Lady Elena for many days now." Her voice was raspy through lack of use.

"We could dispense with the formalities. I am Isabella. And I am grieved to discover you have been here at Wolvesley without our knowledge." Her eyes flashed daggers at Gaunt. "We shall have a chamber made ready for you."

"Once we are finished here, she shall return to the dungeon. She is my prisoner, Lady Isabella. Not yours."

Hamish's hand went to his sword and encountered only air. He opened his mouth, but it was the younger de Neville brother who spoke first.

"Take care, Lord Gaunt, not to overstep the mark. The de Nevilles believe in treating women and children fairly, whether they are prisoners or not."

Hamish's surprise grew stronger when he saw Elena throw him a small smile. He looked again at the man he had originally paid little heed to. Tristan was the son everyone talked of. This was undoubtedly his brother; he had the same coloring and even the same set to his shoulders. He may stand a head shorter than both Hamish and Tristan, but there was no denying the conviction in his flashing eyes.

Lord Gaunt waved a languid hand. "Then you shall appreciate the offer I am about to make."

Isabella audibly tutted as she helped Isabella into a chair and poured the wine which had been hurriedly brought over. "I shall find you something to wear, my dear. When did you last eat?"

Did Elena look again at the younger de Neville brother? Hamish thought she did. But her gaze was fully on Isabella when she answered.

"I have already broken my fast, thank ye milady."

"I am glad to hear it."

Isabella handed Elena a goblet of wine and Hamish felt a powerful rush of love. He had always believed Isabella to be a remarkable woman, but here she was, taking care of his sister as fiercely and instinctively as if she were her own sibling. With her golden hair shining in the light from the candelabra overhead, she could have been a ministering angel.

Isabella turned to face Gaunt. "Let us hear this proposal of yours, and quickly."

Lord Gaunt sat back in the tapestried chair, apparently enjoying the attention he was receiving from all sides. He ignored Isabella's request and a tense silence fell across the room.

Hamish found his fists were clenching once again. His gaze slid over Lord Gaunt and came to rest on the de Neville brothers. Both of them were immaculately turned out, in fur-trimmed cloaks and spotless tunics shot through with gold thread. They looked like men who had never faced the hardships of battle, but he knew, in Tristan's case at least, that this was not the case. Tristan had fought long and hard on battlefields up and down the country, and over the water in France, but his luck had held, and he had never been seriously injured.

Would Tristan's good fortune extend to the McIvor? Could

Hamish count on his support, whatever bold plan Gaunt came out with?

Hamish found the answer would not come to him. But strangely, he sensed he could count, absolutely, on the support of Tristan's brother; whose gaze kept swinging to Elena; whose name Hamish did not even know.

The silence continued; its weight so heavy that Hamish found it difficult to breathe.

The de Neville coat of arms hung over the wide fireplace. Hamish focused on this display of English military might rather than risk his temper spiking at Gaunt's cunning smile.

"Pray speak, man. I have other business to attend to." The earl's voice was gruff with impatience.

"'Tis a delicate matter, my lord. I am only searching for the right words." Gaunt licked his lips with the tip of his tongue and from the corner of his eye, Hamish saw Isabella shudder. "I need a son." He paused. "For that, I need a bride."

Hamish felt a hammer blow strike his chest as he realized with sudden, sickening clarity, when Gaunt was headed.

"I have always appreciated beautiful things," he continued. "Isabella de Neville is a woman of great beauty. But in these last days, I have come to appreciate that Elena McIvor has some share of beauty too. And she is young." His small eyes gleamed lasciviously. "With many childbearing years ahead of her."

"Nay," Hamish said forcefully. "I am her brother and I forbid the match. Elena has seen only seventeen summers."

Gaunt held his gaze, a mocking smile playing about his mouth. "A fine age for a bride."

Tristan cleared his throat. "You are saying, Gaunt, that you will release Isabella from her betrothal contract. And return Greenock to the previous laird. But in return, you claim the hand of Lady Elena?"

"I claim the hand of Lady Elena along with the jewels which Lady Isabella freely offered." He put his head to one side, thinking. "And I will retain Lady Isabella's dower, which is only fair. I doubt the Greenock coffers will offer much coin for the last remaining daughter of the McIvor line."

"Preposterous," exploded the younger de Neville brother.

Tristan turned to him. "Jonah, shall I fetch you a chair. Does your leg pain you?"

Only then did Hamish note that the young man's left leg was narrow and twisted.

Jonah shook his head impatiently. "I am quite well, thank you." But he heeded his brother's inferred reprimand and pressed his pale lips together, saying nothing more.

"You cannot expect that we will agree to these terms," Isabella said calmly. She looked down at the jewels in her hand, as if weighing their value. But from the casual way she had offered them earlier, Hamish guessed that Isabella's real concern was for Elena.

With every fiber of his being, he hoped that were true. For he would rather be consigned to hell than see his sweet sister marry Lord Gaunt.

If only I had my sword.

He was castrated and powerless without it.

"Ye canna marry Elena," he said flatly.

"She is my prisoner under the terms of war. I can do with her whatever I like. Just as Lady Isabella is contracted to be my betrothed." Gaunt smiled at the assembled company. "My terms are generous, under the circumstances."

Isabella pressed her hands together as if praying for aid. She turned sideways to look at Elena and seemed to reach a decision.

"Very well, Lord Gaunt. You leave me no choice. I will honor our betrothal contract on the understanding that Greenock Castle is returned to Hamish McIvor, along with the freedom of his sister." Her voice trembled only slightly.

Hamish felt as if his heart was beating out of his chest. Iron bars clamped around his ribs and squeezed tightly.

"Isabella, think carefully upon this," her father warned.

"There is naught to think about." She stepped out from behind the chair and dropped into a perfunctory curtsy. "I beg leave to rest, these proceedings have quite exhausted me."

"Give us until the morn for our answer," Tristan spoke up. "That is little enough to ask, Lord Gaunt. You may remain here, as our guest. And Lady Elena can also be shown to a guest chamber."

Gaunt shook his head. "Elena will return to the dungeon with my own men guarding her."

"Your men can stand guard outside a bedchamber as easily as the dungeon." Jonah's voice was cold. "I will take her myself to a chamber in the western tower, with a door which bolts from the outside and a window far too high and narrow for anyone to jump from. Will that meet your requirements?" He looked down at Lord Gaunt as if he would like to strike him.

"It will do very well." The earl concluded in a tone that brooked no argument. "Come the morn, I will write to the King myself."

Hamish found he could breathe a little easier at the prospect of Elena leaving the dungeon. He looked for Isabella, but all he saw was the swish of cream silk as she passed out of the arched double doorway leading from the hall.

He reached out for the support of the plastered wall as his heart began to slow.

They had until the morn.

CHAPTER TWENTY

I SABELLA RAN THROUGH the marbled entrance hall and hurried down the wide stone steps to the fountain, only pausing when she reached the bottom and the pervasive chill of the November wind could no longer be ignored.

I should have brought a cloak.

But the cold was invigorating, and she relished the distraction from the claustrophobic circling of her thoughts. So instead of returning to the keep, she pressed on, her long skirts trailing through the damp grass of the rose garden. The wind whistled through the spiky branches of the beech tree, so that it seemed to wave a warning to her. But it was too late for warnings.

The damage was done.

Salty tears burned her eyes before the wind whipped them away. Her goat skin slippers were no match for sludgy puddles of melting snow, and soon the damp had seeped all the way through to her stockings. But she would sooner face mud and cold than the concern and disappointment of the people she loved. She had an urgent desire to visit the lake: perchance gazing out over the clear expanse of rippling water might help to clear her mind. But when she finally reached the shingled shoreline, Isabella saw that a fog lingered over the water, so she could see no further than twenty feet ahead.

Even the weather was conspiring against her.

Uncaring of dirt, Isabella sank down onto a fallen tree trunk and hugged her knees.

She had hoped to be transported back to her childhood, when the lake was a magical place where rules were relaxed and almost anything could happen. The five de Neville siblings had played in the trees along the shore, skimmed stones on the water, paddled and even swam. She recalled one summer when she privately decided to swim out further than either Frida or Tristan; determined to prove to them that she was stronger than they believed. But she had not taken account of the bone-chilling cold of the deeper waters in the center of the lake; nor of the larger waves that washed right over her head. Panic had her in its grip, before she felt the strong arms of her brother pulling her to safety.

Tristan had always been there when she needed him. But he could not save her from Lord Gaunt. As the future Earl of Wolvesley, and the son of the King's judiciary, he could no more break contract with a peer of the realm than she could storm a keep.

She sighed deeply, the pain in her heart far exceeding the numbing cold of her hands and feet.

As powerful as they were, neither her father nor her brother could help her in this. 'Twas all down to her. Isabella would marry Lord Gaunt because saving young Elena from that same fate was the right and proper thing to do.

And because it would be her final gift to Hamish.

At the thought of his name, Isabella's final vestiges of self-control left her, and she began to sob.

"Dinna cry, lass. I canna bear it."

Mayhap the spirits of the lake had conjured the man she most wanted to see. Somehow he was here before her, gathering her into his strong arms so that, for a fleeting moment, she believed that everything may yet be well. He was warm, solid and reassuring.

She sniffed in a most unladylike fashion. "You should not have come."

How could she take comfort from him when she was to marry another?

"I couldna stay away."

She pressed her forehead into the center of his chest and breathed deeply. "You must. We cannot be together, you and I. You have seen how it is."

"I canna let this happen."

She pulled back and looked into his honest blue eyes. What she saw there convinced her that he meant what he said. He was a man used to fighting for what he believed in, using both brawn and brain and never giving up.

But this was a fight he could never win.

A flare of anger shot through her chest. She had been resigned to her fate. What good could it do for him to come here and stir up hope? *Futile* hope.

She pursed her lips, feeling the same flush of defiance as the young girl who had swum too far into the lake. "How can you possibly prevent it?"

He recoiled as if she had slapped him. Slowly he got to his feet, his shoulders slumped.

"Ye are right to doubt me, for I dinna ken what I can do ter save either ye or Elena."

Regret coiled inside her. She rose up from the log and put her hands on his shoulders. "Nay, I am wrong to put distance between us when we have so little time left." She cupped a hand around his stubbled cheek. "We should not spend it squabbling."

"I am so very sorry." Emotion rippled across his face. "And I canna bear the thought of ye and him—"

"Hush." She put her finger to her lips. "There is no more to say."

"Then what can I do to help?" His plea was anguished.

She rose up on tiptoes and entwined her fingers in his tousled hair, so that her lips were all but pressed against his when she gave her answer.

"Love me," she whispered. "No more questions. No more

regrets. Just love me."

Hamish lifted her easily into his arms and carried her to a copse of trees on higher ground, where the melted snow had all drained away. He spread his cloak on a bed of dry leaves and reverently, tenderly, did as she asked. Their two souls joined as lovers, coming together after a storm, each freely giving what comfort and warmth they could. Comfort which spiraled into peaks of pleasure, so that for a long time, Isabella forgot all about the ordeals ahead. There was only now. Only Hamish. His large body covering hers, his lips crying out her name. Their limbs tangled together so she no longer knew where she ended and he began. They were as one, and naught could ever part them.

But after, when their pounding hearts had slowed and their breathing returned to normal, she felt a wave of desolation which was colder than the fog rolling in off the lake. Tears pooled in her eyes but she held herself still and quiet so he would not notice her distress.

Hamish raised himself onto his elbows. "Dinna hide yer sorrows from me. Not ever. I love thee, Isabella. And I would share the burden of any sorrows with thee." Gently he stroked her tears away.

"I love you too," she choked. "But there is no future for us." She sniffed, but her tears would not be staunched.

"There is now. And there are the next hours. Who knows what the future may hold."

Isabella held her tongue. She knew well enough what awaited her: marriage to a man she despised. A cruel man, prepared to bargain with the life of an innocent young woman to get what he wanted.

How could I ever have agreed to marry him?

She closed her eyes, remembering her overriding desire to bear a child: to be married and titled with a proper place in society. Back then, she had not known what it was to love and be loved.

She had not known what it was to *live*.

"Do not let this be it between us." She held tight to his hands. "I could not bear it. Let us have one more night together."

"One more night in the comfort of a proper bed," he smiled down at her. "How can I deny thee? But will yer father and brother not chase me from the grounds if they find out?"

"That is the very least of our problems." She traced a line from his cheek to his jaw. "I will make sure they do not find out."

ISABELLA WENT DIRECTLY to the ladies' solar to her mother to ask for Hamish to be given use of the bedchamber adjacent to hers. By tradition, it was Esme's. But Esme and Adam had already left for Ember Hall.

Morwenna set down her sewing and raised her blonde eyebrows. "That will cause certain people to be upset," she said diplomatically.

"That is why I am talking to you now, so that certain people do not overhear." Isabella remained standing, conscious of her mud-stained gown and the pale cushions on the window seat.

Morwenna patted the cushion beside her anyway. "Won't you sit for a while, dear?"

"There is nothing to discuss." Isabella was nearly trembling with the effort of keeping her emotions in check. "Father must have told you what is to happen. I must marry Lord Gaunt, as agreed."

"Isabella—" her mother began.

Isabella held up her hand, refusing to be interrupted. "I will do my duty to this family. All I ask is for the man I love to be close to me for one more night."

Morwenna's delicate face creased with sympathy. "You love him?"

"I love him." Isabella was firm. She crossed her arms and gazed stonily at the tapestries on the wall. "Remember, Mother, I am no maid in need of protection. I am a widow."

"I do not need to be reminded of that."

Isabella was dangerously close to tears. She thanked her mother, curtsied and left the solar, before anything more heartfelt could be said.

Next, she went in search of Mirrie.

Isabella had always had a fondness for her brother's wife, even if, when they were children, Mirabel had seemed quieter and less courageous than the rest of them.

As she ascended the winding staircase and followed the torch-lit corridor to Mirrie's private chamber, she reflected that it must take a certain type of courage to be married to Tristan. Firstly, because Tristan was a force of nature, like a fierce wind that could not be stopped, or a mountain that could not be moved. Secondly, because as one of the King's favored knights, Mirrie would never know when he might next be called into battle.

And thirdly, because Isabella—along with her sisters—knew that Mirrie had secretly loved Tristan almost from girlhood.

Love, Isabella had recently learned, took courage.

She knocked on the chamber door with more hesitation than she would have done, some days prior. And when Mirrie opened the door, Isabella seized her hands with genuine affection.

"You are recovered from your illness?"

Mirrie quickly recovered from her surprise. "I am quite well now, thank you. Come in, Isabella."

Again, Isabella baulked at tracking dirt along the pretty fur-nishings in Mirrie's chamber, which was hung with silks and finely-stitched tapestries. She held her muddied skirts in one hand and perched on the edge of the couch. Mirrie was wearing a simple tunic in pale blue, knotted at the waist with cream-colored cord. Her long hair was neatly plaited, and her cheeks, though pale, had a tinge of pink about them.

"I am sorry to disturb your rest."

Much as she had with Esme, Isabella felt that all of the usual ways of the world had been turned on their head. Usually, she was the one in control; the one to marry an earl and command a great house. Now, she looked at Mirrie and saw wisdom and experience in her tired eyes.

Mirrie indicated the day bed and, belatedly, Isabella saw the sleeping figure of her nephew.

"I did not realize." She lowered her voice to a whisper, then pressed her lips together at her clumsiness. "Esme said the fever had broken."

"Aye. He is getting stronger every day."

Mirrie crossed the room and gazed down at her son, who was a miniature double of his golden-haired father. From her position on the couch, Isabella could see the upward sweep of thick blond eyelashes. She did not want to move closer, for fear that she would disturb his rest. Having never had children, Isabella was not comfortable around them.

"I should not have come." Isabella made to get up, but Mirrie hastened to stop her.

"Please don't leave just yet. 'Tis lovely to see you. And I have been low on company these last days, looking after Lucan." With a last look at the boy, she came to sit on a chair pulled close to the fire. "Tell me what has been happening downstairs."

Isabella knew a pang of guilt. She had come here for Mirrie's help, not to chatter.

But it was Mirrie who looked embarrassed. "Forgive me, Isabella. Tristan has told me some of your tale. I should not have pressed you for more. I am not quite myself, you see." She wrung her hands. "The world outside this chamber has become small and unimportant by the side of Lucan's health."

"As it should be." Isabella leaned over and clasped Mirrie's hands in a sisterly gesture, albeit one she had not made often. "Naught is more important than your boy."

Mirrie smiled and squeezed her hand. "But Tris has told me that your future husband, Lord Gaunt, is a difficult man."

"That is most restrained of Tristan. I would say that Lord Gaunt is a despicable man."

Mirrie leaned forward. "Then you cannot marry him."

"Nay, Mirrie, you would not say that if you knew what consequences an innocent maid would suffer if I refuse the match." Isabella shook her head. "I signed the betrothal contract myself and now I must make good on my promise. That is not why I am here." She sat straighter. "I have come to ask if I may borrow some of Tristan's clothes."

"Oh." Mirrie thought for a moment. "For the highlander?"

"You are very well acquainted with recent events." Isabella raised her eyebrows.

"Tris is free with his tongue of an evening, especially when he has imbibed strong wine." Mirrie glanced at Isabella then quickly swung her gaze to the fireplace.

"What is it?"

Mirrie grimaced. "I most certainly should not say."

"Mirrie, I am tired and I am dirty. Perchance on the morrow I will be married to a man I cannot ever hope to respect. If you have something to say to me, please God say it now."

She gave a little laugh. "I am not accustomed to you being so direct, Bella."

"Nay, 'tis a habit I have recently acquired." Isabella stretched out her long legs, noticing that bits of leaves clung to her skirts, amidst the mud.

"Tristan believes you to be in love with the highlander." Mirrie's cheeks flushed at her daring. "I cannot believe I have said this to you." She put a hand to her mouth and shook her head regretfully.

"Tristan said that? Tristan noticed?" Isabella was more amazed than embarrassed.

"He sees more than he pretends to see."

"Aye, well, perchance in this case he is correct." Isabella saw no sense in prevaricating. "But it matters not. I am to marry Lord Gaunt. I only wish for my highlander, Hamish, to dine with us this night in the great hall, where he rightfully belongs. He cannot do so in clothes that are torn and matted with blood."

Mirrie gave her a long look before going over to the closet and fetching out a freshly laundered shirt, clean breeches and a plainly stitched jacket. "They are of a similar size, I imagine?"

Isabella nodded and held out her hands for the clothes. "Thank you, Mirrie."

"You are most welcome." Mirrie caught her eye. "If I might say one more thing?"

"Of course." Isabella smiled whilst she braced herself for the blow. How could the future Countess of Wolvesley countenance a dalliance between her sister-in-law and a rebel Scot?

"Do not give up hope." Mirrie clasped her hands behind her back. "There were times when I doubted Tristan and I would e'er be together. Times when it seemed vast oceans stood between us. But somehow, we found our way and I have learned that love is worth fighting for."

Moved by her kindness, Isabella gave Mirrie a kiss on the cheek, but as she took her leave and returned to her chamber, she reflected that Mirrie didn't have any idea what she was talking about.

Whatever challenges Mirrie and Tristan had faced, they most certainly did not involve dungeons and death, nor the ruination of an innocent girl.

Isabella had no hope of a future with Hamish. And there was naught to be gained by pretending otherwise.

CHAPTER TWENTY-ONE

HAMISH KNEW IT was important to Isabella that he made an appearance in the great hall that night. He washed in a bowl of warm water brought to his chamber by a pink-cheeked serving maid, and he carefully shaved, hardly knowing the man looking back at him through the gold-edged looking glass.

Not a man; *a victim.*

No matter what he had faced in the past, Hamish had always believed, deep down, that he would prevail. Hardships he could and would endure, but victory would ultimately belong to him. He was a warrior. The Laird of Greenock. Crops may fail, but the McIvor did not.

Until today.

He placed the ivory comb on the nightstand and sighed so deeply that a nearby candle flickered and went out. His face in the looking glass was now obscured by shadows.

Very appropriate.

From this day forward, his life would be overshadowed by what might have been. Aye, he would return to Greenock with Elena by his side. But not a day would pass without him thinking of Isabella and the sacrifice she had made on his behalf.

Hamish's fist crashed down, and the ivory comb jumped onto the floor. A beaker of ale, also brought for him by the pink-cheeked serving maid, wobbled precariously.

God's blood; it was more than he could endure.

Brianne had not appeared to him since the day on the moors and he missed her. Right now, some sage advice from his wise and witty sister would be most welcome. But the large bedchamber remained defiantly empty. Perchance a Scottish spirit was not able to enter an English castle.

Perchance she didna want to enter.

If anyone had told Hamish that he would sit down to dine with the Earl of Wolvesley; he would have thought that person touched in the head. If Siegfried were here, he would issue some scathing comment. But Hamish had no argument with the de Nevilles. Only with Lord Gaunt.

Blood pounded in his ears. If he thought more on the subject of Gaunt, he would not be physically capable of donning the clothes Isabella had brought for him, nor of going downstairs to dine.

And he owed her that much, at least.

Grimacing, he turned to the canopied bed where, hours earlier, a manservant had laid out his outfit. Deferentially, the man had asked if he should stay and help Hamish to dress, but Hamish sent him away.

He needed some peace and privacy to prepare for the ordeal ahead.

And to process what had happened with Elena.

After bidding farewell to Isabella at the lake, he had gone, somewhat cautiously, toward the western tower, where Elena was now imprisoned. The fact she languished behind a locked door made his blood boil. But it was, at least, a step-up from the dungeon, and for that he was grateful to Jonah de Neville. He was not certain that the guard at the bottom of the tower would allow him to pass. Forsooth, he was not fully certain that he had the freedom to roam the castle grounds, for although Tristan had spoken up on his behalf, he had never spelled out that Hamish was no longer under house arrest. But after a startled look at Hamish's ragged outfit, the guard stood to one side.

Hamish ducked under the low door and paused until his eyes

adjusted to the dim light. Ahead of him was a spiral staircase, lit with flaming torches affixed to the granite wall at regularly spaced intervals. Despite the cramped conditions, the air smelled fresh, and the walls were dry. Swallowing his apprehension, Hamish began to climb; his large feet only just fitting on the narrow steps. Round and around he went, one hand trailing on a wooden banister, until he reached a small gallery with a narrow window and two heavy-looking wooden doors. Between the doors was a wooden chair, and on the chair sat a man, fast asleep and snoring.

Hamish raised his eyebrows at this dereliction of duty from the Wolvesley guard, but on closer inspection he realized the man wore Gaunt's standard—a serpent—on his dark-red tunic. An empty flagon of wine stood by the chair leg.

Hamish's mouth twitched. At long last, Gaunt had dealt him a winning card.

He went to the first door and tried the handle, but it was locked, of course. He looked at the sleeping guard and saw a heavy keyring hanging from his waist. Lowering himself onto his knees, Hamish put an eye to the keyhole and waited until the room beyond came into focus. The floor was bare but cleanly swept. A narrow bed clung to the wall, and a slender young woman with long, unruly hair stood looking out of the window.

Hamish's heart leaped in his chest. He put his mouth to the keyhole. "Elena."

She turned immediately; recognition of his voice evident in her face. "Hamish?"

"Outside the door."

She ran to the door and dropped to her knees. "Are you there?"

"I am here." He flattened his palms against the panel.

"I'm so glad to hear yer voice."

His view of the chamber turned dark, and he guessed that Elena's long hair was hanging over the keyhole. No matter. They could talk. And for as long as the guard slept, they could talk in private.

"Elena, have ye been treated well? Has anyone harmed ye?"

"Dinna fret, Hamish. I am as well as I can be."

His fists tightened. "Has anyone touched ye?" he growled.

"The guards here are kind." Elena avoided the question. "'Twas harder at Greenock. Gaunt's men liked to taunt me. But women from the village smuggled food in. I have ne'er been hungry. And I have ne'er been harmed, not in the way ye mean."

He leaned his forehead against the door, exhaling with relief.

"But I canna stand by and let that man, Gaunt, take Greenock from us. It canna happen." Her voice rippled with passion. "Brianne died for Greenock. 'Tis up to us to make things right."

"I ken so." He wished he could hold her hand, but the keyhole was too small for even his smallest finger to wriggle through. "I will put it right. Ye heard what was said inside, aye? Greenock is ter be ours once again."

"I heard what was said and I saw the way ye looked at the pretty lady in the white dress." Elena sniffed. "I ken ye dinna want her ter marry Gaunt. But ye must let it be, Hamish. We have suffered enough and so have our people."

Hamish's heart beat hollowly. "Dinna worry, Elena." He cast a glance at the guard who was still deeply asleep. "I just wish ye were not still a prisoner here.' Tis not right."

"'Tis a small matter." Elena's small finger appeared through the keyhole and he grasped it. "Ow," she protested.

"Sorry." Laughing quietly, he released his grip.

"As soon as I heard yer voice in the dungeons, I knew that all would be well."

"Ye were in the dungeons at the same time as I?" Hamish recalled the slight figure huddled by the wall.

"Aye. When ye came out with yon English Lord, I covered myself with my shawl so ye wouldna ken 'twas me."

"Why in heaven's name would ye do that?"

"Because I knew that ye would find a way outta this. And ye have."

He bowed his head and sighed. "Ever since ye were captured,

I have been trying to think of a way to rescue ye. Ever since Gaunt's men took Greenock, I have plotted and planned to take it back."

"And ye have prevailed."

Hamish closed his eyes against the pain. Beside him, the guard startled and sank back in his chair, his head nodding.

"I must go," Hamish whispered through the keyhole. "But I will see ye again soon, Elena. And ye will have yer freedom."

Upstairs in the bedchamber which was so grand it could only belong to a family member, Hamish felt again the swirling pain of loss. 'Twas a similar pain to what he had felt the day he failed to protect Brianne. For who was he, *what was the point of him*, if he could not protect the women he loved?

But both his sister and Isabella were convinced he should sit back and go along with this plan.

Hamish gritted his teeth and began to dress.

AT FIRST, THINGS went very well in the great hall. Hamish was uncertain of his welcome, but Tristan himself stood up and bade him sit with the family at the long trestle table on the dais. Hamish found himself seated between Jonah de Neville and a pretty dark-haired lady who introduced herself as Mirrie.

So polite and unassuming was Mirrie, that it took Hamish many minutes to realize she was Tristan's wife. Until then, he had sat in awkward silence, allowing a future countess to fill his goblet with wine.

He apologized for his lapse of manners, but she placed a cool hand briefly atop his and said he should not give it another thought.

"I am not one for airs and graces. None of them are, really, if you look beyond the surface."

Hamish looked along the table to where Isabella sat, beside

her parents, and was not sure he could agree.

Isabella sparkled more brightly than the vast candelabra overhead. She wore an elegant gown of rose pink, with her emerald necklace glittering against her creamy flesh and jeweled rings flashing from every finger. Her golden hair was pinned elaborately about her heart-shaped face and her smile lit the hall more effectively than all the candles and torches combined.

Below them sat table after table of the Wolvesley men-at-arms together with their brightly attired ladies. The hum of conversation, at times, was loud enough to drown out the trio of musicians playing on a small stage erected against the opposite wall.

'Twas all a far cry from the feasting hall at Greenock, with a lone fiddler and one long table set across the unevenly flagged floor.

Hamish took a sip of his wine. Perchance, after all, this was for the best. Isabella did not belong in a draughty Scottish keep. He could never be a proper husband to a woman accustomed to such luxury.

"Isabella is much changed," commented Mirrie, who had followed his gaze.

"She is?" Hamish was surprised.

"Aye. 'Tis as if she has discovered something new about herself." Mirrie gave him a small smile before filling her trencher and indicating he should do the same.

He thought of Isabella serving up the stew she had cooked at Ember Hall. What had she said that he so readily dismissed?

"Perchance I would relish the chance to work and have purpose."

He looked down at the fine array of roasted meats, glazed vegetables and glistening pies, and thought that he had never been less hungry in his life.

Instead of eating, he took another mouthful of wine.

Mirrie grimaced. "I had dared to hope he would not come."

"You and I both." Jonah spoke up for the first time.

Hamish realized that Lord Gaunt was ascending the steps to

the dais. Inside the vast hall, with its high ceiling and majestic proportions, the English usurper looked smaller and scrawnier than ever. He wore a fur-trimmed cloak of deep scarlet, which Hamish hoped he would soon be sweating under.

As Gaunt walked proprietorially over to Isabella, Hamish felt his stomach begin to churn. The wine soured in his mouth and he thought, for a terrible moment, that he might retch. When Gaunt's hand rested on Isabella's shoulder, he knew that he could bear it no longer.

Apologizing to Mirrie and nodding to Lord Jonah, Hamish pushed his chair back from the table and left the hall as quickly and graciously as he could manage.

But upstairs, in the bedchamber set aside for him, Hamish's thoughts still would not settle.

What can I possibly do to save both Isabella and Elena?

One answer presented itself.

God help him, if Tristan had not relieved him of his broadsword, Hamish thought he may well have acted upon it.

Removing Gaunt's head from his scrawny neck would solve their problems in one fell swoop.

But Hamish could not kill a man simply by wishing it.

He paced over the thick rugs and reflected that there must be another way. If only he could think long enough and hard enough over it. As he passed the nightstand, he took another long drink of ale.

The door opened and closed, and there stood Isabella, resplendent in her sparkling jewels and fine gown.

"Thank goodness I have found you."

Hamish put a hand to his aching head. "Ye didna have to leave the meal."

She sniffed contemptuously. "There is dancing. And I had hoped to dance with you, Hamish. But you are up here."

He sat heavily on the bed. "I canna think of dancing now."

"And I cannot dance with Lord Gaunt, betrothal contract or no betrothal contract. And so here I am." She sat beside him and linked her fingers with his, as if she had not a care in the world. Only a slight tremor in her voice revealed the depth of her emotions.

"Isabella." He said her name like a prayer. "What are we to do?"

She hitched herself further up the bed and leaned back against the pillows. For the first time in the long, challenging days of their acquaintance, she looked weary.

"We are to do as we promised ourselves and spend one more night together. I will not think beyond that." Her eyes shone with unshed tears. "Do not make me."

"I willna." He felt as if his heart was being torn from his body. At the same time, the blood in his veins pulsated with frustration. As much as he wanted to lay down beside Isabella and take her in his arms, he needed to move, to pace, to act.

"You are agitated." Isabella's blue eyes followed him up and down the chamber.

"I am beyond that."

"What can I do to help?"

Her words felled him. He sank to his knees and rested his head in her lap. Her fingers entwined in his hair and for a brief moment, he was at peace.

"Ye have already saved my sister. What can I ask more than that?" He sat up and took hold of her hands. "Nay, Isabella. 'Tis a failing on my part that I canna save ye from marrying that foul man."

"I asked you not to speak of him. Nor of what will happen on the morrow." She stroked the backs of his hands with her thumbs. "There is only now."

"How can ye be so strong?" The words burst from him. For most of his life, Hamish had been the strong one. Now he felt as emotionally fragile as a young boy.

"Honestly, I don't know." Isabella bit her bottom lip. "All day, people have been telling me to not give up hope. My sister Esme e'en told me that love has the power to conquer all. But all of this I have dismissed, however well intentioned. Because how can things be made right between us? If I refuse to marry Gaunt, he will take your poor sister in my stead. And as the King's judiciary, my father is powerless to move against him. E'en Tristan, who has once or twice been reckless in the pursuit of justice, cannot risk our family's name by turning on a peer of the realm." Isabella choked on her words and fell to silence. She took a deep breath and continued. "But just now, I hear my mother's words in my head."

Hamish pictured the elegant woman with silver strands in her hair, who had been seated near Isabella in the great hall. Her face had looked familiar to him, although he could not recall being properly introduced to her.

"What did your mother say?"

Isabella gave her head a small shake. "She has said naught of note about you and I. I have not given her the opportunity. But when we were children, whene'er things were tough, she would say *fortune's wheel never stops turning.*"

Hamish considered this. "She is not wrong." He sat back on his haunches and pushed his hair away from his face. "I grew up the son of a laird and thought naught could ever change that. Then my own uncle moved against us, and for two long winters my family and all men loyal to us were forced to live in a cave."

Isabella's eyebrows rose up at this. "Elena too?"

"Nay. Elena and my mother were held captive by my Uncle Donald." He found he had no wish to dwell on what came next. "We successfully recovered the keep and I thought the hard times were behind us. E'en when my father passed on, I became laird in his stead and the harvest was good." He shrugged and smiled, despite the dark thoughts that threatened to intrude.

"And now?" Isabella left the question hanging.

"Now I am in love with Isabella de Neville. And forced to stand by while she marries my sworn enemy."

"But don't you see?" Isabella leaned forward so the glow of light from the wall torch framed her like a halo. "Things worked out in the past. Perchance they will now as well."

He could not tear his eyes away from her. "Do ye really have such faith?"

If Isabella believed, then so would he. For he had lost what hope and faith he had once had. But for the sake of the woman he loved, he might find it again.

She pressed her lips together regretfully and shook her head. "Of all my family, I am the last person to speak of faith. I had so little faith in my future that I agreed to marry Lord Gaunt." She swallowed painfully. "My mother is the one who sees spirits and meaning in all things."

Even in the depths of his despair, her words caught his interest. "Your mother sees spirits?"

"'Tis the worst protected family secret. My sister, Frida, would oft converse with them in her youth. You see, we are not a conventional noble family." She smiled half-heartedly.

Hamish wondered if he should admit to speaking with Brianne. 'Twas a secret he had never confided to anyone, not even Elena. But had Brianne ever been there? Or was she no more than a figment of his feverish imagination?

Or a consequence of his guilty conscience?

For he had let Brianne down, just as he was letting Isabella down.

Frustration pulsated inside him once again. He jumped to his feet, unable to stay still for a moment longer.

"Forgive me, Isabella. I am too out of sorts to stay indoors. I must go outside where I can breathe more easily."

"But it is dark." She sat up in alarm. "And fiercely cold."

"I am a son of the highlands." He leaned over and pressed a kiss against her forehead. "I dinna feel the cold like an Englishman would."

She caught his hands and held them tight. "I want to wake up beside you in the morn. Do not deny me this."

"I willna." His fingers began to tremble as he perceived the depths of feeling in her gaze. "I promise ye that much."

HOURS LATER, HAMISH crept back inside the keep, walking softly so as not to disturb the sleeping inhabitants of the chambers he passed. The guards saw him; and the guards recognized him, but this could not be helped. When he reached his own bedchamber, he paused, seized with fear that Isabella may have grown angry in his prolonged absence and turned the bolts against him.

He would not blame her if she had.

But when he turned the handle, the door opened easily, and he saw the chamber was still lit by the glow of the fire and several candles which had burned down low. Isabella was laid on the bed, under the covers. Her golden hair fanned out over the pillows and her breathing regular and even.

She slept the sleep of the innocent.

Hamish knew a deep pang of regret that he had not stayed with her. But he had returned, as promised. Isabella would wake up beside him.

He could not control what happened after that.

CHAPTER TWENTY-TWO

ISABELLA WAS SLEEPING when the bell began to ring. The sound permeated her dreams as if through rolling waves of fog; undefined at first, and easy to ignore. Then it became loud, clamoring and insistent. She sat up in bed and clamped her hands over her ears.

"What is that noise?"

She thought it must be some time after dawn, for weak sunlight was already peeking through the shutters, but the sight of Hamish stretched out beside her did not bring the glow of deep domestic pleasure she had longed for. She only wanted him to make the bell stop. Or at least, to prove that he could hear it too and she wasn't going mad.

He rolled onto his side to face her, his pale blue eyes sharp with understanding. "'Tis a warning bell. I have heard that sound often enough." He was out of bed and reaching for his tunic in an instant.

Isabella was briefly distracted by his muscular torso. She frowned, trying to make sense of his words. "But Wolvesley cannot be under attack."

Still, the prospect was disquieting enough for her to get out of bed and cover her white night rail with a thick robe that most likely belonged to Esme. Running footsteps sounded from behind the door and her alarm increased.

"We should go down." Hamish hesitated. "But mayhap not

together."

Dimly, she grasped that he was protecting her reputation. "I shall go first."

"Nay." He caught at her elbow. "It might not be safe."

"I am a daughter of this house." She raised her eyebrows imperiously. "And anyway, you have no sword."

"I have my fists," he countered. But then the fight seemed to drain away from him and he sighed deeply. "I am sorry that I was not here for you in the way we both wanted last night."

His handsome face was creased with regret and Isabella found herself softening. "I am more sorry that we have not e'en the early hours of this morn to be together."

He ran his hands up her arms to her shoulders and gently touched her hair. "Perchance 'twas not meant to be, ye and I."

"Don't say that." Her voice was forceful, even as her heart was breaking.

Shouts reverberated up the staircase. A man's voice, loud and commanding, calling for Lord Tristan. Then Tristan's reply and a waterfall of booted feet tramping down the stairs.

Isabella gathered her composure. "We should go. It sounds like the entire household is descending, but you may go ahead of me if you wish."

She smiled to take the sting from her words, which she had meant kindly.

"Nay, ye have yer brother ahead of ye. I will stay at the back."

He pulled on his cloak, his own cloak, which had been re-paired and freshly laundered. Isabella took a final moment to appreciate the beauty of him, from his russet curls to his broad shoulders and confident stance. She had hoped for poignancy this morn, but 'twas hard to think of anything other than the clanging of the bell.

She rose up on her tiptoes and pressed a kiss to his cheek.

Beyond her chamber door, she spied the last of a group of uniformed guards hurrying around a bend in the staircase. The keep rang with noise, despite the earliness of the hour. But although the air was fraught with a nervous excitement, she sensed no immediate threat. She straightened her robe, briefly considered returning to her own chamber for something more suitable, then pressed on into the throng.

At the bottom of the stairs, she found a chattering huddle of men-at-arms and servants, none of whom paid her much attention. The big double doors stood open to the outside, even though the November morn blew cold and damp. Isabella was compelled to pass through the marbled entrance hall and out onto the terrace.

Here was the sense of threat.

She paused, one hand going to the neck of her robe. Now she wished Hamish had stayed by her side, so that she could hold his hand and take comfort from his touch.

The Wolvesley fountain shot foaming jets of water high into the bleak sky, just as it always had. But to the left of the fountain lay a crumpled figure in a scarlet cloak.

Even from this distance, it was unmistakably Lord Gaunt.

And he was unmistakably dead.

Blood pooled around him, the same color as his cloak. He gazed upwards, never to rake his eyes lasciviously over Isabella again.

She took a trembling breath.

Fully dressed and with his sword at his hip, Tristan strode over to the body. He crouched beside it and then nodded to the group of waiting men.

"Dead."

His proclamation, unsurprising as it was, unleashed a torrent of emotion. Isabella came to understand that the soldiers amassed around Tristan did not all serve Wolvesley. Many wore the blood-red colors of Lord Gaunt. And they were angry. She heard the scrape of swords being unsheathed, and before much time had passed, a line of Tristan's men faced an equal line of men sworn to Gaunt.

With her brother at the center.

Isabella opened her mouth but no sound came out. From the corner of her eye she saw her father, stately and tall, descending the steps to join his son. She wanted to shout, to tell him to take care, but at that moment she was more an observer of the scene than a participant, and she could neither move nor speak. Then Mirrie was at her side, with her arm about her shoulders, and Isabella could breathe again.

"Oh, Isabella," her sister-in-law murmured.

Isabella clutched at the blue sleeve of Mirrie's robe. "I am worried for Tristan."

Mirrie said nothing, just held her tighter. Hamish was on the steps, above her father. Isabella wished he had his sword and could swell Tristan's ranks.

Tristan was talking now, his voice too low for them to properly hear what he said. He took a step closer to the man who appeared to be the leader of Gaunt's troops and stood unflinching even as that man pointed his sword directly at his chest.

"He did not put on his mail shirt," Mirrie said in a strangled voice.

Tristan raised up his own sword, then slowly and deliberately sheathed it.

As one, the men behind him did the same.

Gaunt's men still wielded their sharp swords, but the Wolvesley army were momentarily defenseless.

"What is he about?" Isabella half wanted to close her eyes. The chill wind tugged at her robe but anxiety made her almost feverishly warm.

"It is working." Mirrie exhaled with relief as one-by-one, the men in scarlet put down their weapons.

Tristan gestured to his father and the two spoke quietly for a moment.

Angus raised his voice so that it carried through the court-yard. "I bid you all come inside for refreshment whilst my son investigates this matter."

Gaunt's men did not like this. They looked uncertainly at one another, but Tristan glowered at his own men who reluctantly began to lead the way back inside the keep. The red-cloaked leader threw back his head and said something to Tristan, who nodded solemnly.

"They are going in." Isabella breathed deeply to quell a wave of dizziness.

"Aye." Mirrie gave her a small smile. "I shall go and offer my help in the kitchen."

Isabella stood uncertainly on the terrace. Should she follow Mirrie?

She looked for Hamish and saw him walking toward Tristan. With an impatient gesture, Tristan beckoned for her to do the same.

Isabella averted her eyes from the body of Lord Gaunt as she descended the steps. Spray from the fountain covered her face, making her blink and shiver. She dried her cheeks with her sleeve and met the angry gaze of her brother.

"Who could have done this?"

She recoiled in surprise. "I have no idea."

Tristan's piercing eyes moved to Hamish and something cold and heavy slid inside her belly.

"What about you? Do you have any idea?"

Isabella wanted to see shock and innocence writ large over Hamish's face, but the highlander's expression was unreadable.

"I canna say."

"Cannot, or will not?" For a terrible moment, Tristan looked about to reach for his sword. "You have the most to gain from his death." He nodded curtly toward the lifeless figure behind them.

Hamish stayed stonily silent, and Isabella felt the ground shift beneath her feet.

Did he do this?

"Can you vouch for his whereabouts?" Tristan demanded of her.

"I don't know what you mean." She clutched at the neck of her robe, playing for time.

"Do not be coy, Isabella. I am under no illusions about the two of you. I ask again. Can you vouch for him?"

Isabella gasped for air. She wanted to move closer to the fountain, to lean against the solid stone basin, but Gaunt's body was in the way.

"Hamish, tell me, please, you didn't do this, did you?"

Hamish shook his head, but then he spoke and shattered what small reassurance he had provided. "I didna kill him, but perchance I should have done."

"Did he leave your side last night?" Tristan's voice came out in a growl.

"Yes." She wanted to deny it, but could not lie outright to her brother. "I'm sorry, Hamish." She put her hands to her face as she began to sob.

"Ye are only speaking the truth, lass." His voice was gentle.

Tristan dragged a hand through his shock of hair. "I have men inside ready to mutiny over this. They will string you up, man, if they sense your guilt, just as I have."

Hamish stood still and silent. Isabella wanted to fall to her knees and beg for him to deny this terrible charge, but that would draw even more attention from the men-at-arms looking down at them. Time slowed down and she knew what Tristan was about to say, even before he opened his mouth.

"You must leave," he told Hamish. "Take your horse from the stables and ride far away from here. Now."

HAMISH COULD NOT blame de Neville for believing him guilty; in his shoes, he would have done the same. When Hamish had looked down at Gaunt's lifeless body, the question in his mind had not been 'who did this?', but 'why didn't I?'

Still, the shock and horror in Isabella's gaze had left a lasting imprint on his soul. The woman he loved believed him to be a killer. He had, after all, murdered Alaric just a short distance from her terrified face; but only because he had been left with no other choice.

Where Gaunt was concerned, he'd had another choice; a lifetime of misery. And it seemed that even in death, the man had the power to deny him.

Hamish kept his head down as he trudged down the path to the stable yard. Luar whickered a greeting when he turned the corner, but this was not enough to lift his spirits. He looked for his beloved horse and saw that Isabella's mother, the Countess of Wolvesley, was there before him.

Still a few steps away, he paused and bowed.

"Milady."

The countess turned. She was a beautiful woman, despite her age, with eyes that shone with wisdom and kindness. She was stroking Luar's face, and Luar was apparently enjoying it. His usually flighty horse had her eyes half closed and her nose pressed against the countess's shoulder.

"Hamish. May I call you Hamish? You must call me Morwenna."

Hamish thought it unlikely he would ever address her again, but he accepted the compliment with another short bow. They were alone in the well-swept yard, with just Luar and two chestnut carriage horses watching their exchange.

"Your horse is a beautiful creature."

His lips inched upwards. "Aye, she is that." He felt they conversed under false pretenses. "Milady. Morwenna. I should tell ye that Lord Tristan has asked me to leave Wolvesley. I am to ride away this morn." He forced himself to stand tall as he said this, not to hunch his shoulders with guilt and shame.

"Such a shame, when we were just getting to know one another."

Hamish had a distinct feeling she was talking about Luar, but his discomfort faded when she gave him another kind smile. The rings on her fingers flashed in the weak sunlight.

"It will be due to the upset by the fountain. That is why I have come here. Horses are better companions than people, I often find. Especially when people are angry and combative."

The countess was not at all what he had expected. She dressed like a grand lady, in silks and furs, but she spoke with the candor and friendliness of a local Scotswoman. And she had seemingly bewitched Luar, with her gentle voice and touch.

He recalled Isabella's words the night before.

"My mother is the one who sees spirits and meaning in all things."

Words from another lifetime. Sorrow pooled in his stomach at all he had lost.

Morwenna's green eyes looked at him appraisingly. "You do not want to leave?"

He shook his head. "I dinna want to leave with Isabella, Lady Isabella, believing me guilty of a crime I didna commit."

"Ah." Her attention returned to the horse. "So you were not the one to murder Lord Gaunt. But you have no one to vouch for you."

He leaned his arm against the granite wall of the stable and felt weariness wash over him. "The only one who can vouch for me is Luar. 'Twas her I came to see last night. She has long been my friend and companion, milady. And speaking with her soothes my soul."

Morwenna nodded, as if this was perfectly sensible. She stilled for a moment, and Luar's ears pricked forward, so the two appeared to silently converse.

"I believe you," the countess said.

Winter sunlight warmed the back of his head. He folded his arms and looked again at the woman and the horse. "Did ye ask her?"

'Twas a foolish question and he regretted it the moment it left his lips.

But Morwenna only smiled. "Would it shock you if I said yes?"

Hamish rubbed at the stubble on his face. "Honestly, nay, it wouldna shock me." He took a breath. "Oft times I have spoken to my sister."

This was the secret he had never confided in anyone, but it was a relief to say the words out loud to this calm and kind woman. Mayhap he trusted her so implicitly because she had such a strong look of Isabella. Or mayhap 'twas because Luar obviously trusted her. Either way, their strange, twisting conversation on a misty November morn felt entirely natural.

"I presume your sister has passed from this life?"

He nodded. "She died in battle."

"I am sorry for your loss."

"But she has been with me since. I see her. I speak with her. Until these last days, that is." His arms hung awkwardly at his sides.

Morwenna considered this, her small hands still rhythmically stroking Luar's face. "She has been with you in your times of need."

Hamish felt a knife twist inside him. 'Twas true. Brianne had always appeared to him when he was lost and alone. But this insight caused him pain, because in the final moments of her life, when Brianne most needed him, he had not been there.

He doubled over as if winded, putting his palms to the cold granite wall as a wave of grief washed over him.

Morwenna came to stand by his side. Her hand on his shoulder was surprisingly warm.

"I find that those we have loved never really leave us. But perchance, as you find your happiness, Brianne will find her peace."

Hamish swallowed painfully. "I would not deny her peace."

She nodded in agreement. "Nor should you deny yourself happiness."

He would not aim so high as happiness.

The countess's face, so close to his, evoked a memory. He blinked in surprise. "Ye are the one that came to me, in the dungeon." He put a hand to his wounded arm, which hardly troubled him at all now. "Ye healed me."

Her green eyes went to his arm. "Before I came to Wolvesley, I learned some healing skills from my grandmother. My eldest daughter, Frida, has inherited her gifts." She smiled. "I am pleased to see you so much stronger now."

Hamish struggled to properly convey his gratitude. This woman had saved him in his darkest moment. As Laird of Greenock, he would throw a feast in her honor. But what could he do now?

Uneven footsteps broke into his thoughts.

"Mother." The voice carrying across the yard was strained.

"Jonah." Morwenna frowned. "What ails you, my boy?"

Reluctantly, Hamish turned around to behold the younger de Neville brother limping toward them. He looked pale with worry and exhaustion, with dark smudges beneath his blue eyes.

"I need you," he said, "please."

Morwenna put her head to one side and thought for a moment. "I must go," she said to Hamish. "But I wish you Godspeed." She put her hand on his arm. "I will see you again, Hamish McIvor, Laird of Greenock, I am certain of it."

CHAPTER TWENTY-THREE

THE PLASTERED WALLS of her father's solar had never before pressed in so oppressively.

Isabella could not settle, but paced about the rectangular room, so distracted with her thoughts that several times she came close to sweeping piles of parchments from the cluttered desk. Angus sat in his leather-bound chair by the fire, his hands steepled beneath his chin, his blue eyes following her with concern.

"Isabella, dear one, why not come and sit down?"

"I cannot rest, Father."

Forsooth, if she sat down, she might be physically sick. The only way she could keep her rising nausea at bay was by constant movement.

The heavy oak door opened and Mirrie appeared, her cheeks flushed and her skirts dusted with flour.

"I am come to see if I can fetch you anything?"

Instead of answering, her father cleared his throat. "How goes it in the great hall?"

Mirrie grimaced. "We have placated Gaunt's men with strong mead and a ready supply of food, together with a promise to hunt down whoever killed their master."

"And they believe you?"

"Aye. Tristan is planting the seed that it may have been an intruder."

Isabella's heart leaped. She spun around so her robe flared

about her calves. "Could that be true?"

Mirrie avoided her eye. "'Tis unlikely an intruder would gain entry through the main gates. Though Tristan has sworn to interrogate the guards." She made a hopeless gesture.

Isabella sank back against the desk, her hopes plummeting once again. Mirrie darted forward just in time to catch a heavy ledger as it toppled toward the floor.

"I'm sorry." Isabella put her head in her hands. "I cannot do anything right."

Mirrie straightened the ledger and the parchments beside it. "You are tired, Bella. Why not sit down and take some refreshment?"

"I have been trying to persuade her to do that since before noon," Angus remarked, dryly. "But perchance you will have better luck, Mirrie."

"I have no wish to eat or drink, and I cannot sit still." Isabella leaned forward in an attempt to ease her rolling stomach. "I am so worried about Hamish."

"He has had many hours to get away." Mirrie rubbed at Isabella's back, as if sensing intuitively what would help.

"But how could he do that?" Isabella's voice was anguished. "To kill a man, in cold blood, in *my* home."

Angus leaned back in the chair and regarded them both solemnly. "We do not know for certain that he did."

Mirrie opened and closed her mouth. Isabella knew that Tristan firmly believed in Hamish's guilt. Consequently, so did Mirrie.

And mayhap they were right.

"Do not give me false hope, Father," she breathed.

"That is not my aim." Angus poured himself a goblet of wine. "But there are questions we must ask ourselves. Firstly, what was Lord Gaunt doing outside the keep at that time?" He shrugged. "Why was he fully dressed? And why did he wear a sword belt if he was not carrying a sword?"

Isabella blinked in confusion. "How do you know he was not

carrying a sword?"

"There was no sword with the body." Angus sipped his wine.

"Then Hamish must have moved it." Mirrie clamped her lips together. "I mean to say, the killer must have moved it," she corrected herself lamely.

The door opened a second time and this time it was Morwenna who appeared. At Mirrie's sharp inhale, Isabella noted that her mother's neatly braided hair had come loose and her silken gown was streaked with blood.

She gripped the edge of the desk tighter. Would the nightmare of this day never end?

"My love, what has happened?" Angus strode over and took Morwenna's hands.

"I am not injured," she spoke up quickly. "The blood is not mine."

"Then whose?" Angus lowered his bushy brows as he helped his wife to a chair.

Morwenna sank down and put her face in her hands, as if exhausted. "'Tis a long story, husband, and perchance one for your ears alone."

Mirrie did not miss a beat. "I will return to the great hall." She dipped into a small curtsy and left.

Morwenna held up a hand when Isabella went to follow her. "On second thoughts, Bella, 'twould be better if you also heard this."

Nonplussed, Isabella resumed her position by the desk. The weak winter sunlight streaming through the window was barely enough to light the room, and she could not properly read the expression of either of her parents. It was time for the maids to come in and light the candles, but all servants had been asked to stay away from the solar ever since Angus ushered her in here.

It was Angus who finally spoke up. "Morwenna, you know I have never been a patient man."

Morwenna gave him a small smile. "I am also waiting. You see, 'tis not my story to tell."

A knock sounded on the door and it was slowly pushed open.

"It is Jonah's story," Morwenna added as her youngest son walked hesitantly into the solar.

"Father." He bowed. His blue eyes rested upon Isabella and then flickered to their mother in an unspoken question.

"Isabella should hear this," said Morwenna, in a tone that brooked no argument.

"Very well." Jonah shuffled his feet on the rug. His embroidered tunic was crumpled, almost as if he had slept in it. His thick hair was uncombed and there was a smear of dirt on his cheek. "I am here to beg for your forgiveness, Father. I was the one to kill Lord Gaunt."

In the silence that followed, Isabella could hear her heart pounding against her ribs.

Jonah was the one to kill Lord Gaunt!

It made no sense at all.

Her father must have been wrestling with the same problem, for it was some time before he answered. "Tell me how it happened."

"I challenged him to a duel."

A log cracked in the fire whilst they all digested this. "A duel?" Isabella repeated, wondering if she had misunderstood.

"Aye, a duel." Jonah frowned across the room and she realized it was not dirt on his cheek, it was dried blood.

Nausea rose inside her and she pressed the back of her hand to her mouth.

"You killed him in a duel?" Her father's voice was strained.

"I fail to see why that would be so hard to believe." Jonah's eyes flashed and he walked to the window to compose himself, as he had often done as a child. He spoke with his back to them. "But nay, that is not how it happened."

"Why would you challenge Lord Gaunt to a duel?" Isabella felt as if she were stumbling about in some new land.

"For the freedom of Elena, as well as for you, Isabella. Do not pretend you were happy at the prospect of marrying him."

"I was miserable about it," she cried. "But I would ne'er have asked you to put yourself in danger."

Jonah lifted his golden head, apparently staring with great interest at something outside. "I know you would not. There are times when you petition for Tristan's help, but ne'er mine. I long since realized this is because you do not believe me *capable* of helping you." He turned slowly. His eyes were calm, even if his voice shook with restraint. "But you see, there are some things that I can do, that Tristan cannot."

Isabella cast about for an answer to this, but her mind remained stubbornly blank.

"Our father, as Judiciary, cannot act outside the law. Our brother, as the future earl, cannot act outside the law. But I can."

Angus spoke up quickly. "'Tis not outside the law to duel. Not if it was done with honor."

Jonah let out a bark of laughter. "It was not."

Morwenna stood and poured them all a goblet of wine. She passed one to Isabella and one to Jonah, insisting they take them when they both declined.

"For the shock," she said.

"We arranged to meet at sunrise. I gave the guard a bag of coin to be elsewhere." Jonah gave his father a small nod of apology. "I waited for Gaunt by the fountain. But when he came, he was not alone."

At this point, Jonah walked over to the fireplace and took a long drink of wine. Isabella watched impatiently, tapping her long fingers on the silver goblet. Was Jonah about to speak Hamish's name?

"Elena was with Lord Gaunt," Morwenna revealed softly, perchance reading the anguish in her daughter's face.

"Aye. The coward brought Elena from the western tower. He told me that I could only kill him if I went past her." Jonah slammed his empty goblet onto the mantle. "Of course, I yielded straight away. I could not put Elena's life at risk."

"'Twas the right thing to do." Angus nodded with relief.

"I placed my sword on the ground, near the fountain." Jonah fixed his gaze on a finely-stitched tapestry of Wolvesley Castle which had long hung over the fireplace. "And whilst Gaunt was taunting me for standing down, Elena picked up my sword and came at him."

Isabella gasped, slopping wine onto the rug beneath her feet. "So Elena was the one to kill him?"

Jonah looked at her shortly. "Nay, she struck only a glancing blow. Gaunt turned on her in retaliation. And when I saw the devilish intent in his eyes, I had no choice but to step in. I grabbed my sword from Elena and swung it wide. It struck him full in the chest." He picked up his empty goblet, looked inside and placed it back down. Isabella saw that his hands were shaking. "He died almost instantly."

Angus glanced up at his son. "Why did you not stay by the body?"

"Because Elena was injured in the struggle," Morwenna answered for him. She rose from her chair and put an arm around Jonah's shoulders.

"She was most aggrieved." Jonah took a deep breath. "She blamed herself. I was worried she might either bleed out or pass out with distress. And then I heard men coming from the knights' sleeping quarters. I did not think, Father. I simply picked her up and ran."

"You got her to safety," Morwenna said pointedly.

"Is she badly hurt?" Isabella thought of Hamish, who had been wrongly banished whilst his only sister was bleeding.

"She will heal, but it will take time." Morwenna guided Jonah into the chair she had recently vacated. "She can stay here for as long as she needs."

"And I will take whatever punishment you see fit, Father." Jonah nodded firmly as Morwenna shook her head in distress.

"There will be no punishment." Angus dragged a hand through his greying hair. "This changes everything."

"It does." Isabella could hardly breathe for the urgency of it.

"It changes everything. I must go after Hamish. There was no cause for him to leave." She held out her hands as if warding off an enemy. "Don't try to stop me, Mother."

"I have never tried to stop any of my children doing anything they set their minds to," Morwenna said patiently. "But I will say this, in some hours it will be dark. Pray, take the carriage, child."

"But there will not be time." Isabella wrung her hands.

"There will be plenty of time," Morwenna interjected. "Take the carriage and meet Hamish at Ember Hall. You will find him there, I promise you."

HAMISH FOUND IT hard to travel north through England with no sword and only a small bag of coin. Luar had been well-fed and well-rested at Wolvesley; she stepped out with all the enthusiasm of a colt on a spring day. But Hamish felt the dampness of the fog seep into his bones and, as they climbed higher over the moors, the desolation of their surroundings burrowed deep into his heart.

To keep despair at bay, he spoke aloud to Luar; telling her of his plans to rebuild Greenock and make a happy home there for himself and Elena. He did not allow himself to dwell on the detail; the lack of coin, dearth of laborers or the simple fact of Elena still being held captive at Wolvesley Castle. Nay, if he focused on the difficulties ahead, he might find himself unable to proceed.

And if he thought of Isabella, he might seize up entirely.

But even as he conjured a roaring fire for the feasting hall and a new roof for the barn, he kept one eye on the sinking sun. These borderlands were notorious for raids and thieving, and the threat loomed larger given his swordless state.

"We will have to take shelter for the night," he told Luar.

They stopped at a small but hospitable inn by a crossroads,

where Luar was led to a large stable, and Hamish was shown to a cramped chamber with a sloping floor. But the food was edible and the landlord seemed happy enough with the coin Hamish could pay. To his great surprise, Hamish slept deeply on the narrow pallet provided. When he awoke, somehow his heart was lighter. The November morn did not dawn brighter; if anything, the mist hung more heavily over the heather. But a voice spoke in his head, telling him that all would be well. Rather than bracing himself against despair, he found himself embracing the possibilities of the day. Luar whickered to him as he came out into the yard; the sound travelling through the blanket of fog. He tossed a coin to the stableboy, who had brushed her coat to a glossy shine, and bid him farewell.

"'Tis a beautiful horse you have there," the lad opined, giving her a final pat.

"She is that." Hamish smiled.

They trotted off into the mist, Luar's hoofbeats the only sound for miles around. Acting purely on impulse, Hamish took the easterly road which hugged the coast. He told himself that he longed to see the sea, after so long looking only at bleak moorland and barren trees. But the real reason had naught to do with waves, and everything to do with a golden-haired woman whose smile he would never forget.

Perchance he would never again look upon Isabella de Neville. But he could take this final opportunity to look upon the unassuming house where his life had taken such a dramatic turn.

He gave Luar her head as they climbed up a steep road with the mournful crying of gulls echoing around them. Luar was breathing heavily now, her flanks damp with sweat. They had, by necessity, taken the longer route north, following the ancient roads laid down long ago. When they rode this same journey in reverse, Hamish had tracked Isabella's much more direct route directly over the moors. But he did not know these lands as well as she, and could not risk getting lost in a bog.

Nor did he want to come across what might be left of Alaric.

Closing his eyes to such unwanted memories, Hamish breathed deeply, taking in the tang of sea salt as well as the fresh, clean country air.

"Soon we will be in Scotland," he told Luar. "I shall know every nook and valley. And the air will be bitter cold with frost and snow, until spring sunshine turns the glen green and bright with blossom."

Luar's ears flickered back and forth as she listened obligingly to his nonsense.

"Once we are over the border, I will find friends in the lowlands," he promised her. "'Twill not be long until we have the men and provisions we need to recover what is ours."

He recalled Morwenna's words to him, in the stable yard at Wolvesley. She had warned him against denying himself happiness.

Is happiness within my reach?

Nay, he decided. Not without Isabella. But he would have a life of purpose. A life which saw peace and prosperity return to Greenock, for the good of all.

Isabella's sacrifice would not be in vain.

"Ye are tired, lass," he said when Luar stumbled on some loose ground. "We will rest a while at the summit."

He would rest and put his thoughts in some sort of order before travelling the short distance to Ember Hall. He had no intention of going up to the gates, he would just look upon the place and remember.

God willing, Siegfried is long gone, he thought.

God willing, Siegfried would be waiting at the village of Greenock. In less than a sennight, Hamish would bring him the good news. Greenock was theirs, once again.

He dismounted and pulled Luar's reins over her head so he could lead her more easily. She snorted and nudged his stomach, but followed him readily enough. Hamish didn't know why his feet were compelled to lead him forward, away from the road and toward the cliffs. He had never been here before, but somehow he sensed there was something he needed to see.

The ground dipped and Hamish found himself in a small clearing, where spears of sunlight pierced the swirling mist. Far below, he could hear waves running up and down a shingle cove. They were sheltered from the wind and an air of calm prevailed. Hamish felt quite comfortable allowing Luar to crop at the damp grass, while he meandered toward the cliffs.

But after a few paces, he stopped short, all senses on high alert, until his eyes made sense of what was before him.

At first, he thought himself the subject of an ambush, for several men seemed to rear up out of the mist. Next, his mind briefly considered the possibility that he had inadvertently wandered amongst the faerie folk, for some of these ethereal beings stood no higher than his hips. But when none of them moved for several seconds, he realized that they were, in fact, made of stone.

"Standing stones," he said, rotating in a slow circle so he could examine the tall, rectangular stones individually.

Each had a different shape, but together they formed an almost magical whole. He fancied the air felt different here, as if it shimmered with energy which snapped and fizzled between the ancient stones. It could be a place for ritual and witchcraft, but Hamish was not afraid. In truth, he felt more settled and relaxed than he had in many months.

Luar swung her head toward him, her ears sharply pricked. At the same time, Hamish also became aware of someone approaching. Out of long habit, his hand went to where his sword should be and once again, it came away empty.

There was no time to duck behind a stone. But as the mist slowly cleared, Hamish discovered he had no need to hide. Forsooth, he must be dreaming or delirious, for the person walking toward him was none other than Isabella.

She wore a heavy fur cloak and balanced something long and thin across the palms of her hands, like an offering for the Gods.

Hamish gulped. "Is it really you?"

The woman stopped and smiled, and the last of his doubts burned away like. "I could ask the very same question."

"Isabella." He wondered, belatedly, if saying her name might cause this wondrous vision to fade. But she only stepped closer. His eyes widened as he realized what she was carrying.

"I bring you a gift from my brother Tristan." She held his gaze. "Your sword."

He could hardly believe it. His sword had been a part of him for many years and its worth far exceeded that of a mere weapon. He reached out his hand and grasped the hilt, recognizing immediately the familiar feel and weight.

"Thank you." Words were inadequate. He raised his eyebrows questioningly. "How can this be?"

"Tristan sends it by way of an apology. He should ne'er have banished you from Wolvesley Castle." Isabella folded her hands behind her back and gazed around at the stones. "I have not been up here for years, but my sister Frida loved these stones. 'Tis a fitting place for us to find one another, is it not?"

Hamish felt his reason slipping away. "How did ye ken I would be here?"

"I had a vision." She met his eye and laughed like a pealing of bells, which was both delightful and startling after the long hours of fog and near silence. "I speak in jest, Hamish. Although my mother had a strong notion you would travel by Ember Hall, which could be described as a vision of sorts. But 'Twas the lookouts that saw you and Luar arrive at the stones just now."

He sheathed his sword, still shaking his head in wonderment. He wanted to take her into his arms, but there was still too much he didn't understand.

"Will ye tell me what has happened, Isabella? I canna help but think this is some dream."

"'Tis no dream." She closed the distance between them and reached for his hands. She wore gloves, but he could feel the warmth of her touch even so, and it made his pulse begin to pound.

"Ye are real."

"As real as Luar and the stones all around us." A brisk gust of wind snatched at her hood and caused long strands of golden hair to stream out.

"And yer brother has forgiven me?"

"There is naught to forgive, as you must already know. You were not the one to kill Lord Gaunt." She frowned and took her hands from his, leaving him cold and bereft, but 'twas only to fix her hood back in place. "Why did you not protest your innocence?"

He answered simply. "Would ye have believed me?"

Isabella bit down on her lip. "I was desperate to hear you deny the charge. But in truth, I don't know if I would have fully believed you."

Hamish had no wish to apportion blame. He tightened his hold on her fingers. "How did ye discover the truth?"

A tremor passed through her. "Because the real killer came forward. 'Twas my younger brother, Jonah."

"Jonah?" He all but staggered in surprise and wished they stood nearer the stones so he might lean his weight upon them.

"Aye." She took a deep breath. "I'm afraid your sister, Elena, was caught up in the fray. She is injured, although not seriously. My mother is tending to her."

The world tilted around him. "I should go to her."

"Elena has instructed me to tell you to go straight on to Greenock. She wants you to reclaim your birthright with no further delay."

He blinked and tried to make sense of it all. Isabella put her hands on his forearms as if wanting to share her strength with him.

"But who will take care of Elena's interests whilst I am gone?"

Isabella's eyes danced. "I think you will find that Elena has a worthy protector in my brother Jonah. 'Twas for her sake, as well as mine, that he challenged Gaunt."

Hamish recalled the scene in the great hall, when Jonah had

visibly bristled at Gaunt's treatment of Elena.

"The two of them must have met whilst Gaunt had her locked in the dungeon," he said, thinking it through.

"That is precisely what happened. Elena told me that Jonah regularly brought her food and drink."

Hamish had a hundred more questions to ask. But he was satisfied as to Elena's immediate safety. It was time to move on to more pressing concerns.

He cupped her cheek and looked deep into her blue eyes. "And what about ye, Isabella?"

She made a show of pursing her lips, before placing her own hand on top of his and leaning into his touch. "There is one thing you should know about me, Hamish. I am a woman of my word."

His body began to tense and sing at her proximity. Her lips were inches from his. This was not the moment for puzzles. "What do ye mean by that?"

"I mean that some days ago I left my home at Westchester to ride north and become the Lady of Greenock." Isabella rose onto her tiptoes so he felt the warmth of her breath on his face. "That is still what I intend to do."

Could this wondrous future really belong to him?

Joy went into battle with disbelief and came out victorious. A wide smile broke across Hamish's face. "Ye may have to check matters with the Laird of Greenock. I hear he can be a difficult man."

"Nay." Isabella put her head to one side. "He is as loyal and obliging as a faithful hound."

"A faithful hound, ye say?" He lifted her from the ground and spun her in a circle so her cloak flared out behind her. "Not more of a fierce wolf?"

"Nay. A hound stretched out by the fireside." Isabella giggled as he spun her around again. "You will have to put me down sometime."

"I willna," he countered. "For if ye are to be the Lady of

Greenock, ye belong to me now. And I might like to keep you close so ye dinna disappear."

"I will never disappear," she whispered.

Her lips were too close to be denied. He kissed her long and deep, until passion sparked in his belly and he had to place her gently down before his knees buckled. He wrapped his arms around her and they clung to one another as the sun finally broke through the clouds above.

"So what does the Laird of Greenock say?" Isabella asked, her head tucked snugly against his shoulder.

Hamish sighed in contentment. "I say this: ye have given me back my home. But more than that, ye have given me a reason to hope for the future and be happy in the present. I love ye, Isabella. And I will spend the rest of my life making ye glad ye decided to be the Lady of Greenock." He paused and looked down at her upturned face. "If ye will let me."

Isabella nodded thoughtfully. "I think I can allow that. But I must insist on one thing."

"Anything." He meant it.

"Kiss me again."

"Does the lady not wish to go somewhere warmer?" he teased.

"Nay, the lady is growing accustomed to the cold." She pressed the tip of her nose against his. "Do you not wish to kiss me, Hamish?"

Desire flickered inside him. "I wish to kiss ye very much," he said honestly. "I can hardly believe ye are standing in my arms."

"My wild highlander," she whispered.

Hamish decided enough words had been said. He lowered his head and kissed the woman he loved.

CHAPTER TWENTY-FOUR

Six years later...
August 1339, Greenock, Highlands of Scotland.

T HE LITTLE PONY stepped out briskly, with its grey head held high and its furry ears pricked forward. At first, Hamish hardly dared lift his eyes from the pony, and the precious load it carried, but eventually the tension in his shoulders began to drain away.

His daughter was a natural horsewoman. Even though the pony was new to their yard and this was their first foray beyond the castle walls, she retained the confident seat and light hands of a much more experienced rider.

He had naught to fear.

Luar snorted as if in agreement, breaking into a trot as she traversed a ravine and splashed through a shallow river. Brianne squealed and wiped droplets of water from her pink cheeks.

"Can we go to the cave, Papa?"

Hamish reined Luar in until the little pony caught up with her long stride. They were climbing a wide path lined with an abundance of purple heather; the day was warm and birds chirped happily from nearby bushes. Even the incessant buzzing of summer insects could not dampen his mood.

"Who told ye about the cave?" he asked genially, thinking it was most likely Siegfried. The elderly seneschal had a great fondness for Lady Brianne, and they were often found exploring the castle grounds together, her small hand clasped in his.

Brianne tossed back her chestnut curls and smiled over her

shoulder. "'Twas the pretty lady."

Hamish gulped, steadying himself. Brianne was soon to celebrate her sixth naming day, and it had been many moons since she last mentioned a visit from 'the pretty lady' who had been a frequent guest in the nursery. Isabella had long thought this visitor was a product of their daughter's overactive imagination. But when Frida once came to them at Twelfthtide, she'd calmly observed how her niece had the same coloring and impish smile as her namesake. With no likenesses of his sister, Brianne, hanging in the keep, Hamish had opened his mouth to ask how Frida knew this.

Then he recalled the particular gifts of the de Nevilles, and merely nodded in agreement.

"What did she tell ye, about the caves?" he asked.

Brianne clung onto a clump of the pony's coarse mane as he plunged through the heather. "That they are cold in winter and smell bad. But in the summer, they can be a fine place to light a campfire and play games of pretend with a brother." She wrinkled her small nose. "She must mean David, because Adam is too little to do anything but sleep and cry."

"She must be talking of the future," Hamish interjected firmly, knowing that if anyone was determined enough to take a four-year-old boy to a cave, it was his spirited young daughter. A lump formed in his throat as he remembered how he, Brianne and Elena had played together as children, clambering over rocks and chasing one another over the hills. Oft-times he had run so fast he thought he might fly.

"Mayhap." Brianne considered this. "David and Adam will be more fun when they are bigger. That's what Siegfried says."

"Siegfried is usually right." Hamish sat deep in the saddle and reined in Luar. "The cave is up there." He pointed to a grassy promontory jutting out from the rocky cliffs. "We don't have time to go this day, but I will take ye there afore the summer ends."

Brianne pouted. "It willna take long, Papa."

"Aye, but we have the feast to prepare for." He smiled as the spark returned to her blue eyes. "Had ye forgotten?"

"Never," the little girl declared. "'Tis a feast in honor of my naming day."

"'Tis the Lammas Feast, and ye came ter us on Lammas Day, the greatest gift I e'er could have gotten."

His eyes misted at the memory. Baby Brianne had been born almost nine months to the day that he and Isabella had first come together at Ember Hall. He had held his tiny daughter in his arms and thanked God for the blessings raining down upon him.

Brianne beamed up at him, bringing him back to the present. "Can I stay up and join in with the dancing? Please, Papa."

"Ye can stay fer a while," he allowed. Isabella would raise her eyebrows at his leniency, but Hamish found it difficult to deny his daughter aught she desired. It was fortunate indeed that Brianne had a sunny disposition and rarely expressed discontent.

Brianne dropped the reins to clap her hands together, and the pony quickly ducked his head to snatch up a mouthful of moorland grass. "I will wear my new plaid and sit beside Mama who always looks so pretty on a feast day."

"Aye, she does that." Hamish waited until Brianne had gathered her reins again. "Though yer mama looks pretty all the time."

"Less so when she's working in the kitchens," Brianne opined. "If I was the Lady of Greenock, I would do naught but wear pretty dresses and sit in the long gallery and eat sweetmeats."

"Well, mayhap that day will come." Hamish smiled down at her daughter, but she had twisted in the saddle and was looking back at the cave.

"Do ye think we will e'er have to leave Greenock and live up there?" she asked.

"I dinna think so," he answered honestly. "I willna lie to ye. And if I have learned one thing in all my years on this earth,' tis that ye rarely ken what events are ahead of ye. But our castle walls are strong and our guards are stronger. Balliol's troops ne'er troubled us, e'en when most of Scotland fell to them. And now peace is the victor in these lands."

"Good. I wouldna like it in the cave." Brianne shook her head so vigorously her curls bounced.

"'Tis not all bad." Hamish remembered playing the lute on warm summer nights, with his sister singing along beside him.

Brianne's attention had moved to other things.

"Can we race back, Papa?"

"Race?" He feigned astonishment. "All the way back ter the keep?"

Brianne squealed with glee and urged her pony into a gallop. The little creature moved at quite a lick over the moors, but Hamish ensured Luar stayed a nose behind all the way back to the outer walls. The guards saluted smartly as they passed through the gates and a breathless Brianne declared herself the winner.

"'Twas nay fair. Ye started afore I did." He frowned down at her in jest.

"Dinna worry, Papa. We can race again another day."

They trotted into the stable yard where Siegfried was deep in conversation with a young groom. His lined face lit up at the sight of Brianne and he lifted his arms to help her down.

"How is the new pony, Lady Brianne?"

"Fast," she answered with satisfaction. "Faster than Luar."

"'Tis true." Hamish ruefully swung himself down onto the cobbles. "I may have to borrow him."

Brianne looked alarmed. "Ye are much too big for him, Papa."

"Then he will have to grow." Hamish nodded seriously, then ruffled his daughter's hair. "Siegfried, do ye ken where I might find my wife?"

"The Lady is busy in the kitchens."

"Of course she is." Brianne sighed with exasperation. "But she needs to make herself pretty for the feast."

"She needs little time fer that." Hamish waved his hand in

farewell. "But I shall go and hurry her along all the same."

Leaving Brianne in the capable care of Siegfried, Hamish walked briskly over the cobbles to the long and low granite building which housed the castle kitchens. The air was thick with steam and the enticing aroma of roasting meat. Two pink-cheeked maids turned a large spit whilst the redoubtable cook used a long iron handle to fetch bread from the oven. Isabella was in the far corner, biting her lip in concentration as she rolled marzipan for a large fruitcake. She didn't hear as he snuck up behind her, and she gasped in surprise as his hands closed about her waist.

"I am come to steal ye away," he whispered in her ear.

Isabella giggled. "I must finish this cake before I do anything else."

"Ye forget who ye address. I am the Laird of Greenock and my word is law."

"Are ye certain of that?" Isabella turned in his arms and dabbed sugar onto his nose with the tip of her forefinger. "For I am the Lady of Greenock, and 'tis my word that is law, at least in this kitchen."

Hamish guffawed, resisting the urge to kiss her in front of the servants. "Yer word is law, Isabella. In each and every room of this castle and wherever else we may roam together. But I have hardly seen ye this day. Would ye be so cruel as ter deny me yer company, just for a short time?"

She nodded slowly, her long blonde plaits swinging over her shoulders. "For a short time, then. In truth, there is something I must tell you."

Hamish grasped her hand and led her from the heat of the kitchen to the herb garden, pausing only long enough for Isabella to give her instructions to the servants. Outside, the warm breeze was pungent with the scent of mint. Isabella wiped her sugary fingers on her apron and pushed back a loose strand of hair.

"The herbs are flourishing." She turned around slowly, looking at the well-stocked beds with a proud smile.

"We are all flourishing." He pulled her into his arms and pressed a kiss to her golden head. "Thanks to yer tender care."

"'Tis thanks to the mighty Laird of Greenock that we have such a fine and prosperous home." She ran a hand over his cheek and he closed his eyes at her touch. "You have not rested since we wed. Are you not tired, Hamish?"

"Never." He caught her hand and pressed it to his lips. "I have the energy of a boy. Especially since our wool exports to France are doing so well. I ken 'tis likely thanks to the intervention of yer brother Tristan that trade flows so freely from Greenock."

"The unrelenting hard work of yourself, plus the odd word from Tristan, mayhap." Isabella shrugged. "'Tis in the interest of the de Nevilles to stand side-by-side with the McIvors now that we are joined in marriage not once but twice." She smiled up at him, haloed by the noontime sun.

Hamish fought to keep his focus on the conversation they were having, but it was difficult when his wife was so alluring. "Jonah and Elena make a fine couple," he managed. "I ne'er thought I would consider a man worthy of my little sister. But Jonah de Neville has proven me wrong."

"And I ne'er thought to see my youngest brother so happy." She shielded her eyes from the sun. "Remember, they expect to be with us before the harvest."

"So that Elena's first child can be born at Greenock." He fastened his arms about Isabella's waist. "I havena forgotten."

Isabella took a breath. "So it's true, you have not yet grown exhausted by all this?"

He raised his eyebrows. "All what?"

"Everything." Isabella caught at her lip with her teeth and looked away.

Hamish pulled her closer. "What are ye trying to tell me?"

Slowly, Isabella took his hand and placed it on her belly. "By Twelfthtide we shall have another babe in the cradle."

"Ye are with child?" He smiled broadly. "Ye Gods, that is wonderful news."

Isabella inclined her head as a furious wailing erupted from the nearby western tower, which housed the nursery. "I am glad you think so. Especially as our latest babe is hardly out of the cradle. Nor has he afforded us more than one night of sleep since his arrival."

"Our Adam has strong lungs and a strong temperament." Hamish was still smiling; he thought he may never stop. "And the patience of a highland warrior hungry for his supper."

"Your son," Isabella said lightly. "I hope this one may be a girl. A sister for Brianne."

"Girl or boy, I care only that it is healthy."

"Amen to that." She rose onto her tiptoes and kissed him. "I know that Adam is in good hands with his nurse, but I cannot bear to hear him cry. I must go to him."

With some regret, Hamish released her. "I will come and find ye later," he promised. "There is unfinished business between us."

Having taken a few steps away, Isabella turned toward him, her eyes bright with merriment. "Still?" she enquired, one hand lingering over her belly.

"Always," he said firmly.

After six years and three children, he loved and desired his wife more than ever.

"I will hold you to that, Hamish McIvor," she teased.

"I ken ye are a woman who keeps her promises, my lady."

The sound of Isabella's laughter mingled with the song of a blackbird as she resumed her journey to the keep. Hamish put his hands on his hips and gazed up at the granite fortress that had dominated his decision-making almost since birth.

In years gone by, he had felt the weight of history pressing down on his shoulders. But now he looked to the future with a heart that was light and filled with love.

THE END

About the Author

Elizabeth grew up in a rambling old farmhouse high on the Yorkshire moors, where a sense of history was never far away. She studied English at university, specialising in mythology and folklore and often bemoaning the lack of sword-wielding heroines. After graduating, she spent several years moving between northern France, southern Germany and London, where she worked in travel publishing and PR.

She now lives a stone's throw from her childhood home, with her husband, children and a feisty black cat who enjoys interrupting her writing. She plots most of her novels while walking in the rugged Yorkshire countryside, finding endless inspiration in the rolling hills.